I0699666

GOOD

GIRL

GONE

BAD

Also by Emily Kazmierski

Valencia Lamb Series
Good Girl, Dead Girl
Good Girl Gone Bad

Don't Look Series
Don't Look Too Close (a prequel novella)
Don't Look Behind You
Don't Close Your Eyes

Embassy Academy Trilogy
Deadly First Day
Lethal Queen Bee
Killer Final Exams

Ivory Tower Spies Series
For Your Ears Only
The Walk-in Agent (a Julep Short Story)
The Eyes of Spies
Spy Your Heart Out
Spy Got Your Tongue
Over My Dead Body

Other Novels
Malignant
All-American Liars

GOOD GIRL GONE BAD

Emily Kazmierski

Once you find the people in your life worth fighting for, don't
let go of them. Cherish every moment you have together,
because each is a gift.

GOOD GIRL GONE BAD

Fancy Meeting You Here

I DIDN'T SIGN UP TO SPEND TIME OUTSIDE OF SCHOOL WITH my frenemy, but that didn't stop Janice from inviting herself over tonight. Ever since she accused me of helping my father murder a mutual friend, I've spent a surprisingly large amount of time with her. When she arrived, her expertly curled mahogany locks were sleek down her back. She hadn't come to loaf around. The question of how to get rid of Janice without ending up with weeks of bottom-of-the-barrel writing assignments lingers at the back of my mind.

"You are begging for trouble, using this thing. It's so fake. Who sold you this monstrosity?" Janice flips my brand spanking new fake ID card over in her hand a couple of times, amusement sparking in her sharp green eyes.

"Hey!" Embarrassed, I snatch it from her. I've never needed a fake ID, and she's right. This thing looks like a kindergartener made it for an art project. I barely got a look at the card when it arrived, because my mom was snoozing on the couch when I brought it in from the mailbox. Looking it over more carefully, I snort with amusement. The photo and address aren't printed on straight, and the colors are just this side of neon. "Good thing it was cheap. Think it'll work?"

Janice leans closer to the mirror in my bathroom, applying another layer of Christmas red lip gloss. Scarlet mouth puckered in a perfect pout, she winks at me in the mirror. "I'm no expert, but if it won't fool me, it won't fool a bartender either. You know how much crap they catch if they get caught serving minors."

"That's why we're not going to get caught, Jan." She points at me in the mirror with one of her shiny, polished fingernails. The glittery red sweater, black fleece-lined leggings, and furry boots she's wearing are doing her so many favors. My silver sweater and dark wash jeans look pretty cute too. "I'm as ready as I'm going to get."

Janice eyes me with a sly smile. "Maybe we should stop by the station on the way so you can twirl around in front of your ex a few times. Make him regret losing you."

Grinning at her, I pop a tube of clear gloss in my crossbody purse. "That ship has sailed, and quickly hit a sandbar."

"Pretty sure it was an aqueduct."

Our uncomfortable laughter leads us along the hallway. She and I haven't talked much about all that happened the night I almost died, mostly because after hashing out everything that happened between Gus, Portia, and me with Sheriff McCandles, and my mom, and our lawyer, I was tired of talking about it. Janice doesn't talk about her incarcerated dad much, either, but I'll never forget the advice she gave me when I thought my dad had murdered Gracia. *Hold on to the good memories. No matter what happens.*

It was good advice, and these days, I live by it. Carefully steering clear of the memories that are more bitter than sweet.

Not to mention my dad, who I miss so much sometimes my chest physically aches, in spite of his flaws. I'll be driving through town and a memory of him will spark, a sun flare in my mind that sends me back to when he was still alive. The swing set at the park where he used to push me so high I felt like I was flying. The bowling alley where he'd crow after each strike. The drive-in theater where he snuck me in to see *Jaws* against my mom's better judgment.

Spiced warmth guides Janice and I into the kitchen. "Mom, we're going."

My mom stirs a vat of spiced apple cider. She makes it every year, and we take it down to everyone at the station on Christmas Day. This year, she's making a smaller batch first, because she can't wait any longer. The scents of sticky sweet apples and warm cinnamon fill the house.

"That smells incredible. Can we get some cider to go?" Janice peers over my mom's shoulder at the golden liquid in the pot.

"Yes, please." Plucking a cinnamon stick off the counter, I give it a whiff. Heaven.

"Sure. Grab a thermos from that cabinet, there. You're going to the diner, right? I heard they have a couple of delicious seasonal milkshakes but haven't stopped in to try them yet."

Leaning against the fridge, I'm almost mesmerized by the cyclical motion of her hand as she stirs. "Sykes is addicted to the chocolate orange one. He won't shut up about it. He and Kelley got into a tiff about chocolate and fruit pairings the other day."

Janice prances in excitement as my mom fills a thermos and hands it over. Inhaling deeply, she sighs in pleasure. "This stuff is probably habit-forming."

I can attest that it is addicting. My dad used to sneak as many glasses of the stuff as he could before Mom and I took it down to the station. Assuming he wasn't already working. If he was, we would set aside three thermoses of it just for him. Last year, I added cinnamon sticks to each for a little special something. Swallowing against the tightness in my throat, I catch Janice's eye. "We should get going before all the milkshakes are gone."

Having Janice in my house is still a little odd. The first time she showed up just to hang out, we got into an argument about what to watch and ended up glaring at each other through three episodes of the newest fantasy show everyone is raving about. By episode five, we had bonded over cheap-looking costumes and poor weapons handling. Mocking fumbling swordsmen and bad wigs with her is a delight. After that night, Mom had come by my bedroom to warn me not to scare her away. Her hope was that our home would be comfortable for Janice when she didn't want to be in her own. I have no idea how Janice's home is with just her and her mom. Her dad's been in jail for almost a year, and from the little she has said it isn't easy.

Janice hip-checks my mom on the way past, and we go out through the garage to the Corvette. The leather seats are icy-cold, and we squeal and wiggle while we beg the heater to kick in.

Christmas is in three days, and the entire town of Hacienda is draped in multi-colored lights. Red and green and gold glow, making the town festive and cozy. One yard has a tractor parked on the lawn and completely covered in white twinkle lights. Animatronic reindeer pull the reins, and a waving Santa blow-up is perched in the seat.

"I love Christmas." Taking a sip of her simmering cider, Janice watches the lights as we drive. A puff of mist gathers on her window. I used to love Christmas, too, but I'm dreading it. My grandparents aren't coming to visit this year, having promised to spend the holiday with my uncle and his family a few hours away. A billboard showcasing Rudolph the red-nosed reindeer glides past the car window. Without Dad, who is going to suffer through all of the old TV holiday specials with me?

The Corvette coasts past the diner.

Neon orange points the way to our actual first stop. The parking lot at Neil's Bar is surprisingly full for 8 PM on a Wednesday night, despite the squat, uninspiring building. I park in a dark corner of the lot back from the street. With some luck, no one nosy will spot my car and stop in to cause trouble.

Destin made me promise I'd keep him up to date on anything I work on for the newspaper, especially if it was risky, so I shoot him a text. I get it. His first girlfriend, Gracia, worked for the paper, and she kept a lot of dark and juicy parts of her life from him. I'm not going to make the same mistake she did by keeping secrets from Des.

He writes back almost immediately with a thumbs up and an admonishment to be careful. Bert's happy doggy grin lights up my screen. Janice leans over for a look. I get the feeling based on the unmoved slant to her eyes that she isn't a dog person, but she doesn't argue when I assert Bert's cuteness.

Angling my screen away from her, I send my thousandth apology text to Rock. He hasn't responded to a single one.

An email notification pops up, so I tap it. My eyes widen to a bulge as I read. One of my favorite true crime podcasters wants to write a book about Gracia Cuoco's death and my dad's disappearance. She wants me to co-write it with her since I solved both cases. My input will be invaluable, she writes.

I read the email again, blinking in disbelief. A deluge of emotions hits me. Surprise and grief burn in my chest, followed by a twinge of interest. I cut that right off. I'm not a writer, not really. I could never write a book. Shoving the phone into my purse so I can't stare at it anymore, I run my hands down my pants.

Taking another drink from her thermos, Janice keeps both hands cupped around its warmth. Warily, she looks at me. "You ready to pop your alcohol cherry?"

Dropping my keyring into my bag, I eye her smirk. "People still say that?"

"Only when I'm trying to push your buttons. And that full body cringe you just did? Worth it."

"You're the worst." I run my tongue over my teeth to keep from smiling.

"I'm the best! You love me."

"About that…" I can't deny that she has become more than a caustic acquaintance since everything went down with Portia and Gus and Leif Agani.

Look at me: only eighteen and I already have a list of enemies.

Bundled up in a winter coat doesn't make me immune to the freezing cold night, and I shiver as we make for the bar's dimly lit front entrance. Neil's Bar better be warmer inside than it looks, because my nose is threatening to form icicles.

Janice veers toward the side of the building, pulling a surprised squawk out of me. "Where are you going?"

"Follow me and find out."

To one side of the aging edifice is a small square of concrete cordoned off by a barred fence. Inside the enclosure, a door leads from the corral into the bar. The sign over it reads, Smoking Area. No Entrance.

Sucking in a breath, I squeeze through the gate after Janice. Sneaking into bars sounded like a great idea when we planned it a few days ago, but now that I'm standing behind Neil's Bar watching Janice traipse insouciantly toward the smoking entrance, I hesitate. Maybe I'm not ready to pop my alcohol cherry. My dad drummed it into my head over and over that there were reasons the drinking age was 21. Responsibility, impulse control, blah, blah, blah.

Besides, if we're caught... Hoo boy my mom, and the entire department, will be livid. Or even worse, disappointed. Consequences will be levied. Car keys will be confiscated.

"Come on, Miss Goodie Two-Shoes. You're about to learn that breaking and entering can be fun." Janice's teasing smirk and provoking wave spur me to keep walking.

"Is it though?"

"Yes."

Don't get me wrong. This isn't the first time I've broken some rules. When I was investigating Gracia's death and my dad's disappearance, I basically put a baseball bat through the laws about breaking and entering, tampering with evidence, impeding a police investigation... But that was aimed at solving a murder and a disappearance. Tonight's excursion, by comparison, is for a newspaper article.

Janice catches my eye, her hand wrapped around the door knob. "Carpe diem, Val. Journalists have been putting themselves on the line since forever. And you tend to land on your feet. You'll be fine."

She's right. And our article idea is excellent. I jog to catch up. By the door, the ash tray overflows with burned orange and white butts. Ashes and used cigarettes litter the ground. My nose wrinkles at the potent stench. Janice opens the door and pulls me inside.

The bar's interior is gloomy. Red Christmas lights above the bar add a festive touch to the dreary room, but don't do much to provide actual illumination. Neil's patrons are looming silhouettes hovering over the pool tables and bar stools like specters. I half expect them to turn and reveal glowing, judgy eyes.

In the middle, a dance floor pulses with indistinguishable, clumsy bodies.

Janice reels me in by the arm so she can whisper in my ear over an old Christmas carol. "Watch and learn." Taking a quick measure of the room, she skims between tables and plucks a mostly empty beer bottle off an unoccupied high top. She plunks it down in front of the bartender.

Their conversation is inaudible from where I'm standing, but the sleazy way the guy behind the bar homes in on Janice's chest is obvious. The creep takes the empty bottle, dropping it into a bin before fetching a fresh one. His eyes return to her chest as he pops the top and hands it over.

Janice sashays to me, and I try not to look impressed by her casual flouting of liquor laws. She did it effortlessly. We settle into an empty table near the back of the room, under the balcony, and she takes a few sips. It smells awful, so I decline when she offers.

"How did you learn to do that? And that?" I gesture toward the smoking exit, the row of empty glasses abandoned on a nearby table, and the bar.

"I had to grow up quick with my dad. Had to know what I was doing, or get good at faking it."

"You mean you and your parents didn't sit down to a family dinner every night to talk about the highs and lows of your day?" I used to give my mom such a hard time for insisting we all answer her two favorite questions, but the bleak note in Janice's explanation gives me pause. Maybe my mom's cheesy ice breakers weren't so embarrassing or awkward, given what family evenings at home could have been instead. It must have been a rough environment for Janice to grow up in if the lessons she learned involved how to spot a fake ID and how to coax drinks from a bartender.

I doubt Mr. Hill talked much about the highs and lows of his days as a high-ranking member of a local gang, the Snakes. If he did, it would probably be nightmare inducing. Clearing my throat, I scoot out of the cold metal chair. "Ready to go?"

Janice drops her almost full beer in the trash, and we leave the same way we came in. "Anyone who sees us will think we're going out for another smoke break, and they won't realize I didn't pay for the beer."

Plugging the next address into the GPS on my phone, we chat about how Christmas vacation is going by too quickly, projects we're stressing about doing after the break, and a potential change to our school's dress code. Janice is all for the expansion of options when it comes to school blouses.

Our second target of the night is another older, established bar on the opposite edge of town. Sticky floors, darkened booths and alcoves, and pool tables that have seen better days. Janice uses the same trick she used the first time. Scooping up a mostly empty glass, she flirts with the bartender while he prepares a fresh drink for her. Neither he nor the bartender at Neil's asked for an ID, and now I'm curious what her fake ID looks like. Would it stand up to scrutiny, or would they know it was fake in an instant, if they bothered to look?

Janice takes a sip before dumping the glass's contents in a fake plant on her way back to where I'm standing near the back door. "Strike two." She slides into the chair across from me. We sit quietly, watching the dancers for a couple of minutes. People sway with drink in hand. A few couples scoot around the dance floor. One guy who is drunk off his butt sings the wrong lyrics so badly off-key Bert would be howling if he was here.

"Have you seen Rock?" I keep my eyes trained on the rockstar wannabe.

My friend traces a seam in the plank table with a fingertip.

"Not really. We haven't talked much since we broke up."

"That's the problem I'm having."

"Explain."

"A couple of months ago, we had a fight. Destin, and … Portia, and me. And they accused me of being self-centered. Basically, they said that after Gracia died, I wasn't sensitive to their hurts. That I was off in my own world. And honestly? They were right. But in my defense, my dad was missing, and that freaked me the hell out. Anyway, since then I've been trying to be more aware, I guess.

"That day when I went out to the prison, I tried to apologize to Rock, but he wasn't ready to hear me. And he won't reply to my texts, so I have no idea how he's doing."

"Can you blame him? You did get him arrested."

"Yes and no. Did I handcuff him to a pool ladder? Yes. But did he help Leif dump a body? Also, yes."

"Was he under duress? Also, yes."

"Point taken."

Janice runs her hands up her arms and cups the balls of her shoulders. "Give him some time. Maybe he'll come around."

That maybe worries me. I didn't realize how much I missed Rock until we started butting heads over Gracia's death and Janice's former cattiness. He helped me sneak into his brother's apartment. He didn't rat me out when he caught me the second time. Having Rock in my life again felt right. Like we were supposed to be friends, and we'd circled back to each other after all those years of pretending our history away. Now he's back to ignoring me, and it hurts. I just got him back and I've lost him all over again.

Looking across at Janice, I wonder if I ever had him at all. "Let's get out of here. Mr. American Idol over there is giving me a migraine."

Janice eyes me, as if she can see through my flimsy excuse to the real reason I'm suddenly melancholy, but she doesn't call me out on it. If we wanted to, we could both be well on our way to buzzed, and that really wouldn't help my mopey mood. If we'd been inclined to guzzle the stuff Janice has gotten from both bartenders she has charmed so far tonight. Which we aren't.

We're journalists.

"This is going to make a freaking awesome article." Janice kicks her feet and rubs her hands together as I drive. She's right. Since I joined the staff for our school newspaper, the *Herald*, a few weeks ago, I haven't written anything super interesting. The first article Janice assigned to me was the paving of a new parking lot behind the football stadium. I thought it was a joke. It was not. But sneaking into bars to see which ones will serve us? It's making my fingers itch to write about what we did tonight. I brainstorm opening lines in my head, but by the time I pull into the third bar's parking lot, I'm wondering how ethical it is to include all the details in the article. "You think we should leave our methods vague? Or should we put it all in? If we detail it, are we helping other people get drinks?"

"You think too much." Taking another long drink from the cider thermos, she swings her door open. Leaning into the cab, she grins at me. "Your turn."

The third and final bar on our hit list is nicer and newer than the previous two. The building is modern and trendy, with a sleek, black and white color scheme and artfully placed LED lights. We use the same trick to get inside, where the music is bumping and people are much more chaotic than they were at the first two. Dancers fill the floor, their arms waving in time with the techno-remix of a Christmas song.

Ignoring the nervous flutters in my stomach, I finger comb my hair. I left it down instead of putting it in my usual Dutch braid because I hoped it would make me look older. Putting on a confident smile, I march up to the bar and motion for the server with the glass in my hand. A slosh of pink, fruity smelling liquid snags his attention.

"Help you?" he asks, eyeing me over the glass.

"Can I get another?"

His eyes run over me. Sweat breaks out in my armpits. "Got any ID?"

Oh, crap. "Yeah. Right here." Snagging the fake out of my purse, I slide it over the bar's cool surface. Hopefully the bar's interior is dark enough to cover the multitude of fake ID sins.

The bartender holds it up to his nose, scrutinizing the laminated card. He looks at me. Looks at the card. Looks at me again. And shakes his head. Doesn't take a genius, or waiting until he opens his mouth to know I'm busted.

"Aren't you the murdered sheriff's daughter? The girl who almost drowned in the levy a couple weeks ago?"

My cheeks feel like they're cracking around the fake smile still plastered to my mouth. "Yep, that's me. I just turned 21, as you can see on the ID. First time drinking, and this one was so tasty I want another." Someone needs to come along with one of those giant hooks to pull me away from the bar immediately.

"What was this, again?" The bartender gives me a knowing look. He could probably smell my inexperience the second I approached his bar.

"A daiquiri?" A quick look over my shoulder reveals I've got no backup. Where the freak is Janice?

The bartender taps the edge of my crappy fake ID on the wooden bartop. "Nice try, Miss Lamb. You know I have to call this in, right?"

My shoulders sag. I am so incredibly busted. Especially if my mom hears this guy's call over the dispatch. Crawfish on a cracker, I am in deep crap.

The bartender motions for me to sit on the stool at the bar's end while he makes the call.

I take another peek behind my back and clock Janice in the corner, waving at me to make a break for it. The fluttering heart in my chest beats loudly as I wait for the bartender to dial. He pivots away from the noisy room, probably so he can hear whoever picks up. It's the opening I need. Pushing off the stool, I hotfoot it through the crowd. For once, it's a bonus being short. More cover among the taller drunk people bobbing to a country song techno remix.

The bartender is probably already on the phone with one of the deputies, but leaving will give me a chance to practice my excuses before they catch up to me. It's for truth! Justice! The American pursuit of unbiased journalism!

Heh. That's good. Maybe it'll convince my mom not to ground me and take away the Corvette.

Maybe.

Janice shoves the back door wide, and we scuttle outside. "Wow, that was close," she gushes as we jog to the car.

A vaguely familiar motorcycle tears out of the parking lot, engine rumbling into the night. I watch its progress, tracing the figure straddling it. Plain black helmet and jacket, but I can't shake the feeling I've seen the bike before.

We stop in our tracks.

Sheriff McCandles is leaning on my cherry red car, arms crossed. Boots crossed. Lariat necklace dangling over a work-wrinkled khaki uniform. My pit sweat worsens when his steely eyes meet mine. The man's drawl opens a pit in my stomach. "Valencia Lamb and Janice Hill. Fancy meeting you two here."

We're busted. My fake ID is burning a hole in my purse, and my mom is going to blow a gasket.

So much for not getting caught.

A Short Ride Downtown

Sheriff McCandles confiscates my keys and escorts the two of us to his truck. My heart is tapping out a worried rhythm as we climb inside and buckle up. Despite the winter chill, my body is stickier than the floor back at Neil's Bar. Janice's expression remains cool and unruffled, but the tapping of her fingers on her knees betrays her nerves.

Jonesie, one of the deputies, appears at the sheriff's side and receives the Corvette keys. He follows us to the station. Halfway there, the lawman catches my eye in the rearview mirror. "Next time you go off on a crime spree, you might want to take Miss Hill's car. Your Corvette is easily the most recognizable in town."

"Thanks for the tip, Sheriff. And it wasn't a crime spree. It was for an article. For the *Herald.*" Betting it won't hurt to explain that we weren't actually buying alcohol as underaged delinquents, I outline our article idea as he drives. The only feedback I get is a hum once I'm done talking up our idea in the hopes he won't pursue whatever punishment he's thinking of handing out.

A motorcycle zooms by, recalling the one we saw a few minutes ago. My breath hitches. That motorcycle—I remember where I've seen it before. It's Leif Agani's. He bought it with the cash he made for chopping up my dad's Bronco and selling the parts. And since Leif is in jail… Rock must have been the one riding it.

What was he doing at the bar?

Janice has been quiet, but the furtive, wary glances she's been tossing at the sheriff have slowed. The sheriff's lukewarm reaction to my explanation of the article idea makes me hopeful he's not truly angry with us. She sticks her head between the seats into the front. "Want to know how it went?"

Signal light tapping quietly, Sheriff McCandles makes an easy turn. "Wait until we get back to the station, and then I want to hear every little detail. Don't leave anything out, even to avoid getting in trouble. I need to know what the two of you have been into tonight."

"We won't," Janice and I agree at the same time.

At the department, McCandles walks us through the bull pen. Kelley and Gates are arguing about one of the public high school's football coaches. The mention of my ex-boyfriend's name catches my attention, but I hurry to follow the sheriff.

Sykes is drinking another diner milkshake. "Chocolate orange again?" I ask as we hustle past.

"It's the best flavor."

"How would you know? Have you tried all the flavors?" Kelley teases from behind the mountain of paperwork on her desk.

"Go back to your traffic reports," Sykes lobs at her, gesturing with his cup. To me, "I haven't tried coconut yet, because ew."

The sheriff rolls his eyes good-naturedly as he escorts us

inside his office. Janice and I take the tufted chairs facing the large wooden desk. A photo of him with his wife and son, smiling on a Hawaiian vacation, sits on the desk where my family photo used to live. I skim over it to scrutinize the walls, which bear certificates and awards Sheriff McCandles has earned during his years with the department. Beside them is an article printed from the online edition of the town's paper—a write up of my dad that details his dedicated service up until his death. My heart squeezes with pain and pride.

My attention falls back to the sheriff's family photo. I haven't heard from Leander in the last couple of weeks, since we broke up. He's probably still riding the high of having ended the football season by winning the state championship. Remembering the fall nights Destin, Portia, and I spent at the football field cheering for Leander and his team hurts, so I bury the memories and focus on the clunky way Sheriff McCandles uses a computer mouse.

The lawman clicks a couple times and lifts his gaze to Janice and me. "All right ladies, let's do this."

Janice pulls her phone out of her bag and levels with the sheriff. Her bossy attitude used to drive me nuts—still does sometimes—but it's basically impossible to hold a grudge against a girl who just wanted to solve her bestie's murder. "You want a run down from beginning to end?"

The man nods, running a hand down his lariat. We start in on everything we got up to tonight, from our stop at Neil's, to bar number two, and trendy bar number three. Sheriff McCandles frowns as he types, but something about the relaxed tilt of his shoulders makes me wonder if he's not just a little impressed by Janice's ingenuity. And my nose for trouble. Let the record state that I'm impressed with Janice's crafty, devious methods.

"The smoking entrance, huh?" McCandles says once we finish, a glint in his eye. I would bet money that he'll be leaning on every establishment in town over the next couple weeks to secure their smoking areas. "You had a good idea for an article, and you implemented it. For that, I'll say you did nice work. However, it's my job to warn you both to stay away from bars. You're not above the laws, even if you're breaking them in the name of journalism."

I bob my head, surprised at how fair he's being. Still, I'm curious about something. "What's going to happen to the places that didn't card us?"

The sheriff sits back in his chair, hands relaxed on the armrests. "We've had a big uptick in DUIs and related accidents in town in the past few months. Cracking down on the bars that illegally serve minors will help. If you girls are up for it, I'd like to test the liquor stores and gas stations, too. It won't completely stop the problem, but every citation we hand out helps. You two interested?"

Janice and I grin at each other before nodding at the lawman.

He clears his throat firmly. "In the meantime, I have some office work that needs doing. How about you come work for me over the rest of your holiday break? Earn some pocket money."

"I didn't know you were short-handed."

"We're not. I just want to keep an eye on you in case you get any more award-winning article ideas."

I laugh, incredulous.

"I'll be in touch." Sheriff McCandles moves around his desk, swinging the door wide. "Sykes, escort these two to their car, will you? I have a couple calls to make."

"Sure thing, boss." Sykes's feet shuffle, and papers scatter. Kelley curses loudly, yelling after Sykes to watch his back.

McCandles heads down the back hall, and Sykes meets us in the middle of the bull pen. "You girls ready to go?"

"Yep. Got more bars to hop," I quip, pulling my bag strap up my shoulder.

The deputy wags his finger in my face. "Very funny. Don't make me call your mom."

Hooking my purse with a long nail, Janice pulls my crappy internet ID out of my bag and slides it into Sykes's outstretched palm. "She won't get very far. Look at this."

The deputy looks it over, the corners of his mouth turning up. His chuckle is low and amused as he hands the card back to me. "As an officer of the law, I can't condone you carrying a fake ID, so I'm going to pretend I didn't see that. But seeing as how it looks like a kindergartener made it, I'm going to assume it's purely for costume purposes rather than law-breaking. I'm surprised anyone served you after seeing this."

My neck flushes. I bury the offending card in my purse. "The one bartender who actually looked at it was going to report us."

"We might have run out of there," Janice adds.

Sykes nods. "We got the call. Thanks for agreeing to help us out next time, girls. The sheriff used to make me do it, but I can't pass for a teenager anymore."

Janice and I stare at him. My mouth drops open in surprise that anyone would buy Sykes as a teenager. There's no way.

"It's the mustache." Sykes waggles his eyebrows.

"I didn't know anyone wore mustaches anymore," Janice says, eyeing the furry caterpillar on the deputy's upper lip.

"They don't. Sykes is trapped in the 70s."

"Says the girl with a fifty-year-old Corvette." "Hey. You can say what you want about me, but leave the car out of it."

He tosses me a wink over his shoulder, taking a slurp from

his empty milkshake cup as he leads us toward the front door.

"If you're done antagonizing people less than half your age…." McCandles's hands rest on his belt.

"We're going." Sykes takes one more loud slurp from the empty diner cup and drops it in the trash can next to the exit. He walks us out to the Corvette and makes sure we're buckled up inside the locked car before going inside.

Janice watches his back in the side mirror, turning to me when the station door swings shut. Her green eyes slide to mine. "If you want, I could get you a better ID. I know a guy."

"You know a guy," I deadpan.

Janice pokes her tongue into her cheek. "Yeah. I know a guy."

I start the Corvette and pull up to the street, slamming on the brakes when a tricked-out car roars up the street and cuts us off. Janice gasps in surprise. My heart flies into my throat. Bass notes from the approaching car's radio reverberate through my chest and jiggle my bones. Venomous serpents slither over the black-painted side panels and doors.

My brain helpfully tosses out memories of Leif and one of his devilish sidekicks hunting me across the grounds of my school. Cornering me like a prey animal in the gym, my heart beating so rapidly I thought it might burst. Leif's brutal hands holding me under the chlorinated water long enough for my lungs to burn and my vision to go black.

Seconds stretch out as the car blocks our exit. Four guys in the car glare at us through the windows. My blood runs cold. Janice's hands are white knuckled on her knees.

The Snakes rev the engine one more time, its roar pounding in my ears. Then the car coasts past the sheriff's station. The passengers' eye daggers are so sharp I want to look away. But I can't look away. These goons have plenty of reasons to hate me.

Insulting them when I visited Agani Auto, where the gang was based before Sheriff McCandles and a handful of deputies descended on the shop and found piles of stolen car parts. Getting Leif and Rock arrested for murder. No matter the reason for their anger, having it directed so blatantly at me cannot be good for my continued health. And, you know, staying alive.

I've sunk so low in the seat I'm peeking over the dashboard. Straightening, I catch sight of Janice's pale face. And realize I'm not the only one in this car who might be in deep with the Snakes.

"Do you know why the Snakes are glaring at us? Jan?"

She doesn't answer. Her eyes are glassy and unfocused for so long I wave a hand in front of her face. Janice shakes off the trance she sank into, clearing her throat. When she answers, I'm not sure I believe her. "Probably just keeping an eye on me, since my dad's locked up."

A flimsy excuse calls for flimsy belief. I give her a look. "Jan."

The traffic light glows red and I roll up to the line. I stare at her, expectant.

"There are some expectations I've been avoiding, okay? Now, drop it. Please."

My tongue taps behind my teeth. Curiosity clamors in my veins, and I'm not the most patient when something piques my interest. Haring off to poke at something until I get in over my head? Much more my speed. But the ashen pallor of Janice's face makes me pause. "I'll drop it, but try not to get in trouble, okay? If something happens to you, I won't have anyone to fight with."

"Unless Rock starts answering your texts, huh?" She does her best evil laugh, but halfheartedly. We're quiet the rest of the drive to my house, where her car waits in the driveway. She pops her head into the house to say goodnight to my mom before she goes.

I watch the red taillights until she turns the corner out of sight.

I wish I could say it's a relief to know that the Snakes are keeping tabs on her instead of me. A month ago, it would have been, because frankly she made school hellish for me. And I had enough on my plate without being dogged by a bunch of knuckle draggers with punch-now-ask-questions-later tendencies.

But now, after Janice and I have reached an unspoken truce and voluntarily spent some time together? I wish I could say it's a relief, knowing I'm not number one on the Snakes' hit list, but deep down, I know I'd be lying.

Fudge's sake, I'm starting to care about Janice freaking Hill. What could she possibly have done to get on the bad side of her dad's gang?

Exes and Former Frenemies

Breakfast the next morning is only slightly tense, because Sheriff McCandles graciously smoothed over Janice and my bar-hopping escapade with my mom. And by slightly tense I mean I'm still in possession of the Corvette keys, for now. The sheriff kept the peace by promising that I'd be working at the department and not making trouble. Which is why I'm currently at the department, elbow-deep in some of Kelley's paperwork.

Jonesie marches a boy into the building in handcuffs. He can't be more than thirteen or fourteen if the pimples and braces are any indication. The boy is red in the face and cursing up a storm as the deputy maneuvers him into the back hallway. A clang of a cell door closing precedes a particularly loudly shouted expletive. The boy can't be much of a threat, so he must have done something especially stupid to deserve being hauled into the station.

I go back to the form on top of my stack, thankful for the busy work. It's been slow at the station today, and I've only been here for a couple hours. I was hoping something exciting would happen and give me another article idea for the *Herald*, but so far? No dice.

The sliver of me that knows McCandles offered the job so he could keep tabs on me is the only part that isn't totally sold on it. A girl's got to make money somehow, and working among people I consider practically family is a definite bonus. Sykes had a hot cocoa waiting for me when I arrived this afternoon.

"Two days until Christmas. Only two more days." Jonesie collapses into his desk chair with a groan. He's got a bag of frozen peas propped on one shoulder. It must be acting up again.

"Twelve days until the schools reopen," Kelley adds from her desk. She keeps taking sly peeks at Jonesie over her computer monitor. I hide a smile behind my hand as I scan files with a department machine. I've only been working at the station for three hours, and it's already painfully obvious that Kelley has a thing for Jonesie. Jonesie has no idea.

The bag of frozen peas slips down into Jonesie's lap, and he yelps, dropping it to the linoleum floor.

Finished with another file, I add it to the pile and start on the next one. The stack on my desk isn't getting any smaller. In fact, every time I look up it gets taller. I suspect the deputies keep adding files whenever I'm not looking. I don't call them out on it, because I'm honestly glad for the distraction. Otherwise, I'd probably float between the empty rooms at home wondering how long it will be before every memory or reminder of my dad doesn't make my eyes burn and my throat close up. The grief counselor my mom and I have been seeing comforts us with the idea that it will get easier, but right now? It sucks. Last night I watched *The Little Drummer Boy* by myself, and I promptly vowed never to watch it again. That crap is depressing.

McCandles has his son, Leander working the front desk. I

can't keep my eyes from straying to him while I work, wondering how he's doing. He's just as beautiful as he was when we were dating, what with the honey blond hair and puppy dog brown eyes. He's Hacienda's golden boy heartthrob, and I'd have to be blind not to see why.

Even though today has been slow, we haven't talked. Leander has spent the entire afternoon playing games on his phone. If that's an indicator of how every shift is going to be, this job is going to be awkward.

The sheriff's office door opens, and McCandles shuffles to where Jonesie is sitting. "Darren, did you arrest a kid and bring him in here just now?"

Jonesie spins in his chair, shifting the bag of peas. "He pulled a knife on me, Sheriff. I had to."

The pencil in Kelley's hand snaps. She finds a new one in her desk and attacks the paper in front of her as if it is personally responsible for coming at Jonesie. The sharp look in her eyes hints at violence. Good thing she and I are on the same team.

McCandles grumbles something about dumb kids under his breath. "That's the third time this week somebody has gotten into it with a minor. Care to guess why that is?"

Jonesie scratches at his temple. "I'm not a detective, but I'm guessing they're bored 'cause school's out."

The sheriff turns to me. "When does your school start again?"

"We've only been out for four days, Sheriff."

A phone ringing within the sheriff's office sends him in that direction, muttering the whole way. The blinds on the window clack and swing when he jerks the door shut.

Needing to stretch my legs, I take a couple of scanned files back to the cabinet and wander toward the front desk. "Whatcha playing?"

Leander's eyes flit to mine and back to his screen. Is that a hint of amusement in the corners of his mouth? Yes, it is. "Presidential Zombie Slayer. I'm playing as FDR right now. His wheelchair has built-in flame throwers."

He shifts toward me a little, slanting the screen so I can have a look. It feels like an olive branch, and I take it. Leander shows me the controls for the game, explaining the game's backstory about how the zombies were created. Then he lets me play. I choose John Adams as my avatar, because I can't resist the absurdity of weaponized powdered wigs. I die in approximately two seconds and hand the phone back.

Leander swivels on the stool so we're face to face. "How's it going working for your former arch enemy at the school paper?"

"I've written a staggering two articles so far, and my editor is a nitpicker. So not bad."

He chuckles. "Glad to hear it. I, uh, heard my dad caught you doing some undercover investigating the other night. How'd that go?"

"Free drinks. Can't complain."

"Don't make me fine you," Kelley calls from the water cooler.

"You could just let it slide."

The deputy shakes her head, emptying a packet of flavoring into her Styrofoam cup.

Leander bumps my leg with his knee, waiting until I meet his eyes. "You were safe though?"

My heart squeezes at the care in the whispered question. I nod and he mirrors it. His mouth opens to say something more, but the front door swinging open interrupts. A skateboarding bulldog rolls in, followed by my best friend. Destin props his longboard against the wall and scoops up the dog. Bert wags his tail and tries to lick my whole face when I scrub behind his ears, speaking in puppy gibberish.

"No love for your bestie?" Destin bumps fists with Leander and crosses his arms over the counter. His sun-bleached hair sweeps over his forehead and falls over his ears in a too-long cut that his mom complained about under her breath the last time we hung out at his house.

"Bert is my bestie. Aren't you, Bert? Besides, I literally just texted you a funny skateboarding video."

"Yeah, you did." Destin is ticklish, so he screams when I go for his neck with both hands. His body contorts in a futile attempt to escape my relentless attack.

The front door is thrown open so hard it hits the wall and bounces back, almost clobbering the entering woman. Shoving the door open a second time, the lady scrambles to the desk. Her eyes widen in surprise when she registers a pack of teenagers standing between her and the rest of the department.

I stifle a laugh.

The woman looks between the three of us, not sure who to address. "I need to talk to the sheriff. Is he here? I have to know if my boy will be out by Christmas."

"He'll be out in an hour," Jonesie mutters under his breath, tugging his uniform hat down to hide a blooming black eye. The kid really punched him. Yikes.

Sheriff McCandles ignores him, marching through the bull pen to meet the woman, whose hands are wringing in front of her. "Right this way, Mrs. Brock." Even after the sheriff shuts his office door, the woman's semi-hysterical complaining carries.

"He's going to be fun to be around tonight," Leander quips good naturedly. He's pretty tight knit with his parents. Just like my mom, dad, and me were before he died. Oh, I need to text my mom to ask her what takeout she wants me to pick up on the way home. We've been trading off dinner duty, and tonight's my night. She responds immediately, asking for Thai food. Yummy.

"You could always pull out a puzzle. I have about a thousand you could borrow." Destin leans down to pat Bert, who is lying across his feet.

Leander chuckles. "Your folks still on that?"

"Urgh, yes. If I didn't know it would make Bert sick, I'd feed him pieces just to drive them nuts."

Bert's tongue lolls out of his mouth as he pants. Having seen Bert snarf his food so fast it makes him snort, I can totally believe he'd eat a few puzzle pieces. "What got them started on the whole puzzle kick, anyway?"

"Game night got too competitive, but my mom still insists we need family bonding and all that."

Destin and Leander trade stories about their parents trying to force a bond by doing increasingly awkward family activities. White water rafting with one parent who is afraid of drowning. Getting stuck dangling in the middle of a zipline course. Riding a horse prone to biting. I tell them about the time my dad tried to bond with me by taking me to a screening of *American Graffiti* and spouting Harrison Ford factoids the entire time. An usher had to come and tell him to can it.

Wistfulness coats the memory. At the time, I was embarrassed he kept talking, because an elderly couple in front of us kept turning around to glare at him, even though their conversation indicated they were both hard of hearing. Clearing my tight throat, I make an excuse and go back to my desk. Burying myself in mind-numbing paperwork should bury the messy emotions threatening to overflow.

A while later, a cup of hot cocoa appears in front of my scratchy eyes. Destin plants one palm on top of the stack of files I've already scanned. "Hey. You good?"

Sniffing, I wipe my nose. No, I'm not good. My dad is gone, and missing him sucks. Every day, I stumble over some movie or book he loved. Or I remember a story I want to tell him. Or think about milestones in my life he'll never get to see.

You know what else sucks? Being a downer whenever my bestie asks how I'm doing. I promised to try harder with Destin. To be present. To ask how he's doing, too, with all the crap he went through with Gracia, and then with Portia. He deserves to have someone love him without lies or ulterior motives, and I'm trying my best. But sometimes I just want to be okay, even when I'm not. So this once, I lie. "Yeah, why?"

He glances over his shoulder to where Leander is at the front desk, typing something into the computer. "Looked like you were upset earlier, so I wanted to check in. Make sure you're okay."

"I will be. It's a process, you know?" Smiling too quickly, I thank him for the cocoa.

The depth of pain behind Destin's eyes matches mine. Maybe that's why we've gravitated back toward one another in the wake of Portia's betrayal. Our souls match even more closely now than they did before. We've always found ease with each other, and sinking back into that is like being wrapped up in my favorite hoodie.

Destin's fingers riffle one of the stacks of papers on my desk. "We're going snowboarding tomorrow, up at Pearly Gates. A while ago you said you wanted to learn… Would you want to go with us?"

I cock my head, thinking it over. Going along will slow him down. From what he has told me, he loves challenging himself with harder and harder runs and trails. I've never been on a snowboard in my life. I open my mouth to decline, but wouldn't that be doing exactly what I promised not to do? Assuming I know what he wants instead of asking? If Destin is offering, I have to take that at face value. He has to know that bringing me along will affect his plan, and he must not mind. It's only fair that I take him at his word. "Sure, but don't let me slow you down. Point me to the bunny slope, and you can go take your life in your hands. Just don't hit any trees."

He props his elbow on top of my head. "Please. I just got my arm cast off. I'm not gunning for another broken bone, like ever. My mom would never let me out of the house again. But for tomorrow, you're in?"

My gaze flicks to Leander, nursing his own steaming cup of cocoa. "You think he'll mind?"

Destin stretches his arms above his head. "It'll be fine. Trust me."

Trust. It's not something I'm good at. But since I promised to try… "How many hospital visits have you made this year, again?"

"Smarty pants."

"Yeah, but I'm your smarty pants." Again, my eyes are lured to Leander. Caught watching me, he twists away, running a hand through his hair. Yeah, me coming along on their boys' snowboarding trip isn't going to be awkward at all.

Holes in My Pockets

"SHE STILL OUT?" LEANDER WHISPERS FROM THE DRIVER seat.

Janice looks over her shoulder at me. Her face is pale. "She's awake."

Rubbing at my dry eyes, I sit up in the backseat of Mrs. McCandles's SUV. Early this morning, Leander, Destin, Janice, Janice's new friend-who-is-a-boy Ty, and I piled into the black vehicle and drove up to the ski resort for the day. I spent my first ever six hours on a snowboard trying to conquer the bunny hill. I did it, and apparently was so wiped I slept most of the drive home.

Yawning, I untangle a loose lock of hair from my seatbelt. "What's up? Oh, did we stop for snacks?" Wiping my chin to make sure I didn't drool, I look out the window. My hands claw the back of the seat in front of me.

My house has been trashed. The Christmas lights have been cut and yanked from the eaves. Indignance flares in my chest. It took mom and me hours to hang those lights on my dad's old, decrepit ladder a couple weeks ago. One of the front windows is shattered. Graffiti crawls across the closed garage door, harsh black against the tan metal panels.

My seatbelt swings as I jab viciously at the release. "Let me out."

The doors lock with a click. Leander's gaze clashes with mine. "Let me call my dad first. Get him out here to take a look."

"Let. Me. Out."

He chews on the inside of his cheek, eyeing me. Weighing his options.

My arms wave at my house. Someone has desecrated my home, on Christmas Eve, and worry rides me hard. My mom was planning on running some errands today, but what if she was home when this happened? What if whoever did this heard her inside?

What if they hurt her?

Fear rakes at my insides, its claws sinking in deep. My voice is a sharp, thin razor blade. "Let me out of this car, Leander."

His eyes are solid on mine. "Fine, but I'm coming with you." The door locks disengage. Janice climbs into Ty's lap so I can push the seat forward and wedge my body out the door. My foot connects with a spray paint can that skids over the icy sidewalk.

Leander stands stiffly at my side.

My hands shake as I take out my phone and call my mom. It rings. And rings. And rings.

My knees nearly give out when she answers.

"Hi Val, honey. How is snowboarding going?" She sounds breathless. My fear climbs higher. What if she's trapped inside, pretending everything is okay? What if there's a gun to her head?

"Where are you? Are you okay?" I'm shouting into the phone and I don't care who hears.

Her answering tone sombers. "I'm fine. The stores are just busy today, with last minute shoppers and everything. What's wrong?"

Relief pours through me and I collapse back against the SUV. Looking over the house, at the disgusting words defacing it, tightens my ribcage.

"Front door is closed. It's a good sign." Leander points, looking down at me.

That door had better be absolutely freaking closed. Unlike a couple months ago when our house was broken into and ransacked by Leif Agani and Rock. Frowning, I try to drop that line of memory. Rock was trying to help his brother, forced to by Gus. Focusing on the ambient chatter behind my mom's voice, I ask a question I already know the answer to. I need to hear her say it. "You're not home right now, are you?"

"I'm at the coffee shop. I got done with my errands early, and I decided to treat myself to a peppermint mocha. Are you okay? Did you get hurt snowboarding? Do I need to come get you?"

My mom is unharmed. Pinching my eyes closed with my free hand, I turn away from the damage. Destin stands a couple feet away, hands in pockets. Our eyes meet, and he shuffles closer to put an arm around my shaking frame. Tucking me into his side, his chin comes down on my shoulder. His warmth only highlights the cold tugging at every part of me not touching him.

Leander is on his phone, describing the destruction. He's obviously talking to his dad. He hangs up, meeting my eyes. "Help is on the way."

I mouth a *thank you*, and he nods.

"Val, honey?" My mom's concern makes my eyes heavy. I close them to shut out the ugliness in front of me.

"Come home, please? Someone… Someone trashed our

house."

"On Christmas Eve?" She makes a strangled sound and promises to hurry.

After I hang up, Janice slots into place at my other side, so I'm flanked by her and Destin. Her tongue pushes against her upper lip as she examines my home.

Most of the tags are too vile to look at for long, but the largest phrase painted on the garage is, *Snitches get stitches*. I focus on that, wondering what on earth it means. I edge closer to a blackened patch of lawn. Someone tried to set the brittle yellow grass on fire.

"Hey, Val?" Janice rests her head against mine. "What was the nickname Leif used to call you?"

Ice blooms in my veins at the wariness in her expression. "Little bird. Why?"

She points at a smaller scrawl of black to one side of the front door. I flinch hard. *Little bird. Little bird. Little bird.* The derisive nickname repeats over and over, black paint dripping from the letters.

Cursing, Janice taps on her phone. Her mouth is set in a grim line.

Foreboding prickles at my legs like dry straw poking through too-thin clothes, making me go itchy all over. "Who are you texting?"

Her body goes rigid.

"If he asks, tell Rock I'm fine."

My mind goes back to the other night, when some of the Snakes glared at Janice and me outside the sheriff's department. Knots tighten in my gut. We both assumed they were looking at Janice. What had she said when I asked? A thin excuse about her not meeting some of the gang's expectations.

Little bird.

Something tells me the Snakes weren't glaring at Janice that night, regardless of whatever expectations she isn't meeting. It looks like they found out about my part in getting Leif and one of his buddies arrested. By doing some mental gymnastics, they could blame me for the department raid on Agani Auto, too, even though it wasn't my fault they had more stolen car parts under their roof than legitimately bought ones.

The toe of my shoe taps at the burned grass, and it crumbles to ash. The Snakes know I'm at the root of their legal troubles, and from the looks of my house, they're not going to let it go. I've made an enemy of the largest and most powerful gang in the valley. Again.

And the Snakes aren't known for letting insults lie.

New Art and New Enemies

A Christmas Eve of restless sleep isn't unusual. Waking up hoping my house hadn't been vandalized by gang members as a threat to me for getting their walnut-brained leader arrested is not what I expected.

Mom's smile is falsely bright when I enter the kitchen, drawn by the scent of freshly baked cinnamon rolls and hot cocoa. Hugging me tight, she whispers against my cheek. "Merry Christmas."

"Merry Christmas. Love you, Mom."

Her arms tighten around me. "Love you too, honey."

We eat and open presents, quietly balancing equal measures of tentative enjoyment and empty sadness.

With a full stomach and wearing the thick, luxurious new bathrobe I just unwrapped, I take a quick stroll out my front door. My mom follows in her own matching robe and snow boots. We stand together on the sidewalk, examining our poor, beleaguered house.

The late Christmas morning sunshine confirms that yes, my actions did result in retaliation by the local street gang. Yes, they did trash our house on Christmas Eve, a day that is supposed to be for celebrating with family and eating lots of delicious food.

Did I vow to solve my friend's murder and my dad's disappearance, while also ignoring my impulse control and making increasingly bad decisions? Yes. Did I do it and almost get myself killed? Also, yes.

Because of my admittedly somewhat noble actions, the Snakes are out to get me. Kudos to me.

Mom gives me a squeeze and goes back inside to clean up the wrapping paper strewn under the Christmas tree.

Shuffling across the street in my robe, messy bun, and boots, I tap the driver window of the squad car parked on the curb opposite our house. Sykes rolls down the window, taking in my getup. A travel mug steams in the cup holder at his knee. "What are you doing here? Isn't your wife mad you're not home for Christmas?"

The deputy shrugs. "We do our extended family thing on Christmas Eve, and the wife and I moved our fancy meal from lunch to dinner. It gives her more time to sleep after last night, because the baby woke us up at midnight, and one, and two. You get the idea. Don't worry about it."

Rolling my lip, I meet his eyes. "Thanks, for being here today."

"You're family." He sips from the travel mug. "Doesn't look like you got any sleep."

Revealing the paper plate I had behind my back, I wave it toward him, clutching it close when he reaches for it. "You sure know how to sweet talk a girl. I brought you a couple cinnamon rolls, but if you're gonna be like that…"

Sykes laughs, abashed.

Plucking the cling wrap off the still warm and delicious cinnamon rolls, I wave them under his nose. "Care to try again?"

The man manages a charming smile through his two-day scruff and wrinkled uniform. "What I mean is, I hope knowing we were out here all night made it easier for you to sleep."

"You were always my favorite deputy." My heart twinges. That's really sweet. Knowing that Sykes or Kelley or Jonesie was outside all night was reassuring, even if it didn't help me sleep. I pass the plate through the window. Sykes gestures for me to come around to the passenger side and climb in. I hand over a plastic fork, and he eats while I wait for the sheriff to show up to look over the scene and take my statement. It was already getting dark when my friends and I got back from snowboarding last night, so a detailed look had to wait until this morning.

I try not to think about the fact that my actions have yet again taken people from their families. Whoever was outside my house all night. Sykes this morning, and the sheriff, when he shows up.

"Speak of the devil," I murmur as the sheriff's truck pulls up to the curb behind the squad car.

Sheriff McCandles shuffles across the street to stand on my sidewalk, hands propped on his belt. Climbing out of the squad car, I meet him on the front walk. He surveys the house. "I would have come out earlier, but my boy told me you like to sleep in."

That makes twice in one morning these tough law officers have surprised me with a little tenderness. I thank him and aggressively try not to turn bright red.

Leaning inside the front door, I holler at my mom to come out to talk to the sheriff. She wraps up in a puffer coat and a knit hat, and we stand on the sidewalk on Christmas Day, looking at our messed-up house. The sheriff asks questions about my mom's itinerary yesterday, establishing an approximate window for when the house was vandalized.

Arms crossing over his chest, Sheriff McCandles waits while Sykes takes photos. "Make sure you get the back yard, too."

It hadn't occurred to me to look in the back. Instead, my gaze keeps returning to the wall of taunts by the front door. *Little bird.* As if I'm a small, winged creature knocked out of its nest and trapped by a hungry snake. It's the second time in my life I've felt kinship to a small prey animal, and it better be the last.

"Is that some slang I don't know about?" The sheriff gestures toward the front door, eyes resting on me.

I swallow, my attention locked on those two little words. A stubborn streak a mile wide presses me to lie, but I learned my lesson about keeping crap from the sheriff while I was investigating my dad's disappearance and Gracia's murder. Hiding evidence from the man almost got me drowned. Twice.

"Leif Agani used to call me that. It wasn't a compliment." McCandles' frown digs grooves in his face as I tell him about my unbelievably reckless visit to Agani Auto in the fall. "It's conceivable that one of the Snakes who hasn't been arrested yet heard the taunt and has picked it up."

The sheriff runs a thumb along his jawline. "Doesn't seem casual though, does it? A nickname like that feels personal. It's designed to hit you with as much fear as possible. As does choosing to do this on Christmas Eve."

"But Leif is in prison."

McCandles regards the house, chewing on the idea.

"Could someone have visited him, and been told to do this?" My mom chimes in, worried eyes trained on the lawman.

"Could be."

"But that's not what you think it is." I can't explain how, but I know I'm right.

Sheriff McCandles looks at my mom over my head, and must get some kind of go-ahead from her, because he levels with me. "With Dino Agani, Angus Hill, and Leif behind bars, there are holes in the Snakes hierarchy. We've had increased incidents of unprovoked violence around town. Graffiti. Stunts like this. All of it leads me to believe that the remaining gang members are recruiting. I'm guessing that a few of them are gunning for the top spot and are gathering followers. It wouldn't be unusual for them to send their new recruits out to prove themselves by performing acts like this. Usually, they target their rivals, though, not civilians."

My mom wraps her arms around me and pulls my back against her front. Her puffy-jacketed warmth is reassuring and cozy. "But Val isn't only a civilian."

He shakes his head. "That she isn't. Which is why I'll have someone posted outside your house for the next little while. We'll keep an eye out for you."

"It's what Dan would have wanted," Sykes adds. I had forgotten he was here, so focused was I on the bad news the sheriff came to deliver. At hearing my dad's name, my teeth clamp down on my tongue.

"Would questioning them again do anything?" My mom sounds hopeful, but it's without foundation.

I don't need to ask to know that's a non-starter. "Leif Agani would never help me."

Sheriff McCandles runs a hand down his lariat. "I'll send someone out to the prison and talk to them, but don't get your hopes up. Neither Dino nor Leif is willing to talk to me much, these days. I could speak to Rock, see if he—"

"Rock doesn't know anything about this," I bark.

The sheriff's eyebrows twitch, but he doesn't argue.

We thank him as his radio goes off. Excusing himself, the

lawman climbs into his truck and goes.

I turn in my mom's arms and wrap around her waist. "Should we start scrubbing?"

"Let's go back to our Christmas movie marathon. The scrubbing will keep 'til tomorrow."

We go inside, but all the while holiday movies play on the TV, my mind isn't on them. I can't stop picturing the image of our front door defaced with a condescending name meant to scare me.

Little bird. Little bird. Little bird.

If the Snakes are recruiting and sent some of their new lackeys to scare my mom and me, it worked. I hate it, but from what the sheriff said, it was probably a stunt. Nothing to be worried about.

Then why is he having his deputies stationed outside our house around the clock?

Leif Versus the Volcano

My legs are sore from snowboarding, and my arms are aching from scrubbing. I'm not entirely convinced they're not about to fall off. Dropping my hands, I wipe at my running nose with a coat sleeve. "If I ever get the chance, I'm going to find a volcano and drop Leif Agani into it." I'm not even kidding.

Spending hours scouring graffiti off the side of my house, with mixed results, has given me ample time to build a convincing mental argument that penalties for vandalism should be much more severe. This crap is impossible to get off. The more elbow grease I put into attacking the black paint, the more obvious it becomes that we're going to have to repaint the entire front of the house. Black has seeped into the siding and is not letting go.

Hopefully Sheriff McCandles gets some useful footage off our neighbors' security cameras and can put names to whichever jerkwads did this. But if what he said about new gang recruits is true, that will be difficult. Even if there is video footage of their faces, it's difficult to identify anyone without a criminal record.

Plunging my prune hands into the bucket of soapy water, I put every muscle into attacking the black letters beside the front door. Leif's insult isn't the foulest thing the Snakes painted onto our walls, but the cruel nickname bothers me the most. Not only is it an unflattering holdover from when Rock and I were kids, but it reminds me of the day last fall when I marched into Agani Auto without an escape plan and demanded he return my car, or else. The memory is a blur of tense fear, rough hands, and clammy, stinky breath on my skin. Moments of fear that when strung together couldn't have added up to more than ten minutes, but in my head lasted for hours.

Revulsion washes through me and I growl at the paint in frustration, scrubbing harder. How dare they bring their hate to my house.

"How's it going, over there?" My mom asks. She's around the corner cleaning up the pile of chicken bones someone dumped over the fence into our side yard. Neither my mom nor I saw it until this morning, when the droning buzz of a fly army got loud enough to be heard through the bathroom window. I offered to help clean it up, but one look at the pile triggered my gag reflex.

Standing back, I wipe my sweaty forehead with the back of my hand. "I hope you like painting."

Feet shuffle at my back. I pivot to position my back to the wall.

Sykes shrugs off his uniform shirt, leaving a gray tee tucked into his khakis. He doesn't comment on my jumpiness. Tapping a message into his phone, he slides it into his back pocket. "My mother-in-law is visiting today, so my wife told me to get out of the house for a while. Get some air. I've got a few hours, so I'd like to help. What do you need?"

Sykes is definitely my favorite deputy.

He and Mom make a list of supplies, and she leaves for the home improvement store. Sykes and I work on cleaning while she's gone. Giving up, I heat up a couple cinnamon rolls and we eat while making small talk about goings-on around town. He hypes up a new avocado milkshake the diner has been teasing, coming in January.

"That sounds disgusting." We're plopped down on the front step, and I stretch my legs out, careful not to overturn my plate.

"Don't knock it 'til you try it. Seems I remember someone not liking pepperonis on pizza not too long ago." He forks a big bite into his mouth.

"That was turkey pepperoni, and I was seven." Our chuckles mingle as we finish off our pastries.

I go inside to toss our trash, and when I get back out front Leander's truck is parked along the sidewalk. He and Destin are exchanging fist bumps with Sykes. My best friend comes right for me, wrapping me up in a cozy hug that morphs into a noogie. "Heard you could use some extra hands. Get it?"

"Worst joke ever," I complain at him, but I can't bite back my smile.

My mom returns with a trunk full of paint and tools, and the five of us get to work. Mom and I work on the ladder, taking down the ruined Christmas lights and cleaning in preparation for paint. Sykes and the guys pour the paint into trays, and the deputy doles out brushes. Mom uses the paint sprayer to lay down coats while the rest of us do the trim work.

We're all splattered in paint and laughing when Janice shows up. Destin must have texted her. A tingle in the vicinity of my heart makes me hesitate as she crosses the lawn in a dingy white long-sleeved tee and paint-splattered jeans. Even though we've been hanging out, I still don't feel super comfortable reaching out to her. Or anyone, really. My independent streak is a mile wide, and building a bridge across it is taking some time. That might be exactly why I should have texted her. Should've given her the chance to rise to the occasion.

"It's your turn to boss me around, for once. Don't get used to it." Janice takes the big hedge clippers I give her and sets to trimming the hedge that fronts the windows. Her cuts are vicious, but precise.

"That's the bridge troll I know."

She flips me off over her shoulder, her laughter pleased.

A tan truck parks behind Janice's car, and Kelley and Jonesie hop out. Who is calling everyone we know to get them over here? Not that I'm complaining.

Mom hugs them both and gives them the task of weeding the flower beds. I didn't realize until all these people appeared in my front yard how run-down our property had gotten since my dad disappeared. I can't remember the last time my mom did any yard work, and it should have occurred to me to help.

Not letting it get me down, I push the disappointment in myself away. Working alongside my friends and family fills me to the brim with warm mushiness. All of these people have our backs, and they're proving it today by doing the dirty work of painting and weeding and battling back the overgrown hedges along the fences. This show of support is night and day different from last fall, when everywhere I went I was met with hostile stares and serrated whispers. Having a community like this makes every single day a little easier. Spending our first Christmas without my dad was tough, but with friends, we got through it.

Mom must be feeling the same way I am, because she climbs the ladder to get everyone's attention. "Who wants some pizza?

Come inside and have some cider while I order us some dinner."

Sykes whoops. He always loved my mom's cider. His wife and their weeks-old baby show up a few minutes later. Mrs. Sykes hugs her man, even though his pits are stained and his hair is slick with sweat. I'm not a baby person, but the way their little chubbster stares at everyone is kind of cute.

Janice helps herself to my personal space on the sofa, poking at me until I fill her in on the sheriff's visit and his theories about who defiled our house and why. She takes a long drink from her steaming mug. "God, I love your mom's cider. You think he's right?"

I shrug, even as my phone burns a hole in my pocket. I snapped a few photos of the damage and sent them to Rock early this morning, asking if he had heard anything about who might have it out for me. I still maintain that he doesn't know anything, because no matter how much Rock despises me, I can't believe he'd keep it to himself if he heard I was in danger. He promised he would always come for me, and even though I'm not sure I believe him, that promise has burrowed into my heart so deeply I know I could never remove it.

Despite his promise, Rock hasn't broken his wretched radio silence. Trying to hide the hurt in my own when I meet Janice's prying eyes, I confess. "I don't have a clue."

And the only person who might be able to shed some light on my predicament still isn't speaking to me.

Don't Say I Never Gave You Anything

Rock

SINCE I WAS A KID, I'VE LOVED CARS AND MOTORCYCLES. Looking at them. Riding in them. Taking them apart and putting them back together with my dad. I've even done some part fabrication, although that is a much more challenging job.

Normally, digging into a project is an effective way to cut out the noise and pain of the real world for a little while. But today, all I can think about is the little gray kitten hiding behind the shop dumpster in the alley. If my brother could see me right now, it would confirm I'm too soft to be a gang leader. Leif's constant need to one-up me is a big reason I've learned to guard my words.

Tools clang against metal, breaking my concentration on the little furry ball across the alley. One of the guys in the bay next to mine is on a creeper under an SUV, changing the oil. Dude lets out a string of curses and kicks the concrete floor with his heels like one of my baby cousins throwing a tantrum when Granny doesn't agree to mac and cheese for dinner for the third time in a week.

I look up baby cats, and the rescue group I find advises to never rescue a kitten you find abandoned, unless you've watched it for a few hours to make sure the mama cat isn't coming back. Sometimes, mama cats leave their babies in a safe spot to go find food or better shelter.

Sometimes mamas just need a break. That's what my mom told me and Leif before she walked out the door. Naive five-year-old me believed her. Leif was the one who realized she wasn't coming back. When the sunlight faded and the house got dark, she still wasn't home. My brother cooked us boxed mac and cheese on the stove and put me to bed. When I woke up the next morning, I ran into my mom and dads' room to see her, only to find my dad in bed alone.

She never came back.

The kitten I have my eye on has been alone behind the dumpster for almost 24 hours. I've put a can of wet food from the gas station out for it, but the little thing hasn't touched it.

Cracking my neck, I stand. I've been pretending to work on Leif's bike for over an hour, and if anyone was paying attention, they'd notice that my head has been so far in the past I haven't picked up a tool the entire time.

Arching my back and spreading my arms frees up some of the kinks from sitting hunched over a low stool for so long. Checking the alley for approaching vehicles and seeing none, I cross to the dumpster.

The little gray ball of fur startles and scurries under the bin. The dirty, peeling receptacle is overflowing with cardboard boxes that should have been broken down before they were tossed. Packing materials from ordered parts overflow onto the greasy asphalt. I crouch and crane my neck to get a look under the dumpster. The little cat is at the very back, its tiny body pressed against the block wall. Huge green eyes stare at me without blinking.

How to get it out without hurting it.

I pull a few of the larger boxes out of the dumpster and barricade the sides so the kitten can't bolt away from me toward the street. Then, I shred a skinny box, making myself a long arm of cardboard. Pulling my hoodie sleeves down over my hands for protection against sharp claws, I lay flat on my stomach and scoop the kitten out from under the dumpster.

It comes hissing and swiping at me like it's already learned the law of the street: fight or be flattened. She's trying to make himself look as big and scary as possible, and it's freaking adorable.

Wrapping it up in my arms, I hold it close to my body. I take long, slow breaths and hope it'll read my energy. I once heard somewhere that animals are pretty intuitive.

It takes a few minutes, but the kitten calms down once it realizes that A) I'm not going to hurt it, and B) I'm significantly warmer than the metal dumpster it was cozied up to in forty-degree weather.

I hadn't planned on scooping up the kitten today, but it's supposed to be freaking cold tonight. The shop guys keep complaining about having to unload a shipment in freezing temps. No clue what kind of shipment, and I'm not asking.

Thinking about the little gray kitten out in the cold makes

me shake my head. I'm not a monster. Despite my dad and my brother pushing and dragging me to the edge of darkness and trying to pull me down with them. Metal clangs against metal, and my eyes pinch closed. Bars closing around me. Constant catcalls and threats. Pitying looks from hardened security guards.

Breathing out slowly, I open my eyes. I'm not in jail anymore, and I'm never going back there.

I march inside the shop while trying to shield the cat from curious eyes. The clock on the wall reads seventeen minutes to closing, which is close enough for me. Even though my dad and brother are in prison, having my name on the side of the shop still gets me some clout. Since I got out of jail, I've been keeping my head low. Saving that leverage for a time when I need it. With the infighting among the older, more senior members of the Snakes that's been going on in the power vacuum created by my dad and brother's absence, not to mention Angus Hill's, keeping my head down has been all about survival. Some of the old timers expected me to take the reins even though I've always insisted I wasn't interested in the family business.

Others want to knock me off the top of the pecking order and take that position for themselves. They're welcome to it, as far as I'm concerned.

In my back pocket, my phone goes off. A text from Janice.

She's been seeing the smoothie guy from the resort, and it's going well. Relief goes through me at the news. If she hadn't found someone new to cozy up with, I could see us getting back together just because we're a known quantity. Our hearts wouldn't be in it, but I'd do my best to hang onto her anyway. She's all I've got left. Clinging to a past of trauma isn't love, but us together is familiar and comfortable. Janice knows my darkest secrets. I know hers. Neither of us will spill those jagged bits of shame we bury down deep to hide from the light.

Having a ride or die friend like that isn't love, but it's still valuable.

The judgment in Valencia's eyes when she realized I'd helped my brother dispose of her friend's body? It's a cutting weight that will live rent free in my head for the rest of my life.

Never thought she'd look at me like that. With so much disappointment. It tore me apart.

Disappointing my dad? It sucked, but he understood. Disappointing Leif was easier because my brother grew up into a tool.

But disappointing Valencia? She might as well have stabbed me in the heart instead of handcuffing me to that pool ladder.

I frown down at my phone, my eyes devouring the words as Janice's texts come through.

Someone defaced Val's house. Wrote nasty things all over her walls with harsh black spray paint.

My hand clenches around the device. New recruits to the gang is her educated guess.

They threatened Valencia.

Anger burns hot and fierce in my gut, but I keep my hands gentle as I secure the kitten in a small cardboard box with a clean, soft towel inside. Closing the lid and strapping the box down, I climb onto my bike.

By the time I cut the engine a few doors up from the Lamb house, the cleanup crew is gone and the street is dark. A creeping chill is descending on Hacienda, and the shop guys' complaints come to the front of my mind. They're going to be freezing their butts off while they unload Gabriel's shipment.

I'm thankful for the dark. It's where I'm most comfortable. Bruises and hurts that stand out like beacons in the light are mercifully hidden in the shadows. Val doesn't need to know I'm outside her house, checking on her. She'd be pissed if she knew where I was after I've ignored every single one of her messages. The Lamb house sighs as it settles, and my gaze snaps to the front door. It stays closed.

Val catching me is the last thing I need tonight. She has this way of looking through me, seeing all the hurts I'm fighting to hide. Her blunt fingers would poke and prod at all of my bruises until I lashed out at her, or worse. Val handing over a napkin to wrap the cut I got from a rose thorn notwithstanding, the girl has never been subtle. And if she confronted me now? When I'm at loose ends? Those wide eyes would have me confessing all the crap I'm mired in. My life is a giant pit of movie quicksand. The harder I struggle to climb out, the faster it drags me down. One of these nights, I'll drown in it.

Stowing my helmet, I unstrap the box from the back of the bike and sling it under an arm.

A department squad car is parked across from the house. It's impossible to see anything distinct because the overzealous recruits who vandalized Val's house also knocked out the two closest streetlights.

It takes me a second to realize the little pricks in my chest are envy toward the deputy. A not small part of me wishes I had the right to be nearby, keeping watch on Val and her mom.

I don't have that right. Never will. Not with the stains on my soul.

The squad car window whirrs as it rolls down. Deputy Kelley looks unconcerned at my appearance, despite my inheritance of violence. "You here to see your buddies' artwork?"

Her question is cutting, but I ignore it. I'm used to people seeing what they want to see. "Something like that."

An elbow leans on the windowsill, and her mouth twists downward. "You should leave. Nothing good can come of you being here."

Something in my chest drops. The deputy's naked suspicion of me is not a surprise, but it still cools my heels. She may not let me do what I came to, even if I ask nicely. So I don't ask. "Brought something for Val. I'll drop it off, and then I'll go."

She takes a long look at the parcel in my arms. My exhale is loud when she nods.

Holding up my phone, I lie. "She told me to come around to the back."

The deputy gives me another doubtful look but tilts her head toward the side gate.

I drop off the present for Val, hoping it goes a ways to soothing her after yet another attack on her house, courtesy of my screwed-up family. And then I leave, pretty sure I'm walking out of her life forever.

Threats in Dark Corners

Val

MY HEART IS POUNDING AS MY EYES FLY OPEN. There was a weird noise, like rustling paper, right beside my bed. Which can't be right, because there are only two souls in the house tonight, and one of them is asleep. The other is me.

A flicker of movement in the doorway catches the tail of my vision, and my head whips toward it. Shadows dance in the dark, but there's no one there. "Mom? Is that you?"

Nothing but quiet. I must have imagined the figure I could have sworn was standing there.

My entire body seizes when another rustle comes. Right beside my bed. There's something moving on the floor.

Pinching my thigh hurts like hell, but it confirms that I am in fact awake. I'm not imagining the papery scritches coming from below. Fists balled in my weighted quilt, I breathe in and out, not making a sound.

One of the Snakes is back to make good on their threats. He got into my house somehow and is waiting to attack. Waiting for what? I swallow tightly, not sure what to do. Heart thudding, I wait. Listening.

There it is again. Rustling paper.

My phone is inches away on my nightstand, but I can't reach it without hanging my arm out where the monster under my bed could grab and devour it.

Scowling in the dark, I brace myself. I'm being ridiculous. If anyone had come to hurt me, the deputy stationed outside would have stopped them. I'm going to look. In three, two, . . .

Flinging myself across the mattress, I look over the edge. Into two large, glowing goblin eyes. Cue the screaming, cut off with an abrupt slap to my own mouth.

A door down the hall slams open.

"What? What is it?" Mom bursts into the room with her handgun held just how my dad taught her. Pointed at the ground but ready.

"She's pretty cute, huh?" Flicking on my bedside lamp, I hold up the tiny gray kitten who somehow found her way into our house.

My mom's eyes go heart-shaped and soft. She sinks onto the bed by my legs and coos at the kitten. Scratching her soft chin, my mom looks at me. "Where did she come from?"

The kitten arches her back into her hand, loving the attention. Her silvery fir is the softest substance that has ever occurred on this planet. "Found her by my bed. I'm guessing she snuck in this afternoon during all the fun and hid until it was quiet."

Mom hums speculatively. "Smart little girl. It's cold out there tonight."

The kitten jumps out of my hand and curls up between my knees. "Guess she knows what she wants."

"I guess she does."

My mom goes downstairs, checking to make sure the doors and windows are secure. I can't drag my eyes away from the tiny kitten in my lap. Green globe eyes watch me without blinking. Curling up in my lap, she settles into the tiniest ball. Her breaths become slow and even. This little girl looks completely at ease, even though she only met me a few minutes ago. I'm deeply honored to be chosen by such an innocent little ball of fluff. I have a cat now.

Mom comes back in carrying a large cardboard box. "Do you have any idea why there was a box of cat food, a food bowl, a litter box and bag of litter, and a pink studded collar on the back patio?"

"Are you serious?" I take the box from her and pick through it, careful not to disturb the kitten in my lap. My mom is right; someone put a kitten starter pack on my back porch. Lifting out the bracelet-sized burgundy collar reveals a silvery nametag already attached. *Rosie.*

A note attached reads, *Don't say I never gave you anything.*

Warmth flushes my cheeks, and I'm grateful the shadows cast by the lamp on my nightstand hide them. If Mom notices me blushing, she'll ask me what it's about. I have no words to explain why Rock Agani would bring me a kitten.

Once, he told me that if a guy liked a girl, he'd put in the work to show her. But that's ridiculous because he has made it obvious I'm not welcome in his life anymore. Still, I'm confused. The precious kitten's sweet name gives him away as the giver of this precious little soul. This is no rose cut from Leander's mom's garden.

Mom ceases fawning over the gray fluffball to pat my cheek. "Now that I know you aren't being murdered in your bed, try to get some sleep, okay?"

She leaves, and I scoop up my phone. I texted Rock hours ago about the house, and he hasn't replied. No heads up about the kitten either. I own I made a huge mistake when I accused him of helping Leif murder Gracia, but in my defense all the evidence was stacking up pretty high, and none of it looked good. Then there was the video.

Befuddling guilt churns in my gut. I assumed that once I apologized, we could pick up where we left off, wherever that is. Partners in petty, investigation-minded crime. Friendly, maybe. Through working together, I thought we were kind of bonding. Despite the blackmail.

Burying my fingers in the kitten's whisper soft fur calms me. My heart beats slow from a race to a crawl. Relaxing back against my padded headboard, I stare at the silvery ball of fluff in my lap.

I've lost Rock twice now, and both times were my fault. I refuse to let it stick this time.

If Rock won't come to me, I'll go to him. In a few hours, when the sun is up and there isn't a warm ball of kitten in my lap lulling me back to sleep.

Granny Agani smiles wide when she opens her front door and sees me standing on the porch, poinsettia plant in hand. "If it isn't the sweet little girl who used to follow my Rocky around all the time. How you been, girl?"

Her frail arms wrap around my shoulders and pull me inside, where a passel of Rock's younger cousins are playing a racing video game and screaming childish taunts at each other over the game soundtrack.

"I'm okay, thanks. How are you?"

Granny leads me into the kitchen and puts me to work drying dishes as she washes. The easy way she falls into conversation, even though she and I haven't spoken in years, makes my chest squeeze tight. "Got four grandkids living with me, and that creates a whole heap of dishes. Seems like everyone needs a new cup for every sip. It's like in that movie where the little girl leaves half-drunk glasses of water on every piece of furniture in the house. Minus the aliens. You know the one."

I grin, because even though the words coming out of Granny Agani's mouth could be construed as complaint, her love for her grandkids seeps through every syllable. The kiddos in the living room get especially loud, and I wander across the kitchen to peer around the corner at the TV. One of them has smoked the others in a race and is doing the most obnoxious victory dance I've ever seen. Reminds me of the one Leander did when I agreed to go on a date with him after he made a touchdown. Biting my lip, I float back to Granny Agani's side.

"Speaking of grandkids, where is Rocky?" Even though I wished it would, using his nickname doesn't soften it on my tongue. Instead, his name tastes bitter with regret.

Granny clucks her tongue as she loads glasses into the dishwasher. Silverware tinks as she slides it into the tray. A couple of plates clink together as she closes the door and sets it to run overnight. "Want something to drink? I have plenty of tea in the cupboard."

I decline, and she goes about making herself a cup. Steaming mug in hand, Granny leads me to the round table in the breakfast nook and lowers herself into one of the chairs. She's still pretty young and spry for a Granny, but she's moving slower than she did when I was a kid. It's been ten years, so I don't know why I'm so surprised.

One of the cousins comes running into the kitchen and snatches a banana. Granny Agani calls after her to get one for the others, too. Chuckling, she shakes her head. "They keep me young, that's for sure."

I grin. "You don't need help with that. You still look the same as when I was a kid."

"Pretty lies from a pretty girl," she quips. Cradling the mug in her hands, Granny Agani looks toward the hallway to the bedrooms before meeting my eyes. "My Rocky, he hasn't been around much since he got out of prison. I don't know where he goes, and he doesn't say. He's old enough that he doesn't need me to baby him, but I wish he'd still let me sometimes."

That doesn't surprise me either. Rock was locked up for a couple of weeks, but even a short stint like that can change someone. I can understand him avoiding me, but Granny? Seems like he should be leaning into her wrinkled arms instead of making himself scarce.

Granny nurses her tea, her focus wandering out the back window. She misses him. He has lived with her almost his whole life, and his prison stay has turned him into a ghost.

Determination calcifies in my gut. I'm going to pull him out of his shell if it's the last thing I do.

"He isn't here, is he? Rock?"

"I doubt it, but you can check." Granny tips her mug toward the hall.

My fingers brush along the old, familiar dips and whorls in the wall texture as I follow the hallway to the end where Rock's room is. The door is closed. I'm tempted to bustle inside and have a look around, but he wouldn't appreciate that. Knocking doesn't produce him, so I try again. "Rock? You in there?"

I try the knob. It's locked. He's either not home, or he's still ignoring me. Each one of his rejections gets bulkier and harder to manage, like shipping boxes too large and awkwardly shaped to carry. I carry them anyway.

A knock comes at the front door, and Granny answers.

I stiffen when Rotten Egg Breath comes inside bearing armfuls of groceries. "Hey, Granny," he greets the woman, shuffling past her to drop everything off in the kitchen. How dare someone as gross as him be so familiar with the Agani matriarch. He shouldn't be allowed anywhere near her pure, loving soul.

I nearly choke when she greets him. "You're an angel for helping an old woman with groceries. Thank you!"

Pleasant chuckles float down the hallway. He retreats from the kitchen once his arms are unloaded, inching toward the door. "You need help putting these away, or. . .?"

"No, you go on, Gabriel. I can handle these."

"All right." Rotten Egg Breath does a double take when he sees me hiding in the shadowed bend of the hallway. A malicious grin overtakes his features, and he speaks without looking at Granny. His eyes are locked heavily on me. "Okay if I use the bathroom before I go?"

Paper bags rustling in the kitchen cover Granny's response.

REB looms closer, growing taller and wider as he advances. By the time he gets close enough to smell, I feel very, very petite. I usually forget that five foot even is small, but right now I'm keenly aware.

That day when I stupidly ran into Agani Auto without a plan, REB's hands had been almost crueler than the stench coming off him. I press myself into the corner, trying to appear even smaller and helpless. Let him underestimate me. Maybe if he doesn't see me as a threat, he won't try anything. It's a watery, unsubstantial hope, since he's already seen me break a nose and use pepper spray with near perfect aim.

I try not to think about the countless people who have been hurt in homes right around the corner from unsuspecting family members and friends. Unfortunately for me, I know the statistics. If he wanted to, REB could cause serious damage before Granny even realized he was still in the house.

Reciting the kicks and punches I've learned in kickboxing class helps keep my mind focused as Rotten Egg Breath stops an arm's-reach away. "What have we here? Seems like somebody is asking for trouble, coming here. And you know I know how to handle trouble."

Invisible fingertips dig into my sides as his horrible breath washes over me. I try not to gag, and almost succeed. "You should go, before your breath gathers into a toxic gas and poisons Granny and the cousins."

Yes, smart. Irritate the giant, violent man.

He wags a finger at me. "Is that any way to speak to a Snake when you're a helpless, cornered little bird?"

I recoil. "If you were expecting an apology, you'll be waiting a while. I have nothing to say to you."

"Ah, but I have something to say to you. Call it a friendly warning. The Snakes are coming for you, Little Bird. Having some of the newer guys decorate your house was just the start. You think the Snakes would ignore you even after you put both of Boss Agani's sons in prison? After you agreed to sing for a judge? You're a sheriff's daughter. You can't be that naive."

I'm shocked silent. I shouldn't be. I am a sheriff's daughter, and gang retaliation isn't an unfamiliar concept.

The gangster's malicious grin sharpens. He points one long, oil-blackened finger in my face, tracing it down my neck to jab me in the stomach. "Got you. You're afraid. Can't deny it, can you?"

Using a move I learned in kickboxing, I force his arm out and away from me, dashing underneath it. "I'm not afraid of you."

The brute crosses his arms. Shakes his head. "You should be afraid, Little Bird. We're coming for you. When you least expect it." A crisp snap of his fingers punctuates his threat.

I can't look away from the brazen hatred in his eyes. He craves hurting me.

Motion behind him draws my attention. There's a flicker of a shadow under Rock's bedroom door, and then it's gone. It must have been the curtain fluttering or something.

My heart thunders in my chest as I bolt from the hallway. After saying my goodbyes to Granny and the cousins, I run to my Corvette. Dad loved its shiny paint, but maybe Sheriff McCandles is right. It's dangerous to drive such a recognizable car around town, especially if what Rotten Egg Breath said is true. If the Snakes are coming for me, driving the Corvette is like tagging my exact location on social media. It only makes it easier for the gang to find me. To chase me down and hurt me.

Mob Mentality

Rock

I'M TRAPPED AGAINST MY BEDROOM DOOR, SHIRTLESS AND pressed to the flat panels. I was stepping out of the shower when Valencia showed up on my doorstep, and I hid in my room like a coward. I know I'm cute, but that doesn't mean I'm ready for Val to see me clad in only my little cousin's princess towel.

Didn't I decide to stay away from her just last night? The hours since I dropped Rosie by Val's bed and said a silent goodbye have gone by both quickly and slowly. It was the right decision, and I don't regret it. At least not until right now.

What if staying away from Val isn't enough to keep her safe?

My goal was to remove her from the line of fire by staying away. Maybe someday I'll escape the bear trap my dad has me caught in, fighting and bleeding for my freedom. Maybe never, if I can't climb out of the pit my family legacy has dug for me.

But avoiding Val means listening to every word she and Gabriel lob back and forth without interfering. Every word they hurl at each other makes my fists clench and my intestines tie themselves into huge knots.

"The Snakes are coming for you Little Bird," Gabriel hisses so near the door he must have forced Val back against it and loomed over her. That bastard.

That's it. I'm stopping this now.

Tearing into my closet, I yank a shirt off a hanger. It snaps and falls with a dull thud onto the carpet. I yank it down over my head so viciously it almost rips.

That piece of dog filth threatened her, right in my earshot.

Pulling on a pair of jeans, I stalk toward the door. I pause to listen. If Val is pressed against the door, I don't want to fling it open and harm her, even if I am burning to get my hands around Gabriel's scrawny, worthless neck. For the first time, I crave the sound of a bone snapping. My dad used to do it. I've witnessed it more than once.

Never would have considered taking a life, but the way Gabriel threatened Val changed my mind. To protect her, I could make myself do it. Give in to the darkness.

There is no sound in the hallway. Peeking out reveals it's empty. Val and that Snake scum are gone.

Seething, I retreat into my room.

Gabriel threatened her, and I let it happen. I let it happen because my instincts are telling me that if I got between them it would only make the gang even more aggressive toward her. If the more sadistic members of the Snakes realize I care about her, they'll cause her pain. They relish in it.

I won't be responsible for putting a bigger target on her

back.

I'm not anyone's favorite person right now, especially Gabriel and the rest of the Snakes. They don't know the details of how I got out of prison, and I won't be telling them. If they found out I made a deal to testify against my brother and my dad, they'd kill me without hesitation or mercy.

But first, their goal would be to make me suffer.

If they know how much I care about Val, she'll be at the top of their hunting list.

Digging through my dresser, I pull on a thick winter flannel. I haven't had a chance to get a new jacket since the one Janice bought me got shredded the night I helped Valencia break into the shop. The image of her climbing the chain link fence still brings the barest smile to my face. She looked like a natural up there, like when we were kids climbing trees. Until her jeans got stuck on the barbed wire and I had to give her a boost.

Pushing the curtains open, I stare at the fence between our house and the neighbor's. Secretly hoping that Val will appear beyond the glass like she did a few weeks ago. Running a hand through my buzzed hair, I bite my lip. Val appeared at my window, and I caught her staring at my chest. I will never forget the surprise in her eyes. What I'd give to know if the surprise was at being caught, or at liking what she saw.

Drumming my hands against the sill, I close the curtains.

From the little I've heard, and the poison Gabriel was spouting a few minutes ago, the Snakes blame Valencia for the gang unraveling the way it has since my dad and brother were arrested. Under Leif's leadership, the gang was essentially a car theft operation and chop shop. Not nearly as lucrative, or as volatile, as when my dad and Hill were running drugs through the shop.

Since Leif was arrested, the mob mentality of the gang's

members has gotten worse. Gabriel and a couple other guys are locked in a struggle for control. I never thought I'd miss my asshat of a brother, but without Leif, the more senior members of the gang are at increasing odds with each other, arguing about how to make money while slaking their hunger for violence. A few of the younger guys looked to me for leadership, but I've made it clear by my absence since I got out of prison that I'm not interested in being the head of the Snakes. My whole life has been a war—battle after battle in an attempt to get out from under my dad's punishing fist. I want more for myself. I bust my butt at school and keep my nose clean so I can get a good scholarship for college and leave this hole behind.

My nose isn't clean anymore, but I won't let that stop me.

I won't use my dad's dirty money to pay for my escape, either. If I don't get scholarships for my grades, I'll take a gap year or five and work my ass off until I can put myself through college. I have my sights set on a couple of good schools out of state, and once I leave, I'm not coming back. Granny's eyes got teary when I sat her down and told her what I'm planning, but she understood. Watching her son go down the dark path he did must burn holes in her pockets like a drug addict's unspent money. As much as she'll miss me, Granny is rooting for me to make it out.

The thought of leaving Granny's puts an ache in my chest, and I realize I've been staring at my closed curtains for a few minutes. Digging a hoodie out of my closet, I pull it on over the flannel shirt. *You should be afraid, Little Bird. We're coming for you.*

Determination crystalizes in my gut. If the Snakes harm Valencia even though I had the power to stop it, I'll never be able to look myself in the face.

Leaving my phone on the nightstand so I'm not distracted checking it for messages from Val every five minutes, I climb out the window and jog down the street to where I parked Leif's bike. I wanted to go on hiding for a while longer, but the Snakes are threatening Valencia. I have cards I haven't played yet, and the gang's growing volatility is forcing my hand.

Nothing to Do But Cruise

Val

"Told you so." Janice crows as I line up my fake ID next to hers. Janice's fake is legit. It looks exactly like my government issued driver license, down to the special watermarks and holographic details they print on them to make the cards harder to mimic. In comparison, mine looks like a toddler made it.

"Where did you get this, again?" Sliding her ID off the edge of the dining table, I hand it back. Rosie the kitten is curled up in my lap, and I run a hand along her downy spine.

Ty helps himself to another fried crab wonton dipped in sweet chili sauce.

Cartons of half-eaten Thai curry sit open on the dining table next to a pile of paper napkins. We're fueling for another night on the town, poking at sore spots for Sheriff McCandles. Fully sanctioned, this time. Part of me hopes Rock will follow us again. Maybe then I'll be able to thank him for bringing me Rosie, the cutest kitten in the history of the universe.

I mentioned him to Janice this morning when I called to invite her along, and she flat out ignored it. If she knows anything about how Rock is doing, she isn't volunteering any hints these days. His continued silence toward me stings, knowing that he and Janice text back and forth fairly often. They broke up, but they're still in each other's lives. All I did was get Rock arrested, and he won't even look at me, let alone hold a conversation.

I might be minimizing that a little bit.

Okay, I admit it. Getting him arrested wasn't great for our rekindled friendship, but still.

Janice tucks her counterfeit ID into her wallet and buries it in her purse. "Don't look so surprised. I'm the daughter of a gang leader. My ID guy is the least shady shady person I know."

"I don't like you hanging out with bad guys," Ty says, covering his mouth so we don't see sea food. "How old is this guy, anyway? A lot of times, older guys pick on younger ladies when the ones their own age won't put up with their emotional immaturity. This guy, he's not bothering you, is he?"

Janice smiles sweetly at him. "The only guy I let bother me is you."

Ty grins. "If you need help with something, I can do it. My older brother lets me have some of his beer, sometimes."

"That's still illegal, Ty." I meet his eyes over my soda glass, and he reddens.

"Leave him alone, Miss Goodie Two-Shoes," Janice says. "I appreciate he wants to help. I just don't need it."

Ty taps her shoulder and waits until she looks at him.

"You'll let me know if you do?"

"Of course." *No I won't*, she mouths to me. Probably because Janice would be more handfuls of trouble than Ty has hands. I've seen Janice going after something, and that amount of dogged determination… Actually, she's a lot like me when she gets something in her head. Our shared drive for getting to the bottom of things is a huge factor in how we became sort of friendly. Sure, she thought I had helped my dad murder Gracia, and I thought she was a bridge troll, but relationships have to start somewhere.

Clicking my phone to check the time, I wipe my mouth with a wadded paper napkin. "You guys almost done? McCandles asked us to get started pretty soon."

Janice and Ty finish their dinners while I clean up the trash and stow the leftovers in the fridge. I put Rosie in the laundry room where we keep her litter box, water, and a really cute cat bed shaped like a cloud, and lock up. Rosie mewls pathetically as the three of us head toward the door. Tonight is the first night I'll be leaving her home alone, and she lodges her protests loudly.

I make it to the front door before Janice cackles at my thin-lipped expression. "Can't do it, can you?"

Pleased with herself for winning this round, Rosie skitters over the back seat of the car. Lap, seat, floor, seat, lap. Over and over like she's so excited she can't sit still. I may need to get her a carrier for car rides so she's safer.

Since Janice's fake ID is so much better than mine, she takes the first liquor store. She's in and out in only a couple of minutes. The guy behind the counter sold her a six pack without even looking at the card she held out. She drives us to the next place.

Rosie climbs out of the neck of my bomber—I have it zipped most of the way up to keep her warm and contained against my heart—and leaps onto the back of the front seat. Ty scoops her up and rubs her soft fur against his cheek.

"Your turn," Janice says, turning in her seat to look at me. "Try not to get laughed out of the store."

I get laughed out of the store. The clerk spotted my fake ID almost before I had it out of my purse. He told me to scram before he called the sheriff's office. Which is still shady.

I take a couple notes on my phone as I walk to the car. The time, date, and name of the clerk who didn't report me for trying to use a fraudulent ID. Every time I look at the one I have, I get increasingly mortified I paid actual money for it. It makes me wonder how much Janice's guy charges for a good one. I squash that thought right down.

As the night ages, traffic and noise around town get thinner. I lean against the window, holding Rosie and listening for the telling rumbles of motorcycle engines.

"What are you dreaming about back there?" Janice catches my eye in the rearview mirror.

Sitting upright, I run a hand down my seatbelt. "Nothing."

Her only answer is a smirk.

Ty doesn't have a fake ID, so he stays in the car while she and I team up for the next couple of stops, a string of gas stations. The clerk at the first one sells us a bottle of whiskey.

Our night doesn't get interesting until we approach clerk number five. A middle-aged woman in a black-collared uniform shirt frowns at us from her stool behind the counter.

"We'd like a bottle of pineapple vodka." Standing to my full, less than impressive height, I smile placidly.

The woman eyes the two of us. "ID?"

Taking out my half-baked card, I hand it over. The woman's eyes skim the card. Sighing, she pulls a small cardboard box out from under the counter and tosses it in. "Nice try, but I don't sell alcohol to minors."

"I was born in 2002."

"And I'm Jessica Chastain."

"I loved you in *Molly's Game*," Janice quips.

"Get a move on, before I change my mind and report you to the sheriff. If you show your face in here again, I'll make the call. And take care of yourself. I was always a fan of your dad's. Hate to see you acting up, now that he's gone."

The tenderness under her gruff warning is like a rifle shot through the spleen. I practically run to the car, breathing heavily. Once I'm inside, Rosie pokes her head out of my collar and licks my clenched jaw with her sandpaper tongue.

"Did you see that box of fake IDs that lady had under the counter?" Janice slides into her seat. Buckling, she turns around to gush at Rosie. "When can I get another turn?"

I want to be selfish with the kitten, since she was a gift from Rock. I want to keep her all to myself and pretend he gifted me a tiny piece of himself to keep with me always. But that would be ridiculous. I have no idea why Rock gave me the cutest kitten in existence for Christmas, but it wasn't because he wanted to be friends. If he'd been extending an olive branch, he would respond to my texts. Or my photos of Rosie sleeping curled up in my mom's house slippers. Or her looking teeny tiny perched on top of the fridge.

But since that's ridiculous and Rosie isn't a piece of Rock, I hand her over. Let Janice enjoy a few minutes of her sweet meows and warm, cotton ball fur.

Rosie bats at the keys dangling from the ignition while Janice drives. Ty scoops her up and rubs her face against his cheek.

Another engine rumbles nearby. A loud one. Pretending to push my hair away from my face, I squirm around in my seat to scan the dark street behind us.

Two bright spots appear in the distance. My traitorous heart pitter patters more quickly.

The lights split into four. A pair of cars.

Not Rock then. I sink back into the seat, glad Janice and Ty can't see the disappointment on my face in the murky evening.

The rumble grows to a roar as the cars close the distance. They're not slowing down, instead coming in hot.

Janice frowns into the mirror, her eyes trained on the growing headlights. They loom closer and closer, their engines roaring like thunder. They drive side by side, blocking both lanes. It looks intentional. They're boxing us in.

"Janice?" Tyler asks, voice strained.

This is the longest red light ever. I'm staring at it, willing it to turn green. Because those two cars boxing us in can't possibly be good news. More like bad, bad news. The kind that threatens with black paint and fingertips burned by struck matches.

"Run the light, Jan. Just do it."

Her hands tighten on the wheel just as the train crossing barriers lower on the opposite side of the street. Because of course there's a train coming right now.

A pulse taps in my throat, speeding up as the cars' headlights fill the rearview mirror. Their engines drown out the Christmas music filtering from the car's radio as they separate, each taking up room on either side of our car with aggressive jerks of their wheels.

We're trapped between two cars full of gang member wannabes out to prove themselves, and a lumbering cargo train.

The drivers on either side rev their engines, drowning out the train's horn with even louder, headache-inducing growls. Janice's hands are fused to the steering wheel.

The light turns green, but the train is still eating up the crossroad.

I lean forward, gripping the seat back. "Put it in reverse and gun it."

She doesn't move a muscle. Janice is frozen in place. I have never seen fear in her eyes, but when she meets my gaze in the rearview mirror, it's there. Icy chills behind her usually confident demeanor. For the shortest of seconds, I let my mind conjure reasons the Snakes might be angry with her instead of me. But now is not the time to drop my guard.

She and I both know the Snakes are here for me.

Windows on the cars flanking us roll down. I move to lower mine, hoping to draw their attention from Janice and Ty.

Hissing like an enraged cat, Janice jabs the window lock button.

"I'm not going to sit here and do nothing. Trust me." As smoothly as possible, I take the pepper spray out of my purse below the window line. A bad feeling is billowing in my gut, making my stomach slosh. My fingers claw around the canister, hovering over the trigger.

Janice scoffs. "Trust you? The girl who has had more murder attempts than my dad, a known gang leader? I don't think so."

I glance at the car on my left and immediately wish I hadn't. As soon as the guys riding in it see me looking, they hoot and gesture for me to roll down the window. Both cars are all flash and muscle, but the guys inside look young. Barely old enough to drive.

Gritting my teeth, my hand hovers over the window. "Disengage the lock, Janice."

"Bad idea," Janice warns, but she does it.

Hand still on the pepper spray trigger, I suck in frigid late December air. "Nice evening, fellas. Normally, I'd call you gentlemen, but anybody who drives around town with their brights on doesn't deserve that respect."

"We're not gentlemen," one of them crows. Another engine rev, longer this time. "Want to race?"

"Into a moving train?" Janice mutters. Then she calls out the window. "No, thanks. Not in the mood."

"What, are you chicken?" the passenger calls back.

"Playing it safe isn't being a chicken." Ty has relaxed in his seat some, but we'd be stupid to let down our guard. Most of the passengers in both cars hang out their windows, watching us with moonlit, predatory eyes.

"You know who doesn't know how to play it safe?" The driver of the car on the right dangles the question in front of us, and everyone in both cars cranes to hear our guesses.

The pulse in my throat has kicked up from a tap to a thump. Wariness crawls along my nape with its many, many hooked feet.

I hate where this conversation is going, but I have to know. "Who?"

They look at each other, winking and nudging. My pulse? It's a gushing waterfall of doom.

"Your boyfriend, Rock. His sense of self-preservation is broken. One of these days, he's gonna get himself seriously hurt."

"Or killed," someone else says through a gleeful snicker.

My free hand tightens on the seatbelt strap across my chest. The thin woven strip is the only thing keeping me from throwing myself out the car window and demanding they tell me what all this teasing and taunting laughter is hinting at.

With one final short horn blast, the train disappears into the night. Lights flash as the barriers rise, clearing the road.

"Go, Janice. Go," Ty urges her. She shifts in her seat, as if preparing to put the pedal to the metal.

"Not yet," I hiss. We can't leave yet. I have to know what

these idiots are driving at. Turning to the car next to me, I opt for cool disinterest. Maybe if they think they're boring me, they'll offer more information to force me to react. "He's not my boyfriend."

More whispers and elbow jabs. "You sure about that? Because he sure acts like it. He heard about how our boss had a chat with you at Granny Agani's, and he came tearing into the auto shop, ready for a fight."

I suck in a breath, surprised at the strength of the protective wave that rises up in my chest. If they hurt Rock, I'll make them regret it.

"He told us to stay away from you, or he'd make us."

"Yeah, but we sure showed him," another chimes in.

Blood rushes in my ears. Janice gasps.

"Yeah, we did." Their gleeful laughter digs under my skin. They're ticks sucking my blood and making my entire body itch at the wrongness of their bites.

My tongue sticks to the roof of my mouth as all the moisture in my body converts to cold sweat in my armpits. I knew it. Rock was listening the other day when Rotten Egg Breath cornered me in Granny's hallway. It was his shadow coiled under the door.

If Rock was so concerned, why didn't he show himself and scare off my stinky antagonist right then? As soon as I ask the question, I know the answer. Granny and the cousins. Rock wouldn't have wanted to make a scene in the house, with innocents nearby. That house has always been Rock's shelter from his dad's storm, and it still is for his little cousins who call it home.

Rock waited until I was gone and his family was safe. Then, he went to the auto shop.

Worry is a sickness in my stomach, and the only cure is

knowing what happened to Rock. "What did you do to him? If you hurt him, Dino will have your heads."

Their heady pause makes my worry grow, helpless to stop it. Baleful grins glint in the moonlight.

Up to this point, this conversation has been unpleasant. Now it shifts to nightmare. A figure hidden in shadow in the back of one of the cars leans forward, shoving aside the younger guy next to him. How did I miss an entire other person in that car? My pulse thrums in my throat.

REB grins sadistically, settling the full weight of his malevolence squarely on me. "Mr. Agani doesn't show mercy to traitors, even if they are his own blood."

One single sentence siphons away every ounce of blood in my body. The granddaddy of all blood suckers drains me dry. I didn't get it directly from the sheriff, but one of the deputies told me in confidence the amount of dirt Rock had to fork over to make his deal with the DA. If Dino Agani knows his youngest son worked with the law to get his older brother tried for his crimes, he'll be furious. If Dino Agani has found out, even blood ties might not be enough to protect Rock.

In a gush, the blood returns, making my head spin.

"Rock is no traitor," Janice says, voice deadly calm. She and I both know she's lying. The question is whether REB knows, or if he's baiting us. "Where is he?" I ask in a strangled tone.

"Like we'd tell you," one of them retorts.

REB runs his tongue over sharp teeth. "All in due time, Little Bird. We've dealt with Rock, and next we'll deal with you."

The light turns green again, and both of the Snakes' cars peel out, leaving a smoky trail of burned rubber in their wake. Choking on the noxious fumes, I roll up my window. My mind is caught in a loop, circling the drain over and over again.

Rock tried to protect me. He went to the Snakes to stop

them. They did something terrible to him. If Dino Agani found out about the depth of Rock's supposed betrayal, there is no telling the lengths he'd go to to punish his younger son's disobedience. He could have discovered Rock was helping the District Attorney and allowed any amount of retaliation against his own son.

"He isn't answering his phone. He usually answers when I call." Janice jabs at the device in her lap, trying to reach Rock. A second time. A third.

With a gentle hand, Ty takes the phone from her. "You drive. I'll keep trying."

I stare, blinded by fear, out the window. Rock tried to protect me.

If Dino found out about his son's betrayal, is there anything he wouldn't let the Snakes do to him?

"Is he answering?" I ask, even though I already know the answer. Through my panic haze, I recognize it's sweet that Ty is showing concern for a guy he's probably never met and doesn't have cause to care about. He shakes his head, expression grim.

Janice guns it, driving like a madwoman all the way to Granny Agani's house.

We jump out and run around the side of the building to Rock's window. It's dark and empty, the curtains pulled wide. The bed hasn't been slept in.

Rock went to the auto shop to protect me. He put himself on the line for me, and now he's missing.

High Value Targets

I never thought I'd say this, but Christmas vacation needs to end.

Every day since Rotten Egg Breath bragged about taking care of Rock, I've been obsessed with finding him. A deeply embedded need to make sure he is okay drives me to go to Granny Agani's house a bunch of times. Every single time after the first she greets me with a hug and the news that Rock isn't home. He hasn't been back in days. Worry lines around Granny's eyes break my heart. I don't know what to say to her. Platitudes about him being fine would be just that: empty words. Because REB was incredibly smug about what the Snakes did to Rock, and the evil behind his eyes was obvious. The man is capable of doing damage. I know he is.

Worse, Janice hasn't heard from Rock either. He's been ignoring her texts and calls too. I've been listening to the police scanner to make sure they don't find a body. Rock's body.

My eyes pinch shut as I work to rid myself of that horrifying thought.

I'm parked outside Granny Agani's house, hoping by some miracle Rock will show up and I can see him with my own eyes. It's been a week since my midnight ride with the Snakes, and worry is riding me hard. Losing Gracia and my dad in the same night did a number on me, and the risk of losing Rock, too… Grief wells up in my chest, suddenly overwhelming. Folding my arms over the steering wheel, I bury my face in the sleeves as tears stream down my cheeks. Shuddering sobs rack my shoulders, slowly gentling to a wash.

Digging a couple paper napkins out of the glove box, I mop up my eyes and nose. Letting all that out has loosened some of the worry woven through my ribcage. As much as I hate crying, that was cathartic.

Blowing out a breath, I sweep my fingers under my eyes.

Still no Rock. There has to be a way to coax him out of hiding. Because he is in hiding. I won't accept any other reason for his silence. Staring at his house, my eyes narrow. Snapping a photo of Granny's house, I text it to Rock.

Where the hell are you?

The answer is harsh and immediate.
Stay away from Granny's house

I'm so shocked he replied, I stare at the message for a minute before it computes. Stay away from…? Looking up at the house reveals no clues as to why Rock would want me to keep my distance. Everything looks fine here. The cousins are visible through the front window, playing video games. Smoke from the chimney hints at a warm, cozy fire in the living room hearth. The grass is a little long and brittle, but that's probably because Rock hasn't been home to mow, and Granny doesn't trust any of the littles with the mower yet.

Stay away from Granny's.

Understanding makes my breath stutter. Granny Agani's house has been untouched by the Snakes. No one has sent their underlings to deface the front or yard. No one has been sent to deliver threats. Rock must be staying away because he wants to keep Granny and his cousins out of whatever disagreement he's having with the gang.

Guilt builds behind my eyes, making them burn. I have a giant, bright neon red target on my back. The Snakes have it out for me, and I've been visiting Granny Agani every single freaking day. What happens if the Snakes decide to come for me, and a sweet old lady and her grandkids are caught in the crossfire? It wouldn't be the first time gang violence has ended innocent lives.

I won't allow my impulsivity and recklessness to harm Granny and the littles. Starting the engine, I tear out of the neighborhood with my heart pounding a bass rhythm in my chest. I won't go over there again. I won't put them in danger.

At a red light, I text Destin and ask him to go over to Granny's and mow their lawn. He hits me back right away, promising to go over later today. Then I text Rock back to let him know I left and won't go back. He doesn't reply. Shocker. It still stings, no matter how many times he ignores my messages. I've never done something so bad that a relationship was irreparable before, but I'm beginning to fear that is exactly what happened with Rock.

Good thing school starts back tomorrow, and he'll be forced into the same room as me. Maybe I can get him alone long enough to apologize, again, and make sure he's still in one piece.

I can't stop my fingers from rapping on my desk. My leg jiggles under the desk. My head is on a swivel between Miss Wayne and the classroom door. Our first day after Christmas break began fifteen minutes ago, and Rock isn't here. He hasn't shown up to school and I'm trying not to panic.

Okay, I'm panicking. A little.

Janice sits hunched over her desk, eyes trained on Miss Wayne. In her lap, she texts furiously without looking.

I'm texting him.
He's still not answering.
I'm going to make myself throw up so I can leave.

And go where?
You don't know where he's hiding.
Leaving now won't do any good.

We go back and forth about it for a couple minutes, until Destin gets my attention with one hand tapping on my desk. Meaningfully, he shifts his eyes from the phone in my lap to where Miss Wayne is squinting at me from the board.

Sliding the phone between my thighs, I give the teacher my full attention. I do not want my cell confiscated during first period, because Miss Wayne's policy is to keep them until the end of the school day. No, thank you.

Janice meets my eyes over her shoulder, her expression drawn. This standoff with Rock has to end. The two of us care about him, more than I'm willing to admit out loud, and not knowing where he is, or what state he's in, is making us crazy. I didn't sleep a wink last night because I was too consumed with what ifs about how school would go today. All of my guesses were wrong. It's hard to check up on Rock when he. Isn't. Here.

Miss Wayne claps her hands to get everyone's attention. Once we're all looking at her, she gestures to the classroom door. A familiar profile appears through the glass, and my eyebrows go up in surprise. "I have a special treat for you today. Sheriff McCandles is here to talk with our class and answer any questions you might have about what it's like to work in law enforcement."

The man himself enters the room, bobbing his head in thanks for the introduction. He aims a stiff smile at the class, eyes landing briefly on Janice before scooting to me. Clearing his throat, the sheriff sinks onto the high stool Miss Wayne keeps near the interactive smart board. "Morning, like Miss Wayne said, I'm Sheriff McCandles. It's my job to serve all the parts of our county that don't fall under an incorporated police district. I've been in law enforcement for 20 years, so I've seen a lot of interesting things. I could talk at you for the entire class period, but I'd rather hear from you. I'll do my best to answer your questions."

For a few seconds, everyone simply stares at the law man. He waits. It's a technique my dad used to use when he wanted to have a conversation with me. Wait until the other person is so uncomfortable with the silence they start talking. A small smile crosses my face.

To my utter surprise, Destin is the first to ask a question. "So, uh, if someone wanted to go into law enforcement, what do you recommend they study in college? Or do I need to go to college first?"

I pivot toward him, eyes wide. I had no idea Destin was

interested in going into law enforcement. Having spent a ton of time with me and my parents, he was always close to my dad. They did guy stuff together I wasn't interested in. Still, this is the first I'm hearing about it.

Sheriff McCandles looks pleased with the question. "Destin. Good question. If you're interested in going into law enforcement, I recommend…" He makes an explanation, ending by encouraging Destin to stay after class to touch base with him, and he moves on to other raised hands. Destin's inquiry broke the ice, and my classmates pepper the sheriff with comments and inquiries.

Bridging the gap between our desks, I tap the back of my best friend's hand. "I didn't know you wanted to be a cop."

He pushes his bleached blond hair off his forehead. "Yeah. Been thinking about it for a while. You remember when I went on that ride-along with your dad a couple years ago?"

Of course, I do. I wanted to come, but I came down with the flu at the last minute and my dad didn't want me yacking all over his Bronco. I nod for him to continue.

"It was a great day, and it got me thinking. I don't know if I'm really cut out for normal four-year college, but I've been thinking about a two-year criminal justice program. That stuff fascinates me, especially since, uh… Gracia. Cops see a lot of people on their worst day, whether that's criminals or their victims. I figure, if I become a cop I can help people going through their worst days. And maybe prevent some of those worst days. I know it sounds idealistic, but is it too much?"

I shake my head in fervent disagreement. "It doesn't. Not at all. I think that's the noblest thing you've ever said."

Destin's cheeks color. "You think I could do it?"

The vulnerability behind his question cracks me open. Destin has been my friend almost my entire life, and even though

I never considered him going into law enforcement, I could see it fitting him. He's athletic, outgoing, and he cares for people. "I think you could be great at it."

He catches my eye. "You ever consider it? Going into the family business?"

I never thought of it that way, but it is kind of the family business. My dad was in law enforcement his entire adult life, and my mom has worked at the emergency dispatch for over a decade. "I've never considered it, to be honest."

Miss Wayne appears at our shoulder. "Is there something I can help you two with?"

Chastened for not listening to the sheriff, we tune into his conversation with the rest of the class. My eyes keep drifting to the empty desk where Rock should be. Having the sheriff in class has been a distraction and a mental break from worrying about Rock constantly around the clock, but now I'm back on that train of thought.

I'm tired of worrying.

I'm done waiting for Rock to reappear.

I'm going to find him.

Rain, Rain, I Hate You

A TORRENT OF RAIN HAS KEPT ME INSIDE ALL WEEK, but not today. Cloudy skies are losing the sky to the sun, and I have people to see. Pulling the car over on the side of a country gravel road, I sit for a minute in the dim light of dawn. Ahead, the aqueduct rises between the fields. I haven't been out to this place since the night Gus tried to drown me in the irrigation water.

The downpour over the past couple of days has filled the levies, swelling their currents until the aqueduct is brimming with brown water. The chattering of the waters as they pass inches from my booted feet sweeps away the swirl of thoughts keeping me up at night. Fed up with lying in messy flannel sheets unable to close my eyes, I admitted defeat early this morning and climbed out of bed. Donning sweatpants and the burgundy leather bomber jacket that used to be my mom's, I coasted the Corvette out to the aqueduct.

Mom and I laid my dad's coffin to rest in the plot they bought in the cemetery, but that isn't his final resting place. It's here, beneath the levy waters.

I climb the bank, and the burbling grows louder until I'm standing over it. Mesmerized, I clutch the bouquet I bought at the gas station tighter in my hand. It sounded like a good idea when I was still half asleep this morning. Buy flowers. Come to the aqueduct. Spend a few minutes thinking about my dad before tossing the flowers over where his body was swept under and reclaimed by nature. Now, being here, I can't move. My hands don't want to let go of the flowers. I know he's gone. I know it. But it's still hard to make myself accept that I'll never see him again.

The night Leif almost drowned me in the gymnasium pool comes to the front of my thoughts. Leif held me under the surface with cruel, unyielding hands. I had fought, pushing and scratching, but he didn't yield. I couldn't get out from under his hateful pressure long enough to take in air. As my lungs emptied and my body slowed, I had seen my dad. He'd come to me under the water. I thought he'd jumped into the pool to save me, and I'd craned toward him. Seeking the safety of his protection.

In this misty morning, clarity provides an explanation for what I'd seen at the bottom of that pool. My mind had pushed past the fear, emptied of the terror and the questions to a plane where I could accept that my dad was gone. Deep down, I had known. As I was drowning, he had come to say goodbye.

Pale, orange blossom sunlight seeps over the horizon, staining the few lingering storm clouds in oranges, pinks, and purples. *Wherever you are, Dad, I miss you.*

My phone vibrates. My mom, checking in. She must have seen the note I stuck to the coffee pot before I left. I'd have texted her, but sometimes she forgets it on her nightstand for hours. The note was quicker.

Taking a quick photo of the bouquet, I let her know I'm

with Dad. She sends back a heart emoji. She hasn't come out here, for a lot of reasons that I could probably guess. This aqueduct is where she lost my dad, and where she almost lost me. To her, this place represents loss and death. For me, this aqueduct represents my dad, yeah, but it also reminds me of Destin pulling me out of the water. Of Sheriff McCandles showing up just in time to save my life. Of Sykes and Jonesie and Kelley, who came tearing down here that night to see with their own eyes that I was okay. This spot on this aqueduct will always hold bittersweet memories for me.

Mom's little heart emoji loosens my fists and unlocks my knees. Untying the bouquet, I drop the flowers into the swirling water one by one. For a few quiet minutes, I watch them float away, twirls of white bobbing over the currents.

My booties crunch over the gravel as I walk down the ramp to the Corvette and slide into the driver seat. Turn the key. A rattling noise fills the cab. I withdraw the key. Try it again. More rattling.

I did not expect that sound to come out of my car. Drumming my fingers on the steering column, I stare out the windshield.

Rock didn't show up at all the first week of school, which is partly why I couldn't sleep again last night. It's a major reason I'm at the aqueduct at 6:30 AM on a Saturday morning. He still hasn't answered any messages. Janice poked and prodded at some people until she found out that yes, Rock is alive. And two, that he got a job at a different auto shop in town.

Which means he really has been tossed out by the Snakes.

With a finger tap, I dial the auto shop to request a tow.

I'm sipping my still-warm cocoa when the grumble of a truck over the country road gobbles up my attention. A white tow truck with *Nik's Towing* in blue letters on the side rolls up behind the Corvette. The engine cuts off, but no one gets out.

I wait a beat. Still no sign of movement from the tow truck.

Rock's buzzed head is unmistakable in the early morning light, and he knows my car on sight. As soon as he drove close enough, he must have realized it was me who had called for assistance.

According to Janice's source, Rock is the newest employee at Nik's, which means he gets the crappy shifts. Like the butt-crack of dawn on a Saturday morning. Rock is working this morning, and conveniently I need a tow. Can't ignore me now, Rocky.

The sunlight warms as the glowing orb rises, painting the surrounding fields with an indiscriminate brush of gold. It would be breathtaking if I wasn't currently in a standoff with my former friend turned stranger turned accomplice turned stranger again.

There's still no movement from the truck. My heart speeds up. I assumed he was avoiding me because of the whole getting him arrested thing, but what if he has other reasons I've missed?

Suddenly nervous, I take another sip of cocoa. Now I'm the one stalling.

This is ridiculous. Dropping the cocoa into the cup holder, I swing my car door open and get out.

Rock is scowling at his steering wheel when I appear in his window. There's a ring of purple around his left eye, and a cut through his eyebrow that only gets uglier as he rolls down the window.

I've never been so reassured to see a black eye in my life, because it means Rock is here. He's alive. He's still mad at me, but he's alive.

My fingers curl around the sill, almost like I'm afraid he'll drive away if I don't hold him here. Licking my dry lips, curiosity eats at me. I'd love to know who gave him that black eye so I can return the favor, but I doubt he'd tell me, since Rock is clearly avoiding me using every trick he knows. "Well, look what the cat dragged in."

Rock's eyes flick to me and away. "Dragged is about right."

"I need help and I'm hoping a young, healthy car expert like you can help me." I give him the most sickeningly sweet eyelash-flutter he's ever seen.

His scowl flickers for the quickest second. Or maybe I imagined it.

Even sporting a wicked black eye and a scarred eyebrow, I'm so relieved to see Rock that I have to suppress a grin as he gets out of the tow truck and ambles over to the Corvette. His solid body moves in that calculating, assured way I'd know anywhere. "What's wrong with your car?"

"Allow me to demonstrate." I turn the key, and Rock grimaces at the nasty rattling sound clanking around my car's innards. With experienced hands, he cracks open the hood and props it up. I meander closer to see what he's looking at.

It only takes Rock a second up in the engine before he stands to full height, leveling me with a suspicious squint. "Did you disconnect your own battery, Valencia?"

I make my best clueless, doe-eyed expression. "Where's the battery, again?"

Sighing, he runs a hand down his face. "Don't feed me that bull. You've watched your dad tinker with this car all your life. You probably know more about vintage engines than most of the guys at Agani."

"You really think so?"

"Wouldn't say it if I didn't." Rubbing his hands on his jeans, he looks out at the horizon. His eyes are full of emotion I don't see on him much. Yearning. And oh, it aches.

For some odd reason, I want his attention back on me. "I

disconnected the battery."

"Missed me that bad, huh?" He quips, but his heart isn't in it. And that makes teasing him no fun.

"Desperately," I deadpan.

Muttering under his breath, Rock reaches into the engine cavity and reconnects everything. He goes over every connection and belt and plug to make sure it's all exactly as it should be. Each movement is measured and sure. He doesn't miss a trick.

I don't either. Rock is favoring his left arm. Every move he makes is with his right hand. He reaches with his left for one of the tubes, but a wince cuts off the movement.

My feet are dragged toward him, and I only manage to stop myself when I'm less than a foot away. "You're hurt more than just a black eye. What happened?"

Rock closes the Corvette's hood and leans his palms on it. He's still not looking me in the eye. "Nothing I can't handle."

Hopping up on the closed hood, I slide close enough that he can't avoid my gaze. "Rock."

He stares at me, and I stare back. We used to have staring contests as kids, and he always won because eventually I'd get embarrassed of him looking at me like that and I'd blink away. But not today. Today, I'm winning.

Growling, he pushes off the car and rakes a hand over his shorn hair. "You really want to see?"

"Yes!" I hop off the car and circle around to his front.

"You won't like it."

"I already don't like it."

"Promise you won't do anything stupid."

"I already did that."

"And broke it immediately."

"What's your point?" We're toe to toe and chest to chest, our breaths puffing in the morning air. Rock's eyes are wild on mine and I probably look just as untamed to him.

"Why you gotta be so stubborn? You are some kind of something, you know that?" Admiration flashes in his eyes, which he tries to hide by ducking his head. Shucking his sweatshirt, he folds it in half and tosses it on the car's hood.

I grin. "Did you just compliment me? That's so— Wait. Stop. What are you doing?"

He pauses with his Henley halfway off. "You want to see or not?"

"Yes?" I don't know anymore, because Rock is pulling his shirt over his head and my brain is not functioning properly. I stare at the large bandage over his heart, my own in my throat. That is a large bandage. Judging by the looks of it, he could have been shot or stabbed. But if he had been injured like that, he'd be dead. The blade or bullet would have gone straight through his heart. A kill shot.

My throat bobs as I try to force my heart back down where it belongs.

"Take a picture; it'll last longer." Rock's chiding snaps me out of whatever zone I was in. Shaking it off, I mince my way closer. Glancing around, there aren't any other people or cars or anything around. Sleepy Saturday morning, it is.

Thinking back to the vision I saw of my dad, I poke Rock in the arm with one finger. Just to make sure he's real and standing in front of me.

"Hey."

"Just checking. Did you… get stabbed or something?"

"Or something."

"Meaning?"

With an annoyed huff, Rock peels the bandage away from bronzed skin, revealing large, calligraphic letters over his heart. The word *Traitor* spelled in a beautiful, flowering font. Whoever inked this into his skin took their time and did it well. Despite the dirty word they've permanently embedded in his skin, it's a stunning tattoo.

"Traitor? I don't understand." Dragging my eyes up to his face doesn't work because they sink right back down to the ink over his skin.

He passes a hand over his chest, brushing careful over the bandage.

I cover my eyes with one hand.

"The Snakes were getting out of control, so I went to knock some sense into them. They didn't listen very well. Hey. Val. Look at me." He peels my fingers away from my face with his gentle ones and lets go.

"You let them ink you?"

The careful restraint Rock has been holding himself with since he arrived breaks. "No, I did not *let them* ink me, V. They were threatening you. They thought you were the reason Leif is in so much trouble, and they were coming for you. So, I went there and told them to leave you alone. That you had nothing to do with it. The bunch of hyenas didn't believe me. They knocked me out. When I woke up, my eye was throbbing, and some guy was tattooing my chest."

Stunned silence unfolds between us. Rock stands like a pillar with his hands on his hips. Goosebumps break out over his exposed skin, but he ignores the cold.

I've completely forgotten how to move. Rock heard the Snakes were threatening me. He heard about it, and went there to talk them out of it, and they beat him. Tattooed him.

"What did you say to them? To get them to leave me alone?" My heart is pounding in my chest. I know what Rock must have told them, somehow, but I need to hear it from him. Because it's been a week, and the Snakes haven't come anywhere near me.

Rock meets my eyes, staring into my depths that he knows better than anyone else. Rock has seen my worst, and still he went to the Snakes to protect me. And they hurt him. Marked his skin forever with a word most foul. *Traitor.*

"I told them it was me who gave everything to the prosecution. That I'm the reason Leif is going to be in prison for a long ass time."

A curse parts my lips. "Now who's being stupid. They could have killed you." I want to move closer to him, drawn by some invisible, powerful force, but he still holds himself rigid. Holding himself apart from me. I won't impose myself on him when he clearly doesn't want me any nearer than I am already.

The derisive snort that Rock lets loose almost makes me flinch. "I'd be dead if my dad hadn't given a direct order. The only reason I'm standing here right now is because my last name is Agani. Blood still means something to my old man, even if I've tainted it by cooperating with his worst enemies. Even though I helped the daughter of the man who doggedly pursued him for years for breaking as many laws as he could."

The sun is brighter now, making me squint to meet Rock's gaze. Yellow sunlight spews over us, over the car and the aqueduct and the fields that surround us for miles in every direction. And even in all that light, I'm confused. "Why'd you do that? Tell them it was you."

Rock's eyes are heavy on mine. "You know why, Val."

"Tell me anyway."

This time the waters draw Rock's attention to their swirling, early-morning dance. His throat bobs as he gulps down crisp, cool air. "I had no choice. There was no other option."

It's not the answer I wanted. Disappointment swirls in my belly.

Besides, there were options. Rock could have kept his head down and let the Snakes go on thinking I alone was responsible for Leif's arrest. Let them blame me for everything that has gone wrong in their organization in the past year. Rock could have kept his mouth shut and let them come for me.

Looking at Rock, I know what he means. There was no other option.

Because if it were me keeping my head down as I watched a pack of Snakes stalking toward Rock with the intention of hurting him, I would have done everything I could to keep them from getting to him. We haven't been friends in seven years, but the truth is we never stopped looking out for each other.

My eyes watch his tattoo disappear under the shirt he puts back on. "What do I owe you? For the engine check."

Rock shakes his head as he moves toward the tow truck. "Don't worry about it."

"Seriously. What do I owe?"

His hands rest on the tow truck's window well, in the exact same position mine were in minutes ago. "Just promise you won't disable your car and strand yourself out here again."

"A girl has to do what a girl has to do, especially when one of her friends is avoiding her."

He doesn't look at me as he climbs into the truck. "We're not friends, V."

"Your mouth is saying we're not friends, but your actions say we are."

There's a murmur of a smile on his face as he drives away.

We Used to Be Friends

"NEED HELP WITH THAT?" LEANDER LEANS A HIP AGAINST the department desk where I'm sitting, scanning more files. I'm convinced I could make a full-time job of this and still be at it when I graduate from college in four and a half years. If I go to college. I haven't decided yet.

The front desk is bare, and no one has walked into the sheriff's office in the past hour. It's oddly quiet for a Tuesday afternoon in January. Leander is supposed to stay at the front, but when I glanced in his direction a while ago, he'd slumped forward on the stool, chin resting in one palm. Faint snores had floated through the bull pen.

Sliding a paper clip onto a stack of documents, I crane my neck to look up at him. It's unfair how cute he looks even under the ugly fluorescent lights in the department. Even in the dead of winter, his skin has a healthy glow from time spent on the football field, and his puppy dog brown eyes are hard to look away from. I manage it, eyes dropping to the half-scanned file lying open on my desk. "That bored, huh?"

"I'm so bored it's terminal. Which ones still need doing?"

I show him the pile that I carried over from the filing cabinets when I got into the office after school. Already, a couple hours have passed, but the pile doesn't look any smaller. "I'd take you up on the offer of help, but we only have the one scanner."

Leander taps the rectangular shape of a phone in his front pocket. "There's an app for that."

Taking half the stack of files, I expect Leander to plop down into the next desk over, but he doesn't. Scooting Sykes's rolling chair closer, he sits opposite me at the unclaimed desk I've been using for the past couple of weeks. We both get back to work scanning files, and I show Leander where to save them in the system.

We work in quiet tandem for a few minutes. It's easy, like how easy it was to confide in Leander back when I was investigating Gracia's death and trying to find my missing dad. Our first date had been like that, too. Effortless. Until Rock crashed it and stole my root beer float.

I flip to the next sheet and feed it into the scanner.

"Care to make it interesting?" There's a mischievous twinkle in Leander's eyes when I look up.

"Meaning?"

Leander's smile quirks upward. He knows he's got me. "Let's see who can scan more files faster. Winner takes all."

"There's nothing for me to take but your dignity, and that's not very satisfying when there's no one here to witness it."

He laughs. "First, you're going to lose. Second, I was thinking of a yummier prize."

"Yummier?"

"I win, you owe me a milkshake from the diner."

"And if I win?"

"I owe you one."

Intrigued, I nod my head. "You're going down, McCandles Junior."

"We'll see. Start in three, two…" He snaps a few photos with his phone before he even finishes the countdown. It's hilarious how much faster the app is than the department's ancient scanner. He is going to wipe the scuffed linoleum floor with my butt. Already, he's finishing a file. The only thing that slows him down is having to save each doc before starting the next one.

Pushing a paper through the scanner, I squawk. "Hey, no fair! You knew this would happen."

Leander tosses back his head and gives his best imitation of an evil laugh. His caramel blond hair looks so soft. My fingers remember the feel of it when he kissed me. Focus, brain! This is not the time for daydreaming.

I yank a page out of the scanner and put a new one in as Leander plops a second file down on his stack of finished ones. This is going to be a bloodbath.

Leander finishes his stack of files in less than an hour, while I still have a handful to get through. We pass the time trash talking and chatting about football and movies and my latest true crime novel. "Double or nothing?" he asks as he approaches my desk after returning his finished files to the cabinet bank across the room.

"I don't make enough at this job to owe you two

milkshakes."

His smile softens. "I'm not really going to make you pay for it, Val, but if you're game we could go over there after work and—"

The department door swings open, admitting Sheriff McCandles and Jonesie. "You sure you didn't see where they came from?"

"I'm telling you, sheriff, those hooligans came out of nowhere. One second the street was clear, and the next they'd poured buckets of red paint all over the intersection and were tearing off in the other direction. Someone started screaming it was blood, and then all hell broke loose. We were lucky that diesel truck was able to stop in time."

The sheriff's frown etches deep lines on either side of his grim mouth. "You think it was more Snake recruits?"

"I didn't get a good look at anyone in the truck, but yeah. The only thing throwing me is the red. Don't the Snakes usually use green as their color?"

Sheriff McCandles hums, opening his mouth. When he catches Leander and me watching with interest, he thumbs toward his office. The two men shut themselves inside where we can't hear anything more about the incident.

"More gang pranks?" I whisper, eyes glued to the office door.

Leander is more worried than curious. "So far it hasn't been violent, but my dad is worried it'll turn."

I run fingers through my hair to work out a couple of tangles at my nape. Once it's smooth, I braid it deftly into the Dutch braid style I prefer. "Pretty soon pranks won't be enough to get attention. He's right to be worried." My dad's time as sheriff taught me some about street gangs, none of it good.

A few years ago, a rival gang encroached on the Snakes'

territory. At first, all it was was a graffiti war. A tag placed in the other gang's territory. Two more in retaliation. But it spread across every overpass in town and ended in a shootout at a drug house on the outskirts of the next town over. The shooters were never caught, but my dad always suspected Leif Agani had been involved. He'd been the Snakes' heir apparent, and my dad had floated the idea that Leif would have been looking for ways to make himself indispensable to his father. Getting rid of rivals would have been one hell of a way to do that.

"You're thinking about that time with the Scorpions, right?" Leander's look is knowing.

Chewing on my lip, I get up and creep closer to the sheriff's door. Not until I press my ear against the glass can I hear anything.

"I'm worried, Sheriff. We've got pranks left and right that are edging toward dangerous. What are these recruits going to do next?"

"Not to mention the uptick in overdoses we've seen over the past month."

My eyebrows rise. That's news to me, although I'm sure my mom would know about it, given her job at the dispatch. Not that she'd tell me. She's had to learn to compartmentalize so she doesn't worry about her callers all day every day. Sometimes, the deputies share the good news with her, and those days she comes home beaming.

Leander hovers at my side. I expect his hand on my shoulder, pulling me away from his dad's private conversation with the deputy, but instead he leans closer, pressing his ear against the door seam.

My smile goes unnoticed, tucked into my own shoulder. It appears I'm not the only nosy kid of a sheriff in the place.

"We need to find a way to trace the source of the drugs, but if it's the schools, I don't know where to start. We could station deputies on campus during the day, but that wouldn't cut off the source. Only the customers."

"What about parties? Back in my day, if anyone wanted an illegal somethin' somethin', they'd find it at a party."

"New Years was last week, Jonesie."

The office goes quiet, but my mind leaps from rock to rock, making connections. I haven't been able to come up with any compelling ideas for the *Herald*, and Janice has been riding me the past few days. I'm her news reporter, so I need to find some juicy news to report. Eventually, her holding over my head the fact that I solved Gracia's murder is going to get old, but it hasn't happened yet. Besides, I give as good as I get, reminding her that if she hadn't been such a bridge troll about it, I wouldn't have solved it nearly as quickly.

But if I could figure out where people in town are getting the drugs they're overusing, that would be quite the story. It would help the sheriff, too. Killing two birds with one stone. I'm so busy pondering how to float the idea to McCandles that I don't hear him approach the door until it opens inward, leaving me hovering awkwardly in the doorway.

"Aren't you supposed to be scanning files?" The lawman asks, expression stern.

"I can help," I blurt. "With tracing the drugs."

Sheriff McCandles shakes his head. "Absolutely not."

"What, are you going to make Jonesie shave his stubble and go undercover at the high school?"

Jonesie laughs nervously, eyes jumping between the sheriff and me. Sheriff McCandles scrutinizes him for a beat, his hand rubbing at the silver bead on the end of his lariat.

The deputy's ruddy face bleeds of color. "You can't be serious, Sheriff. You know I hated high school."

"He won't pass, anyway." Surprised Leander is backing me up, I meet his eyes. He winks at me. A warm rush of gratitude brushes the inside of my elbows.

"He's right, sheriff. I may not be old, but I don't pass for a teenager anymore either. She is one, though. It could work."

Sheriff McCandles looks me over, wheels turning in his head. Finally, he gives a decisive shake of his head. "I'm not doing it. Come in here for a second. Jonesie, go make yourself useful."

I follow the lawman into his office, and he sinks into his chair. Through the blinds separating the office from the bull pen, Jonesie finds his desk. Leander slides in the open door and stands beside my chair. I'm hyper aware of his hand resting on the high back behind my head but force myself to focus on the sheriff. He looks at his son for a beat before turning his attention to me. "I know your dad used Gracia as an informant, and I know he let her do some dangerous tasks for him. I'm not that guy. I can't deny that she got some results, but in the end, she died, Valencia. I won't put you at that kind of risk, not even for something like this. If your dad were here, I believe he'd say the same. So don't ask me."

I suck my teeth, annoyed that he's being so bluntly stubborn after the results I got. "That isn't fair. I'm not dating a gang member." When I asked Deputy Kelley about how Rosie had gotten into my house, she'd confessed she'd let Rock around back because he said he had something for me. Rock, sneaking into my backyard with a kitten in a box.

It's incredibly sweet, but it doesn't count as dating. Neither does incapacitating my car so Rock has to come help me. Although that was pretty sweet too. My smile turns upside down. Until it wasn't.

Leander shifts on his feet.

"I know more about how to protect myself than Gracia did. I keep pepper spray on me at all times, and I've been taking kickboxing."

Sheriff McCandles steeples his fingers. "That's all well and good, but if you bring that spray to a gun fight, you'll lose. I won't have that on my head. The answer is no."

Illusions of getting Janice off my back in the newspaper office dissolve under the quick and efficient dousing the sheriff just gave me. Worse, he has good points. Damn him. I slump back in the high back chair. "Fine. I'll drop it." For now.

"Come on," Leander says. "Let's get back to scanning. I'll give you a head start."

"Don't do me any favors." He wins handily, even when we switch and he mans the ancient scanner while I use the app. My head isn't in the game. It's stuck on drug overdoses and kittens in boxes.

That's My Cue

CHATTER IN THE NEWSPAPER ROOM QUIETS WHEN JANICE walks in. Everyone on staff snaps to attention, waiting for our taskmaster of an editor to begin our weekly meeting. It only took me a few days on staff to realize that I'm the only one not afraid of locking horns with Janice. It's not a terrified fear, mostly. More like a robust respect for preserving their bylines. Last week, one of the sports writers turned in a subpar piece, so Janice rewrote it and put her own name on it. It was fair, since she'd done the real work, but the sports writer left in a huff. This week, he's back, but he doesn't look happy about it. He's also a senior, and I'm betting he needs this class to graduate.

Janice may be a taskmaster, but she puts out a good paper. Since I joined, I've actually read it. More people on campus are reading the *Herald* than I can remember since I started at St. Vivian's as a freshman. This semester, Janice has ramped up her lectures about putting in the work and putting out the best paper possible. She wants to enter the *Herald* in a country-wide contest toward the end of the semester. Which is a huge reason she's been riding me to find newsworthy articles to write. I'm supposed to help her win this award. The problem is all of my ideas either get shot down for not being big enough, or I get blocked by our well-meaning but also incredibly annoying sheriff.

Crossing my arms on the table, I rest my chin and listen to Janice's scary motivational speech to open the meeting. Then, assignments are doled out. A string of damaged traffic lights in the town center. A profile on the new school librarian with questions about recent book bans.

I'm trying to figure out how to change the sheriff's mind about using me as an informant when Janice turns her hungry eyes on me. "Valencia, what have you got for me?"

I sit up straighter, hoping it truly is better to ask for forgiveness than permission. "It feels like there's growing tension in town between the different classes. The poorer neighborhoods have seen a lot of upset from recent gang activity, and the richer neighborhoods are sequestered behind their HOA gates."

"I've noticed increased security at the mall on that side of town," one of the other reporters puts in. "I was thinking about interviewing the guards."

Janice nods, clapping her hands together. "Tracy. Interview the guard. Ask them about any increase in theft and vandalism. Get some juicy details if you can."

My jaw loosens. "What about me?"

"We'll find another angle for you to take. Tracy is better at interviewing people."

I'd be offended, but Janice is right. Tracy's interviews always shine with a finesse that I flat out don't have. She always gets her subjects talking about their secrets in a way that feels honest without being pushy.

Janice wraps up the meeting, bustling around the newsroom to straighten up before we leave. She links her arm in mine. "Come on. I'm ready for my daily smoothie."

I follow her across town in the Corvette to the resort. Inside, lights flash and slot machines jingle. Greasy pizza and soy sauce smells linger in the air close to the food court. Despite having to hustle over from the weight room to start his shift, Ty already has Janice's drink prepared and waiting when we stroll up to the smoothie hut. Two umbrellas sit prettily on the rim.

Janice bats her eyelashes at her boyfriend. "You forgot the extra cherries."

"Oh shoot. Sorry. Here you go." She beams as he places five plump, red cherries on top of her drink.

Claiming the next stool, I drop my backpack. "What, my drink isn't ready yet?"

Ty slides mine in front of me, and I smile. "You. I like you. Janice, you should keep this one around."

She watches him from under her perfectly curled eyelashes. "Maybe. Until I get tired of smoothies."

Ty points a finger at her. "You love my smoothies."

I get the feeling based on the way Janice and Ty are staring at each other that we aren't talking strictly about smoothies. Waving my hand in front of Janice's face snaps her out of it. She makes a show out of enjoying the cherries, and I try not to gag.

"If you don't want me to write about increased gang activity around town, what should I write about then?"

Janice plucks the paper umbrella from her drink, wipes off the end on a napkin, and slides it into her sleek ponytail. "I've been thinking about that. Everyone was crappy to you last year because they assumed your dad was a pedo and a murderer. You should write about what that was like for you. Tell everyone your side of the story, so they know the whole, ugly truth. You know, something like, *The Real Truth About What Happened When My Dad Went Missing*, by Valencia Lamb."

"Pass."

"What? Why? You love true crime, and you were caught smack in the middle of the biggest story our state has seen since the Gemini Killer consumed the news cycle. Your story has it all: lust, murder, betrayal. It could be an amazing piece."

I take a long drag of my smoothie. I don't know how, but Ty makes freaking delicious smoothies. "What do you put in these? A gallon of ice cream?"

Ty's cheeks redden as he smiles. "The secret ingredient is love."

"Aww, I'm touched. But you're dating my frenemy and she's scary."

Janice cackles. "Don't change the subject. The article. You'll write it?"

I hook my thumb at her. "You just want to win an award."

"That is not a crime."

"What did I miss?" Destin slides onto the stool next to mine, and Leander takes the one on his other side. The collar of his letterman jacket is damp, his hair wet, probably from a post-football season workout, same as Ty. Leander greets the smoothie king with a fist bump, even though they were at school together less than an hour ago. He and Destin order smoothies, and Ty gets to work. The loud grinding of the blenders gives me a second to gather my thoughts.

"So?" Destin prods my side with an elbow, glancing past me toward where Janice is breaking a handful of health codes by stealing cherries from the bowl behind the counter. "Did she go for your idea? For the article?"

I spin around on the stool to watch old people play the slots.

One old lady hits a jackpot and whoops as she holds a popcorn bucket under the coin slot to catch her winnings. "She gave it to someone else. It was probably the right call."

Destin glances at Janice over my shoulder. "Sure."

"What idea?" Leander spins to lean his back against the counter, following my gaze. The old woman toddles toward the cashier with her bucket rattling.

"I may have mentioned the tension in town. With the Snakes recruits making trouble."

"Enjoy." Ty sets smoothies down in front of the guys and wipes down the workstation behind the counter.

Janice elbows me, crowding my space so she can talk to Leander over Destin and me. "You're the sheriff's son. What's your take on all this? I bet he tells you all kinds of interesting tidbits."

Leander's eyes meet mine. I shrug. "She won't quit until you tell her. Resistance is futile."

Janice's wicked grin is probably visible from space.

Clearing his throat, Leander's eyes slide to hers. "How involved are you with the Snakes, since your dad?"

She waves her hand in a middling gesture, and he continues. "Without your dad and Dino Agani around to create order in the gang, my dad thinks there's a power vacuum. All of the remaining gang members are jostling for control. We don't know exactly how many there are, but a good number of them have been in the Snakes for years. Some of them are vying for the top spot, and part of that is recruiting new members. They'll each try to gather a large enough following to force the rest of the gang in line."

Ty arches over the counter, forcing me to slide further back on my stool. "So, all the stupid incidents around town—"

Janice bobs her head. "They're power plays, yeah. They'll

only get worse until the gang crowns a new leader."

Nudging Janice with a shoulder, I drink my smoothie. My mind is cycling with all of this information. Asking questions and putting together possible conclusions. "And the drug overdoses play into that how?"

"Without a leader, the Snakes are getting bolder. Sloppier. They're probably being less careful about who they sell to, and it's causing increased issues. That's my dad's guess, anyway. He was talking to Kelley about it yesterday."

"McCandles Junior, were you eavesdropping?" Janice's question makes Leander scratch at the back of his neck.

"Maybe."

Spinning on my stool, I watch a little girl beg her dad to let her play a Barbie slot machine, even though that would technically be illegal. After a shifty look around, he lets her. Spinning away from them, I look to Leander. "I still want to see if I can figure out where the drugs are coming from."

Janice pokes my cheek. "Where would you start?"

Leander's stern expression dominates my field of vision, jaw set in a frown. "My dad said no."

I don't meet his eyes, transfixed by the flashing lights. "I'll be careful."

He wags a finger, putting himself between me and the slots. "You? Careful?"

I cup my smoothie with both hands. "I will. Are you going to tell on me?"

Sighing, he shakes his head. Damp, honey-blond hair falls over his forehead.

Looking at Leander, freshly showered from a workout gives me an idea. "I know it's a cliche, but athletes and drugs sometimes mix. Have you seen anything?"

He blows out a breath, sharing a look with Ty. "I may have

noticed a couple of guys flying red flags during practice. It's my job as captain to pay attention to that kind of stuff."

Ty raises his hand. "One of the guys is throwing a party next Friday night. You could start there."

Janice pulls his hand down and holds it over the countertop.

I rub my hands together and give an exaggerated scheming laugh. "Perfect. You'll come with, right Des?"

He frowns, pushing his hair off his forehead. "Family game night. I can't."

"Your family and puzzles. Bunch of weirdos." My lighthearted eye roll lifts the corner of his mouth.

Leander grips my stool, spinning me to face him. The look in his eyes is so intense I have to fight to hold it. "If you're going to that party, you can't go alone."

Janice waves her hand in his face. "Hello? Ty and I are coming. Oh! He'll bring a friend for Val. Right, Ty Ty?"

Ty looks bemused at Janice's gleeful clapping, but agrees.

"A blind date?" Leander couldn't sound more horrified if he tried. Des rests his hands on my shoulders, notching his chin on top of my head.

"You sure about this?" my friend whispers in my ear, ignoring Janice naming all of the football players she can remember.

"Yeah, okay. Sure. Fix me up."

Leander keeps shooting down possibilities for dumb reasons. Too Tall. Too clumsy. Too pretty. Finally, Janice names one that has Ty nodding in approval. He shoots a look at Leander, whose mouth is a tight line of displeasure. He doesn't voice any objections, instead meeting my eyes. Something passes over his eyes, but I have no idea what it is. I choke down the last of my smoothie, and try not to cough when I get a brain freeze.

Janice watches our wordless exchange with interest. She

taps her smoothie cup against mine. "As your editor, I approve of this plan. That award is as good as ours, as long as you don't screw this up."

I stoop to grab my bag. "You're so inspiring. No wonder everyone at the paper loves you."

"I'd rather be feared than loved."

"Mission accomplished." I toss her a sarcastic salute.

Janice pops another cherry into her mouth. Ty's cheeks go red when she presents him the stem tied in a knot.

Destin pulls his bag onto his shoulder. "That's our cue. You coming?"

I find an easy pace at Destin's shoulder. Leander falls in on my other side. "It was getting awkward back there."

The days are still short, night already falling when we step outside. My best friend and my ex walk me out to the Corvette and wait while I unlock it and climb in. Leander gestures for me to roll down the window. He braces his body with a hand on the roof. "About this party."

"Yeah?"

Leander sucks his bottom lip into his mouth, leaving it puffy and red. "Never mind."

It takes the entire drive home to convince my slippery heart that Leander didn't just almost ask me to cancel the blind date. That he'd go with me instead of whoever Ty can convince to go on a blind date with the former sheriff's daughter. Leander and I have already tried dating, with explosive results. No matter how good our first kiss was, we probably shouldn't repeat it.

This party, however, is my chance. Sheriff McCandles doesn't want me involved with investigating, but I've never let that stop me. I'm doing it. He won't be able to argue when I present him with a solid lead.

It's a house party. What's the worst that could happen?

Drunk and Disorderly

"I CAN'T WEAR THIS. MY ARMS AND LEGS WILL FREEZE OFF." Blinking at myself in the mirror hung from my closet door doesn't change the halter top and short skirt Janice stuffed me into. Her mouth opens to balance as she adds the perfect winged eyeliner to the smoky eye look she did on me with an eyeshadow pallet she pulled out of her purse.

"Beauty is pain, Val. Don't stick your tongue out at me. I don't mean your pain, I mean theirs. Every guy at that party is going to suffer when they see you like this."

"Do I want them to suffer?" I eye her nervously, not entirely hating that idea. I took a lot of crap when the entire town thought my dad was a pervy murderer, and showing them that I'm still standing—and looking fierce—makes me feel taller. And pop a hip like Janice is fond of doing.

"Yeah. You do. Look." She ducks out of my view, and I stare at my reflection. I look like me, but shinier. Mature. More feminine than my usual jeans and bomber jacket.

"I don't hate this."

Janice grins like a cat who has cornered a mouse and is having a ball playing with it. "Duh. I am an expert at makeovers. Don't pick at those nails. The polish should last for at least a week."

Janice didn't give me a manicure. She gave me ruby red claws like the ones she favors. They click together at the tips of my fingers. "How do you use your hands with these?" I complain, but secretly? I flex my hand in the mirror, pretending to be Wolverine's girly counterpart.

Getting ready to go out with Janice is a lot different from going with Portia. There aren't any weird middle names being tossed at me, and she isn't trying to talk me into wearing more glitter. Actually, aside from that, it isn't that different. Janice forced me into an outfit that I'm pretending to hate but secretly love, and then she did my makeup and nails. My eyes pop wide and I spin on her. "Oh my god, we're friends now."

"You're just now figuring this out?" Janice cackles all the way down the stairs and out the front door to the gorgeous Corvette swanning in my driveway. She got a wash and detail yesterday, and she looks as fierce as I do.

Even though driving the recognizable car around town has drawn a lot of unwanted attention from guys I have to assume are Snakes, I haven't looked into painting the car. A pang throbs in my chest. My dad picked the paint color. He loved it, and I can't bring myself to change it.

Sliding into the driver seat, I take a whiff of the air freshener hanging from the rearview mirror. It's the same kind my dad always used. Fake chemical pine and warm memories. I ordered a box of fifty and stashed them for when this one runs out of juice.

Janice turns classic rock on the radio and sings every song

as I drive to the party. It's in one of the pricier gated communities on a hill at the edge of town. Someone must have given out the code because a line of cars streams in the open gate.

I park and we follow the crowd to a large, two-story house already packed with people. Energy pulses from the gaping front door, pouring onto the sidewalk with an electronic soundtrack that blasts so loud the windows vibrate. Despite it being weeks past Christmas, there's an inflatable snowman lording over the front lawn.

Scaling the front walk to the door involves dodging clumps of people so inebriated their inhibitions aren't even visible in their rearview mirrors. One group of guys chants as one of their buddies sticks his tongue out to lick the metal mailbox.

Whistling, I pause, interested in seeing natural consequences at work, but Janice wraps a hand around my arm and tows me in her wake. Inside, sweaty, humid air coats my skin. She was right; a coat would have been stifling.

"Yes! How many people do you think are here?" Her eyes gleam, energy crackling off her as we wade deeper into the sea of inebriation. Being short, I can't tell where she's leading us until we find the staircase. Ty stands on the landing, gesturing for us to join him. He yells something, but it evaporates in the din of off-key singing and shouted conversations.

Janice climbs to the landing and sashays in a circle so he can admire her outfit. Satisfied with Ty's open-mouthed staring, she grins. "So, where is Val's date?"

The lit disco ball hanging over the middle of the vaulted room sends sprays of pink, blue, and yellow light over the dancing crowd. A quick perusal of the room yields heaps of people, some I recognize from school and many I don't. None of them appear to be battling toward where I stand with Ty and Janice on the stairs. The music's plodding bass settles under the soles of my cute booties.

Ty turns sheepish when I meet his eyes. A tinge of disappointment settles low in my stomach. Pity in a friend's eyes is a potent kind of poison. "He's not coming, is he?"

Janice's boyfriend scrapes the back of his neck, tousling his hair. "No, but it's not what you think."

My bare skin prickles, making me feel too exposed standing above the crowd in my skirt and shoulder-baring top. Despite Janice's non-stop teasing this week, I refused to admit I'd been looking forward to seeing who Ty picked out for me. Ty is sweet, and I had hoped his friend would be similar. Easy to be around, sans strings. Now I get to third wheel all night. Yay for me.

Janice sends Ty to fetch us drinks, standing at the railing like a queen overseeing her subjects. I slide into place next to her, close enough that she can hear me. "Maybe I should just—"

"Don't even say it. There are hundreds of people here. We'll find you someone to flirt with while you look for leads for your article. Easy."

Someone vaults over the banister and straightens. Leander, dressed in a gray button down and jeans and looking really nice. He approaches me, half a smile curving his lips. "Sorry I'm late."

Janice claps her hands. "See. Found one."

My heart is jumping to the rhythm of the bassline. "Wait. Did Ty. . .?"

Leander's half smile is a beacon in the ocean of strange faces. "Ask me to be your date? No, but the guy he asked is kind of a flake. He here yet?"

I click my heels a couple times. "He flaked."

Leander bops our shoulders together, and it's so cozy I don't pull away. "I missed a lot of things when we were together, but I won't make that mistake again. Plus, I'm team captain. I know my teammates."

Tilting my head to look up at him makes it obvious that we are awfully close together. "That still doesn't explain what you're doing here."

My ex-boyfriend looks out over the crowd before his eyes settle on mine. "I didn't want you to be alone, Val."

Rosie gets a lot of hairballs, and watching her hack them up is gross. But right now? My throat feels like there's a hairball wedged inside, sucking all the moisture out of my throat and making me wheeze.

Ty climbs the stairs, handing drinks to Janice and me. "I just threw these together with stuff they had out on the counter, so they're probably not good. But they came out pink so. . ."

Taking one of the glasses with a quick "Thanks," Janice tosses it back. "Damn, that's good." Holding the empty glass aloft, she shouts, "To the party gods!" The crowd cheers as she crunches the plastic and tosses it into the writhing mass.

I look down at my own pink drink, trying to figure out what would have made it that color.

Janice hooks an arm around Ty's waist. "Drink up, Val! We'll investigate later. First, we party!" She leads Ty down into the middle of the mosh pit under the disco ball. A few beats of the music are all it takes for the chaos to swallow them up.

I take a sip, watching the crowd. So, this is what it feels like to be at a rager party. I've never been invited to one, maybe because my dad was the sheriff. Take out food and a B movie is more my speed. Looking closer at the outfits on the nearest dancers, I'm glad Janice insisted on picking my outfit. The clothes on these people have more sequins and flair than I've ever seen in one place. Body spray hangs heavy in the air, doing little to cover the dank smell of sweat.

Since I'm here, I might as well try it out. Downing the pink drink, I set the cup on the landing. Leander grins when I rise on tiptoes to make him hear me. "Wanna dance?"

Tunneling through the crowd, we find Janice and Ty in the eye of the storm. She whoops when we appear, and I abandon myself to movement.

"This is so much fun!" I shout over the music so Leander can hear me. He and I have been on the dance floor for four or five songs, and even though it was awkward at first, we're having a blast. Whatever was in that pink drink has morphed me into someone who is loose-limbed and giggly.

Leander agrees, one of his hands skimming down my arm. He yells back, "I'm glad I came."

"Me too. Woo!" Whirling around makes the disco ball spin into a pretty tornado, and I am loving it. Until I almost trip over an abandoned shoe and Leander catches me with an arm around my waist.

"You're such a lightweight." His teasing laughter should probably embarrass me, but I just don't care.

"I'm Mighty Mouse! And you're one to talk. I don't see you with a pink drink."

"I'm more of a soda guy." Leander does a smooth roll of his body that is so cool. I try to do it, and only manage to make him bust up laughing even harder.

"Rude. If you can't appreciate my moves I'll find someone who will."

Destin is probably in the middle of a rousing family puzzle right now, but I wish he was here. He's an even worse dancer than I am. Plus, if anyone could use a chance to cut loose and be silly, it's him. Whipping out my phone, I snap a photo of me grinning and sweaty. Leander photo bombs, giving me bunny ears. My laughter swirls through my streaming hair as I spin.

Janice and Ty are killing it with their dancing. I have no idea what she's doing, but I want to do it too. Imitating her, I pop my knees and snap my arms. Leander's eyes sparkle as he keeps doing his own thing.

The song transitions, and Ty throws up his hands. "I love this song." He pulls out a fake fishing pole and attempts to reel Janice in. I goggle at him, secondhand embarrassment making me cringe. There is no way she is doing that. I squeal in surprise when she hops toward Ty. Good lord, he's reeling her in like a fish! Janice Hill is allowing herself to be caught. Something about it tickles my funny bone, and I dip into a giggling fit. "Did you see that?" I shout in Leander's ear.

His chuckles are warm puffs against my ear. "Let me get you some water or something."

I ricochet off his chest like a dodge ball. "You dance. I'll get more pink drink!"

Grasping my wrist as I twirl, he pulls me into him. "I think you'd better let me get you a water bottle. You're drunk."

"Am not. Maybe you're drunk." I put the tip of my finger in the indent of his chin. His warm hand closes around mine, drawing it down and away from his face. Drawing me along after him, he nudges Ty with an elbow. He asks him something about keeping an eye on this one, but I'm too busy tossing my hands in the air to pay close attention.

Gentle hands cup my cheeks, waiting until I meet puppy dog brown eyes. "Stay here, okay? I'll be right back."

Lights flash in my eyes, painting Leander's face blue. "What if I get lost?"

Calloused thumbs caress my cheekbones. "I'll find you." Then he's gone, swallowed up in the sea of gyrating bodies. For a split second, a familiar recently buzzed head, hair already hinting at a slight curl passes under the disco ball a few feet away. Dark eyes brush against mine.

In a breath, Rock is gone.

I must have imagined it, but the longer I dance and he doesn't appear, the less I feel like dancing. A quick glimpse of Rock has killed my buzz stone dead.

A slow song comes on, and the entire crowd boos and crows at the DJ. That's my cue.

"I'll be back. Bathroom!" Ty is wrapped around Janice, her hands petting his hair, but she gives me a quick thumbs up.

Pushing through the crowd of awkwardly paired dancers and groups of people who are sitting out the slow, depressing song tripping through big speakers, I make for the hallway. There's got to be a bathroom somewhere. Sweaty hair sticks to the back of my neck. I should have brought a hair tie so I could put it up. Maybe I'll find one in the bathroom.

I pass a couple of shut doors, and stumble into a line of people. Jackpot.

By the time I get my turn, the DJ has cycled through a couple of electronic mashups and is playing something that consists mostly of what sounds like dogs howling. The dancing crowd tosses back their heads and howls along. The wild calls, but I'm in no mood to answer. I might as well start poking around this place for useful information.

Ducking into the kitchen, I spy a huddle of people around a beer keg. On the counter, a honking large plastic pitcher of pink is mostly empty. Sad news.

Tingling on the back of my neck makes me pivot slowly, looking for whoever is shooting daggers at my back. Angry heat splashes down my spine, pulling it taut. Beyond the keg worshipers, Rotten Egg Breath leans against a closed window, arms crossed. He's watching me carefully. When our eyes meet, his upper lip curls, baring teeth. Beside him, a freshman boy from St. Viv's is chatting up a girl. So quick I almost miss it, she hands over a wad of cash. He whispers in her ear. She melts into the crowd.

I take a step closer without thinking. It was a mistake.

The Snake pushes off the window, marching toward me with clenched fists. Uh oh.

Back peddling, I trip over someone's leg. My stomach lurches as I fall on my butt. Someone throws an elbow. There's a bellow and a scream.

A fight breaks out right on top of me.

Blood pounds in my ears. I push up, but a large body slams into me, putting me back down on the sticky floor. I try again, but trip over an empty bottle and fall to my hands and knees. A high heel pinches my finger, and I yowl in pain. If I don't get to my feet, I'll be trampled.

My eyes skitter around as I avoid stomping feet and flailing arms. At least REB is buried in a scrum of swinging fists and slapping palms. He roars angrily over the music. His eyes still target me.

A hole opens in the scuffle, and I seize the chance to escape. Scrambling to my feet, I push away from the fight. An elbow jabs into my side, making me double over. Son of a motherless goat, that hurt. Fingers dig into my hair, yanking me back by my skull.

"Valencia!" I can't see Leander through this mess, but the panic in his voice cuts through the white noise my fight or flight response is creating in my head.

"Here!" I spin around, aiming for his voice. Jabs and kicks I learned in kickboxing class flow through me. Scuffling and scrapping, I manage to free myself from the melee in the kitchen. People shove and sweep, trying to get closer to the center of the fight. Sharks scenting blood in the water and craving a bite for themselves.

"You're dead," comes a mortal grumble in my ear. An arm like a steel band shoves me against the wall, yanking the breath from my body. My heart tumbles around in my chest, pinned by the hand at my throat. I try to scream but can't. Just like in my nightmares, when I find myself trapped in Agani Auto, surrounded by Snakes with no chance of escape.

Hate-filled eyes zone in on mine, blocking out everything else. Sharp teeth bared, the villain cocks his fist. "You're mine now, little bird."

Chasing a Ghost

I BRACE MYSELF FOR THE MIND-ERASING CRUSH OF PAIN, but I refuse to close my eyes. I won't let fear control my actions. If Rotten Egg Breath is about to pummel me, I'm going to take it with my eyes open, so I can remember every second while I plot my revenge.

The fake nails Janice glued on dig into my palms. Crap, they're sharp.

They're sharp.

Opening my palm, I rip and drag at the Snake's hand, trying to loosen its grip on my throat.

"You bitch." REB growls. His eyes shimmer with hatred as he looses his fist.

A blurry, red and black-clad figure smashes into my attacker, propelling him to the ground. Rock lands on the Snake's stomach, punching and growling so fast I can't see what is happening. REB fights back, jabbing and landing a few blows. He bucks and kicks, trying to throw Rock off him. Rock is unmovable. His closed fist lands a visceral sucker punch that knocks the gangster's skull against the ground, and he stops fighting. Wiping blood off his lip, the Snake promises death with eyes flashing red.

Pushing off him, Rock gives him his back. Arrogance well earned ripples over his sturdy frame. He put the Snake down with so much strength and efficiency, he's confident the belly-crawler won't come back for round two. My mouth gapes in shock.

On the other side of the wall in the kitchen, the screams and thwacks of flesh pummeling flesh have stopped. Voices chant, "Chug, chug, chug." The fight is over as quickly as it began, but my body is thrumming with unspent adrenaline.

Wiping a trickle of blood from under his nose with the back of his hand, Rock prowls close to me. He stops a foot away, eyes assessing my body. "You okay?"

Breathing hard, my eyes slide between him and REB, who comes slowly to his feet. Did that really just happen? Rock's hands boast red, raw knuckles.

Clearing my awed expression, I meet Rock's eyes. "Yeah, I'm okay."

"This is becoming a pattern. You getting into tight spots and me rescuing you." His mouth flattens as he looks down at his bruised and bloodied hands.

"That supposed to impress me?" Because I am deeply impressed. And a little sweaty from the fight. I blow out a slow breath. Watching Rock tackle that Snake to get him off me? Seeing that protective side of him in the flesh? For a second, I saw the boy who used to take my part against his brother's cruel taunts. Only he's not a little boy anymore.

Rock huffs, leaning an arm on the wall at my shoulder, shielding me from the room. "Wasn't trying to impress you."

"Sure, you weren't." It takes an effort not to stare at the split in Rock's lip, so instead I look up at his too short but growing curls.

He huffs. A quiet second passes. Another. Neither of us says anything, but neither of us moves away, either.

A gorgeous girl appears out of the throng and wraps herself around Rock's free arm. Her beautiful smile aimed to attract him. "She's crazy. I'm super impressed."

He straightens, taking his warmth with him. Gently but firmly, Rock brushes her off. "Not interested. Thanks."

Oddly, a ripple of pleased gratification warms my cheeks. Which is dumb. I banish it.

"Whatever." The girl recedes into the crowd.

Rock's eyes come back to mine, searching deep into my heart and soul. I stare right back.

"Oh my god. Valencia! Are you okay?" Leander grabs me out from under Rock and runs trembling hands down my shoulders to my hands. He's breathing hard. Checking me over for injuries. "I saw you fall, and then I couldn't find you. I thought you'd been smashed."

"No, I'm fine. Rock helped me out."

Leander starts, just now noticing that Rock is right beside me. "Agani."

Rock swipes at his split lip with his thumb, then checks it to make sure there isn't any fresh blood. "Junior."

Their mutual dislike makes me roll my eyes. Sliding my hand out of Leander's, I tuck it into my skirt pocket. "Thanks for finding me, but I'm okay. Kickboxing saved my butt."

Leander's mouth kicks up in a relieved smile.

"Good thing Rock was—" I look over my shoulder, but Rock is gone. Whirling around, I search the party. He's not anywhere. As quickly as he appeared, he vanished. Like a fire spark that flickers with light before disappearing into the air. Carried away by an invisible breeze.

Leander waits for my eyes to find him again. "Still. I'm sorry I left you. I won't do it again."

"Don't worry about it." I can't stop myself from scanning a second time. My search is fruitless. Rock only shows himself when he wants to. His knack for disappearing is becoming deeply annoying.

Leander and I tramp through the house to find Janice and Ty on the front porch, making out in a porch swing. I wish I had driven separately, because I don't want to interrupt all that. Thankfully, Ty spots us coming and peels his face off Janice's. She pouts at first but brightens when her eyes land on me.

"There you are. Tell me. Was coming to the party worth it? Did you get some juicy info for your article?"

I think about Rock pummeling my would-be attacker. The fierce look in his eyes when he backed me against the wall. My pulse zooming through me like a roller coaster cart on a free fall. "Say that again?"

She arches an eyebrow. "Did you get any leads on the drug situation?"

A girl and a boy. A wad of cash passed between palms. The girl's' disappearing act. "Oh. Oh, yeah. I saw a transaction in the kitchen, but I was interrupted by my favorite member of the Snakes."

"Gabriel was here?"

"That's the one. I keep forgetting that's his name." Because giving him a name dignifies him above the rats, and he doesn't deserve it. He'll always be Rotten Egg Breath to me.

Janice minces over Ty's feet to stand closer to me. "So, who was selling?"

"Some Snake peon, but the girl who bought… I've seen

her before, I just can't remember where."

"Well, remember."

"Just like that." I smirk at her.

"Yes. Just like that." We say good night to the guys, which involves Leander and I carefully avoiding Janice and Ty while they kiss goodbye with too much tongue. They wave from the lawn as us girls drive off in the Corvette.

I rack my brain the entire drive to Janice's house, where I drop her off, but I can't finger where I know the girl from. I obsess over the familiar face all weekend, trying to place it. Mom calls me out on being unfocused during our Jane Austen movie marathon, but I still miss all the swoony parts. I keep having to rewind my true crime podcast because my mind wanders and I miss important clues. Basically, my tunnel vision is extreme.

I know I've seen that girl somewhere, but I can't put her anywhere concrete. The diner? A football game? I come up empty.

Not only did I not get any chasable leads for the article, I almost got my nose bashed in. And that look in his eyes when he slunk away after Rock bested him? Pure, unadulterated hatred.

I haven't seen the last of that guy, and next time Rock may not be there to save me.

When that day comes, I'll find out if I have what it takes to save myself.

Don't Be Suspicious, But Be Suspicious

MONDAY MORNING, ROCK IS ALREADY SITTING AT HIS DESK when I enter first period. There he sits, relaxed in a neat uniform, tie draped untied around his neck. As if he hasn't been absent for over two weeks and out of touch with his friends. Like a freaking ghost.

A tingle goes through me that I'm labeling as irritation. Irritation at Rock for ghosting me, saving me, and then ghosting me again. Irritation and a tiny bit of interest. Purely in watching him put my attacker down again, of course. I am definitely not interested in being caught between Rock and a wall again. Or in the way his eyes latched onto mine and didn't let go until Leander interrupted. Nope.

Moving on.

Janice is in her desk next to Rock's. They're chatting back

and forth as if he hasn't been hiding from the Snakes for weeks trying to keep them away from Granny and his cousins. To keep them away from me by avoiding me.

Rock hasn't earned the flare of frustration that rears its ugly head inside me. He never asked to be put in the middle of the Snakes' current power struggle. That dubious achievement award goes to his father, who thank fudge is in prison and will be there for the foreseeable.

Miss Wayne walks in and Rock meets her at her desk. They speak for a minute. She doesn't seem surprised to see him. Which means that he probably made arrangements with her to turn in his classwork while he was away from school.

For as long as I've known Rock, his goal was to go away to college and never come back. His worst nightmare was sinking so deeply into the Snake pit that he couldn't climb out. With Leif around to take up his dad's thorny mantle, it looked like he'd pull it off. Now that he's been outcast by the gang, Rock's escape is even more likely.

Janice grins at me, making a ta da gesture toward Rock as he slides into his desk.

His imposing figure is impossible to ignore. The entire classroom tilts toward where he sits at its center, making it an effort to walk anywhere but straight to him. This must be how a salmon swimming upstream feels, defenseless against its ingrained instincts and the call of the river. My feet stop right in front of Rock's desk.

Two pairs of eyes slide up to my face, Janice's at ease and Rock's wary.

"Morning," I say when nothing brilliant comes to mind. "You're going to have a hell of a time catching up on work."

"I have it handled." So, I was right about him making arrangements with Miss Wayne. The same way he handled that

Snake. With a single-mindedness I didn't know he possessed.

"No doubt."

Around us, everyone is talking and laughing and goofing off in the scant minutes before class starts. I stare at Rock, thinking about Friday night. The bone-deep pulse of the music. The hatred in the REB's eyes. The promises in Rock's, after he removed the threat and inched closer to me. Blowing out a breath, I offer Rock a smile. "About Friday, I never got to say thanks, so thanks."

Rock dips his head, but before he can respond, the bell rings. Miss Wayne wishes everyone a good morning as I hustle into my seat.

At lunch, Destin is in the middle of telling me about a skateboarding trail he tried out with Bert over the weekend when Rock slides into a seat at our table. I'm tempted to steal his brownie again, because that was amusing last time, but I can't bring myself to reach across and take it. After his absence, after Friday night, something has changed between us. Something that makes me squirm whenever I find his eyes on me.

I, being super mature, mostly ignore him in favor of my bestie. Destin and I complain about how much homework our Calculus teacher is giving so early in the semester, and make plans to work together on a project in a few weeks. Destin is a great partner because we're pretty evenly matched, skills wise.

I keep a sliver of my attention on Janice and Rock. She tries to goad him into explaining why he missed so much school, but he dodges her questions expertly. Surprise lines his mouth when she asks, his gaze shifting to mine for the barest of moments. I give half a shrug. I could have told Janice he was trying to protect his family by staying away, but his motives felt private. Like they weren't mine to share. So I kept it to myself despite Janice's needling. Rock doesn't explain beyond the fact that he can't miss any more if he wants to graduate on time.

The hint of a smile around his mouth is all the vindication I need.

After school, I cross campus to the newspaper room, but stop abruptly. Rock is standing sentry by the door. "What are you doing here?"

He shrugs. "Waiting for Jan."

They're so easy together.

The friendship Rock and I have is never easy.

Leander and I have gotten to an easier place since working together at the sheriff's office over the past month. My cheeks warm at the memory of his gentle hands cupping my face Friday night. The panic in his voice when he found me after the fight. The clear care for me in his eyes was touching.

Same with all of the texts he sent me over the weekend. Funny football gifs and kitten memes in exchange for cute photos of Rosie playing with an actual ball of yarn.

Janice brings the newspaper staff to attention with a few claps of her hands. Everyone goes around the table updating her on articles they're writing, research they're conducting. She and one of the editors work a plan to fill holes in this week's layout.

When it's my turn, I embellish how well my writing is going. Because I have nothing. Every time I sit down to write about what it was like to be the town pariah last year, my mind goes blank. It devolves into a primordial pit bubbling with loneliness and hurt. Not a fun place to be, which is why I keep procrastinating.

Add to that the madness of trying to remember where I've seen the party girl, and let's just say I have been impressively unproductive this week. Janice's disapproval is apparent in the thin line of her mouth as she listens to my non-update. "Get some words down, Val. I want to see a rough draft in two weeks.

In the meantime, you can cover the freeway cleanup effort they're doing near the airport this weekend."

Groaning, I slide down into my seat. It's a punishment assignment. Janice hands them out to members of the staff who aren't pulling their weight. I can't say I'm a fan. Schlepping out to the freeway exit to talk to the road workers is going to be riveting.

Zoning out, I stare through the glass pane in the classroom door. A blond ponytail skips past, and I perk up in my seat. That ponytail. I've seen it before. At the party. It's the girl who tried to buy drugs from the Snakes Friday night.

I jump out of my seat, ignoring Janice's indignant bark as I push out the classroom door and scan the courtyard.

Breaking into a jog, I follow the line of buildings, looking around every corner. I can't lose her. The girl must be a lower classman, meaning I've seen her a couple of times around St. Vivian's, but not enough to know her name.

I jog past the gym and slow when I reach the banks of lockers. Blond hair disappears into one of the rows. I pick up the pace, finding her back pressed against a wall of lockers.

"Are you following me?" she squeaks, eyes wide. Her feet shift, and she glances past me. This girl is jumpy. My curiosity rises.

Realizing my own body is wound tight, I force my muscles to relax. "I have a couple questions for you."

". . . Okay." Pulling her ponytail forward, she twists it through her fingers. She won't meet my eyes.

"I saw you at the party Friday night, talking to a member of the Snakes."

Her toe nudges at a dried wad of gum on the concrete. "I don't know what you're talking about."

"Did you miss the whole, 'Say no to drugs' thing the school

has been doing?"

Indignance sparks behind her eyes that snap up to mine. "I don't do drugs."

"Come on. I saw you giving that other guy a wad of cash."

She pulls the lock of hair tighter around a finger, making the tip go white. "I—I wasn't buying drugs."

Frustrated that she's sticking to her lie, I crowd into her space and shove my phone in front of her face. On it is a photo I snapped of her talking to that new Snake recruit. Her hand meeting his, a wad of green passing between them.

The girl's face pales. She swallows a couple times. "I wasn't buying drugs. I swear."

My eyebrows rise at her continued denial. She's either naively stubborn, or telling the truth. Interesting. "Then what were you buying?"

She digs through the books in her locker, plucking one out and dropping it into her backpack. Weighing her words. "I like this guy, and I was trying to impress him. I heard about someone who makes really good fake IDs, so I tried to buy one. I was hoping he would think I was cool if I could buy us some drinks. The guy I talked to at the party said to give him the money, and he'd pass along my info. I'm waiting on a text message letting me know it's ready."

Fake IDs. Huh. I did not see that coming. I probably should have, since the sheriff and his deputies have been reporting a notable increase in DUIs, underage drinking, and drug use. "How long is it supposed to take?"

"A week or so? He didn't give me a specific time frame."

This isn't the lead I was looking for, but I can't pass it up. I'm too curious. What are the odds the person she's buying an ID from is the same one Janice used? I have to know.

"Here's my number. Text me when they get back to you,

will you?"

The girl relaxes a little. "You want a fake ID too?"

"Something like that."

"And you won't tell my parents?"

Holding up my phone, I delete the images of her.

She smiles. "Thanks. You're not as mean as everyone says."

I laugh in surprise. "Thanks, I guess?"

She smiles. "I'm Bri, by the way."

"Nice to meet you, Bri. Don't forget to text me."

With a promise to let me know when she hears from the fake ID guy, Bri turns to go.

"Hey Bri?"

The girl meets my eyes over her shoulder, nonplussed.

"If you feel like you have to do something shady to impress a guy, he's probably not worth it."

Her mouth drops open, but she nods. Then she's gone.

I return to the newspaper office, excitement thrumming in my veins. The tidbits I learned from Bri may not be the lead I had in mind, but I'm on a story trail, and I can't wait to see where it takes me.

Avocado Monopoly

Rows of white tents line the drive-in movie theater. January is wrapping up with more freezing cold days, but the frigid weather hasn't stopped people from coming out for the first farmer's market of the year. Lemons, oranges, and grapefruits are piled high like softballs on vendor tables. Handmade birdhouses sit waiting for tenants. Funnel cakes sizzle, filling the air with sugary sweetness.

Bri texted this morning that her fake ID is ready to be picked up. She gave me the when and where: 7 PM at the farmer's market. I invited Destin to come with, but he's going on his first ride-along with Sykes. He'll probably take Destin to feed the trash pandas behind Twinkle's Ice Cream Emporium.

I stroll along the rows, my stomach growling in want of the delicious foods on offer. The spicy heat of kebabs draws me down one row and up the next. Rosie shifts her tiny weight in my kitty backpack, and I picture her goblin eyes peering out of the clear portal in the back with a smile.

Destin surprised me at school with the backpack earlier this week. He used it when Bert was a tiny squirt. The bag is the perfect size for Rosie. My mom snapped a photo of her in it before I left the house, and it's the cutest thing ever.

There's an hour before Bri is supposed to pick up her ID, so I snag hot-from-the-grill pork pupusas and find an empty seat at one of the picnic benches in the food court. From this vantage point, the market stretches out across the lot, with the nearest stall being the largest and longest-running fruit stand. At 7 on the dot, Bri is supposed to buy three pounds of lemons and a jar of raw honey. With her shopping bag in hand, she was directed to walk from one end of the market to the other, leaving the bag open for someone to drop the fake ID into it. It's a risky way to deliver an expensive product, but what do I know? I'm not the criminal mastermind behind the enterprise.

I'm going to be the one who catches the guy.

I didn't mention it to Janice, because the forger is a sort-of friend of hers and I didn't want her caught in the middle. From everything she has said, her dad puts her in the middle enough.

A booth with custom-painted skating helmets draws my eye. Destin would love them. Finishing my pupusas, I wander over to the mini donut booth. Cinnamon sugar donuts with spiced apple pie filling are calling my name.

"I want to marry you," I whisper to my third donut.

"That's not legal in California yet, but maybe someday…" Leander's broad laugh announces him as he eyes the helmet in front of me. It's matte white with a blooming barrel cactus painted on one side. Destin's mom has a couple of large cacti just like it in her front yard, and their blooms last approximately two seconds. They're gorgeous.

Leander takes a bite of gyro that is bigger than Rosie. The wrap is fragrant but doesn't look as appetizing as my fried rings of deliciousness. "If your wrap was as good as my donuts, you'd understand."

"Maybe. Can I have a bite?"

I hesitate, because I'm down to two mini donuts and I was planning on eating them all. Plus, the idea of sharing food with Leander makes me squirm. Leander's mouth curves up.

"Please? I don't bite. Very hard." His cheeky wink loosens me up. It's just a mini donut. Handing over the sugar-coated ring, I take his gyro. Fair is fair. Hot, herbed chicken and feta cheese hit my tongue.

"That's good, but mine is better."

"Too bad," Leander crows, plucking the last donut from the paper cup. "It's mine now."

"You give my fiancé back!" I lunge for it, but he pivots out of my reach. Rosie meows loudly at the jolt to her perch.

"No chance." Dropping his head back, Leander holds the donut poised over his mouth.

Rosie shifts in the bag, giving me an idea. "Hey look, a cute kitten." Turning the bag toward Leander distracts him long enough for me to snatch my donut. Doing a little victory bob so I don't knock Rosie over, I eat the last donut in one cinnamon-sugary bite. "Sucker."

Huffing a laugh, Leander regards me. "Your victory dance looks like the tin man when he hasn't been oiled in a year."

"You weren't complaining about my dancing last weekend."

"I'm not complaining now."

"But you said—"

His eyes are warm and steady on mine. "Your dancing is one of my favorite things about you. It's the only time you completely let go and have fun. Mostly, you're so controlled. I wonder what's going on in that pretty head of yours."

I don't know what to say. We sit while he finishes eating,

the hubbub of the market around us. I pull the bag around to my front and unzip it to pet my kitten. Rosie climbs up my arm with her tiny claws and perches on my shoulder, nestling in the crook of my neck. It's her favorite place to snuggle. Mine, too.

Holding up my phone, I snap a photo of the two of us and send it to my mom.

My phone pings with a message. Bri has arrived.

Leander and I people watch for a few minutes before Bri comes into view. She meets my eyes through the crowd but keeps going. I told her not to approach me here, because I don't want anyone who might be watching to see us together and connect the dots.

"Oh my god that is the cutest kitten ever." Kelley swoops toward me, heart-eyes homed in on Rosie. "Can I pet her?"

I agree, and Kelley lets Rosie sniff her hand before rubbing her tiny little chin with gentle fingers. Over her shoulder, I spot Jonesie ambling closer to hover beside Kelley. Both of them are dressed casually in jeans and warm winter coats. She has a full face of makeup on, which she doesn't wear on duty. Lady wears it well.

Jonesie carries a couple of canvas bags loaded down with fresh bread and produce. Are they on a date?

"What's the baguette for?" I ask, looking from the laden bags to Kelley's smile. Reluctantly, she drags her attention away from Rosie. "Jonesie wanted to learn how to make spaghetti, so I offered to teach him."

Leander's eyebrows rise, and he catches my eye. I'm not the only one who has noticed Kelley's crush on the other deputy during shifts at the department. He ribs Jonesie for not knowing how to cook, but I lose the conversation's thread. A blonde head passes in the tail of my vision, and I spend the next couple minutes watching Bri weave in and out of the stalls. She pretends to shop at several of them, killing time until seven.

The two deputies leave just before show time, Jonesie practically dragging Kelley away from my kitten. At 6:59, Bri enters the fruit vendor's tent. Purchasing the honey and lemons only takes a handful of minutes, and she strolls down the aisle again. My eyes are trained on her, waiting for the fake ID seller to make a move.

In uniform, Sykes walks by with a bag full of avocados. Destin trails him, surveying the market in a button down and slacks. I whistle at him, and Destin laughs when he spots me. He and the deputy change direction to where Leander and I are sitting.

Sykes holds up his produce bag. "If you want any avocados, better buy some now."

According to the deputy, a drought has significantly lessened this year's crop and avos are about to be scarce.

I wrap an arm around Destin's neck. "How's it going with this guy? He keeping you safe from the evil raccoons?"

"It was one time!" Sykes sighs, resigned. He knows as well as I do that he'll never live down the night he got scared of a pack of raccoons behind the ice cream parlor.

Destin grins. "No evil raccoons so far, but the night is still young."

"How'd you talk your mom into letting you do ride-alongs, anyway?" Leander reaches for Rosie, who clings to my arm. She knows who her person is, this one.

"She made the sheriff swear a blood oath that nothing would happen to me. It was all very serious."

"I bet she's at home cuddling Bert and wishing she hadn't agreed." Rubbing Rosie's silk-soft tail, I scan the market for Bri. All of my friends have distracted me from watching her.

Des tilts his head. "Maybe. Probably. I'm stopping at the

store on the way home to get her some flowers or something. As a thank you."

I reassure him that his mom would love that, and his smile widens. "Riding along is freaking sweet. Not much has happened so far, but listening to the radio is pretty cool. And we got to give a traffic ticket to this truck full of dairy cows. That was cool. Reeked though."

Saying goodbye, Sykes and Destin leave.

My eyes find Bri, who looks away quickly. The tiny shrug she gives indicates nothing has happened yet.

Leander announces he's going to buy a couple avocados, and I ask him to grab me one. Avocado toast sounds delicious, and if avos are going to be scarce, I'll enjoy them while I can. I'd go myself, but I don't want to take my eyes off Bri. It's been about fifteen minutes since she made her fruit purchase, and something is bound to happen soon.

When it does, I'll be ready.

A bubble of commotion at the fruit stand bursts, begging for attention. Leander is at the checkout, but I can barely see his blond head over the mob of people swarming the white tent. In minutes the mountain of avocados dwindles to nothing. Sykes wasn't kidding about the scarcity.

Fudge's sake. I've taken my eyes off Bri. I scan the crowd for her, but she isn't in the first aisle. Standing up, I power walk to the next. Irritation at myself firms my mouth into a line. I've lost her.

Stopping in the middle of an aisle, mouth thinned, I pivot in a circle. No Bri anywhere.

A wadded-up paper bounces off a pole and lands at my feet. At first, it looks like someone's garbage tossed over an uncaring shoulder, but it's a sheet of lined paper. Suspicion creeps in as I unfold it.

Nice try, but you can't catch me.

My eyes fly wide as a trill of trepidation goes through me. Whoever was supposed to hand the fake ID off to Bri caught me watching.

"What the hell?" Leander's breath puffs against my cheek as he appears at my shoulder. "Where did you get that?"

"I'll explain in a minute." Zipping Rosie safely into her pack, I make a beeline as casually as possible down the aisle. Baseball cards. Resin jewelry. Freshly baked bread. No Bri.

The next row also lacks one strolling freshman.

Did something happen to her? Guilt creeps in. If my plan to tag the forger got her scared or hurt… I shut that thought down. She's in a public market. Bri is fine. She has to be.

If that's true, then where is she?

A tap on my shoulder makes me spin. Rosie lets out an indignant meow.

Hand still outstretched, Bri motions me to follow her into a tent bursting with tie dyed dresses and hats. A quick look over her person proves she's fine. Not hurt or scared.

She waits until we're tucked inside the booth to open the bag slung over her shoulder. "Look."

In the bag, next to a few pounds of shiny, yellow lemons and a jar of honey, is a padded envelope. Lifting it out, she shows me the fake ID card nestled inside. It's expertly made, with Bri's photo alongside her own address. Only her date of birth is a lie, indicating an age of twenty-two.

"When did you get it? Where were you?"

She frowns at my stern expression. "I don't know. I wandered around the market, just like I was told to, and when I checked a minute ago, it was there."

Groaning, I swat at a blue and orange tie dyed skirt monstrosity.

Bri shuffles closer. "We failed, didn't we? To catch them."

The vulnerability in her expression pulls a reassuring smile out of me. Judging by the way her eyes widen, I didn't quite manage it. "We didn't fail. I did. You did great."

Her relieved sigh is both sweet and a stark reminder that I let myself get distracted by Destin and Sykes and Leander and avocados. Some investigative reporter I made tonight. Feeling like a clueless dupe, I thank Bri for her help and wander back to my Corvette. The handwritten note taunts me the rest of the night.

Paying the Devil a Visit

Rock

A motorcycle rumbles closer, louder, forcing my attention away from Leif's old bike. I'm in the process of stripping the asinine flames off so I can repaint it. Every time I look at the flames and think of my brother, my mood turns bleak.

For the entire two weeks I was incarcerated, he wouldn't communicate with me. Wouldn't speak to me over the phone, answer my emails, or open the one ink-to-paper letter I sent. In his mind, it was my fault he was in prison. I screwed him over. Forget all of the illegal crap he did—drug dealing, running a chop shop, and trying to murder Val—his being behind bars was all me.

He isn't even wrong. I'm the one who gave the DA every

dirty secret I had on my own brother. To keep him behind bars and away from Val. My hand runs through my growing hair, its ends curling over my ears. For a girl who isn't in my life anymore, she occupies a huge chunk of my brain.

Darren, one of the old-time Snakes, coasts his bike up his driveway and cuts the engine in the space next to mine. It's his garage I'm crashing in, since I won't risk going home to Granny's. Granny Agani has been around forever, and everyone in the Snakes knows who she is. But the new recruits don't. Since the players wrestling for control of the Snakes have repeatedly threatened to kill me if I show my face, I stay away from them.

My dad's protection has held up to this point, even though I refused to speak with him while I was locked up. I never want to speak to him again. Years ago, he had a chance to get out of the gang when he met my ma, but he didn't take it. Instead, he dragged her down with him, setting up Leif and me to rule the viper's den after him. Every message he sent me while I was locked up was short and to the point: come back into the fold, or he'd withdraw his protection. Dino Agani could overlook my disobedience, but only if I repented and returned to his side.

I will never accept the role he has prepared for me. Sleeping on a cot in Darren's garage isn't great, but it's better than stepping into the legacy of violence my dad bought and paid for with his blood and pain all those years of leading the Snakes.

"Honey, I'm home." Darren's chuckle lingers as he shrugs off a broken-in leather jacket and lays it over the seat. The matte black helmet follows.

The middle-aged gang member's eyes rove over my bike's half-stripped body. The acrid stench of paint thinner fills the garage, even with the door up. Following an itch up his arm, Darren's eyes turn to mine. "Making good progress."

I lift a shoulder. Everything in me would love to ditch this bike. Sell it and buy a cheap car to fix up so I have a ride that doesn't make me think of my sick and twisted brother every time I look at it. Even more tempting is the idea of selling it and leaving the money in an envelope on Val's doorstep. Leif bought the bike with money he got from selling her dad's vehicle, after he scraped the former sheriff's body out of the interior. By rights this bike should be hers. A half smile creeps over my face at the idea of Val trying to convince her mom to let her ride a motorcycle. Being a dispatch worker, Mrs. Lamb has probably talked people through the aftermath of so many bike wrecks she'd never consider it.

"What're you thinking about?" Darren leans back against his workbench with a smirk.

My grip tightens around the paintbrush, and I work the condemning smile off my face. One thing I've learned at my father's knee is that showing visible signs of affection is dangerous. Setting my heart by any one person is a great way to lose them. My mom was first, but others have followed. Buddies who got arrested and come out different. Some are still inside. Some dug themselves too deep into the gang and paid the price with their lives. In my world, showing affection for someone like Val would be painting her with a target and handing out loaded guns with her name soldered into the grip. "No one."

Darren fake coughs into his hand. "Liar. You're not fooling me, boy. I watched you two when you were wee little kids. Even at seven you were smitten with her. Now, you're old enough to have deeper feelings, and you're shit at hiding them."

"You're delusional, old man."

The seasoned gang member runs his tongue over his teeth. "Gabriel is tired of her interfering with his plans."

"He can't do anything without permission from Dino, and Dino won't give it. Killing her doesn't do anything for the

Snakes. In fact, it would be like sending an engraved invitation to the entire sheriff's department to be up their butts all day every day, just waiting for them to slip up."

Darren looks over my bike in progress, tapping the front tire with the toe of his boot. "Your dad has a lot of power, but he's still behind bars. You want to risk your girl on the chance that Gabriel will stay on his leash? That's up to you."

Wiping the paintbrush off on the edge of the can, I make a few passes over the prepped metal.

"It doesn't matter to you that Gabriel is threatening to put a price on her head? 'Cause I could use the money. Bonnie wants to remodel our bathroom."

My paintbrush slops to the ground, fallen from nerveless fingers. Flecks of paint thinner splatter over the bike, the floor, and both our feet. "What did you say?"

The old man's eyes are steely on mine. "You heard me, boy. Only question is, what are you going to do about it? Maybe it's time to visit your pops."

Teeth clenched in my skull, I shove to a stand. I vowed never to go visit him. But for Val? I'm beginning to wonder if there's anything I wouldn't do to protect her.

I've seen photos of prisons in other countries, and they don't inspire the dread that standing outside the local joint does. It's tall and gray with arrow slits for windows. That might be because I spent fifteen days inside, and I know way more about prison than I ever thought I would.

Ten minutes have passed while I sit on Leif's bike staring at the big gray monstrosity I'm about to walk into, and my hands won't let go of the handlebars. My body fights every step to the building. I might as well be walking on sand dunes in oversized tennis shoes.

In too few minutes, I'm sitting at a round table in the visitor's room, waiting for the door on the far end to admit my dad. He enters following several other inmates, his eyes finding me immediately. A new tattoo on his neck peeks out of the prison jumpsuit that is not wide enough to accommodate his wrestler's body. We Agani men aren't tall, but we're wide, solid folk.

Forcing all emotion down deep where he won't be able to see it, I put steel in my spine. Any sign of weakness and he'll pounce on it. Use it to make me do what he wants. Step up and lead the Snakes while he and Leif are indisposed, as he'd put it. Can't blink. Can't flinch. Can't feel.

The bench across from me creaks as my father lowers his weight onto it. Hands capable of unimaginable evil land heavily on the tabletop. "It takes ten months for a boy to come visit his dad now?"

"Been busy."

Thick forearms bear his weight. My father has bulked up since I last laid eyes on him. "Your brother came to see me every week."

It's a guilt trip, and not a surprise. My dad expects us to be obedient and dutiful always. He's never said, but his regret that I'm so soft was evident every time he pushed me harder than he did Leif. My brother was all too willing to follow ugly orders, while I resisted at every turn. "Leif was running the Snakes for you. I'm just trying to graduate."

He stares at me, and I know what he's about to say. *I've built a legacy for you, son.* A legacy of violence I don't want.

"I've built a legacy for you. All you have to do is step up. Take your place at the head of the Snakes, and you'll have everything you ever wanted. Family. Protection. Money." He pauses, studying me to see if his lecture will finally sink in.

I don't react. He already knows I'm not interested in any of the benefits the Snakes have to offer. He knows, and he chooses to ignore it. We've been around this racetrack a hundred times.

"Ah, I forgot. You don't want any of that. What might entice you? Maybe a woman? I heard you and the Hill girl are no longer seeing each other. She has a new boyfriend. Ty, was it? If you want her back, I can have someone remove the boy from the picture…"

Shaking my head, I keep my face carefully blank. How can I have a father so evil he would murder an innocent teenager without even blinking? "She and I had a mutual breakup. I'm not interested in getting Janice back."

"As you say."

"I'm serious, Dad. Janice and I want different things. We're not good together anymore."

His thick fingers lace together on the table. "Where have you been staying?"

I don't answer. Selling out Darren isn't on my list of to-dos for today. The guy has been a Snake as long as I can remember, but he was always kind to a scared little boy who lost his mother. A little boy who fought like hell not to be dragged down into the pit with his father and brother. Darren has done more to earn my loyalty more than my father ever did. "With a friend."

My father mulls over my bland statement, a muscle ticking in his jaw. Annoyance that I'm still pushing back against him. "From what I hear, Janice has no problem helping out the family. You, on the other hand… You hurt me deeply when you spoke to the DA. I never thought a beloved son of mine would take up against me. It almost killed me to hear you had betrayed not just your brother, your own blood. But me, too. Your Father. The man who stuck by you when your mom abandoned you. What did I ever do to deserve such disrespect, Rock?"

My dad fires guilt from all sides. Preying on my years of conditioning and programming to look to him for everything. To be thankful that he kept me after my mom left, as if that made him Father of the Year. It didn't. Doing the bare minimum doesn't make him a good father. It makes him someone who sees Leif and me as an extension of him. A man who had to save face by spreading lies about my mom after she ran scared. A man who simply doesn't understand how I, his son, could want anything different than the life he built for himself.

"I did what I had to do. You should understand that. I learned it from you."

A gleam in his eyes appears, and the calculating edge to it sends a frisson of fear through me.

"You may think being confined within these walls limits my reach, but it doesn't. I hear everything. Such as how much time you've been spending with Daniel Lamb's daughter, Valencia."

Hearing her name from my father's mouth blows a hole in my composure. I flinch. He doesn't miss it. He doesn't miss anything. I should have known better.

"Ah, now I see. I could give her to you, if that's what you want. I can make sure she is yours, son. Come back into the den, and I'll see it done."

My hands clench into fists under the table where he can't see. How sick is he that he thinks he can manipulate someone as good, or as stubborn, as Valencia. He'd try, and he'd only end up crushing her. She'd fight like hell, but it wouldn't be enough. "I'm not interested in her."

My dad's mouth splits in a knowing grin. "If that's true, why can't you look me in the eye when you say it?"

Jaw popped, teeth gritted, I lock eyes with my father, the king of the Snakes. "I'm not interested in her."

One thick eyebrow twitches. "That isn't what Gabriel says, and since you've proven to be disloyal, I'm inclined to believe his word over yours. Much as that hurts me."

"I mean it, Dad. Leave her out of this."

Vision tunneling in on the ropes of muscles scrawling up his arms, the wide shoulders the same shape as mine, the neck thick from lifting weights for too many hours each day. Shaved head. Fresh snake tattoo on the right side of his neck to match the cobra on the left. His mouth moves. "No."

"What?"

"I want you at my side, once I get out."

"You're never getting out, Dad. Your sentence—"

"Once I get out, you will be at my side. And if I have to leverage the Lamb girl against you, I will. Gabriel would jump at the chance to remove her as a stumbling block."

I jerk back from the bench, losing the battle against my father yet again. I walked in here determined to keep my cool, but he always knows exactly which button to press to undo me. He does it effortlessly.

Glaring at him, I come as close to ordering him down as I dare. "You can't. If you do anything to her, it will bring the entire sheriff's department down on you and the Snakes. They'd tear apart everything you've built."

My father leans back on the bench, as if he's above even the almighty power of gravity. Lording over its weakness against his bulky frame. "You have no idea of the power I hold. Come back into the den, and I'll call Gabriel off. If you refuse, my hands are tied. Her safety is in your hands, my son."

I've already lost, so I throw at him the one bomb he never

expected me to deploy. "If anything happens to her, I'll give the DA everything I held back last time. I know where all of your bodies are buried, Dad, and I'll lead them to every single one of them."

His mouth flattens. The first outward sign of his displeasure. I'm surprised to see a flicker of hesitation before his eyes go flat, but then it's gone. "You displease me, son. If you won't listen to me, hear this. Learn to sleep with one eye open."

I make it out of the visiting room before nervous energy floods my body. Every muscle in me fires and quakes while I wait for the woman behind the desk to return the items I had to check in before seeing my father. Darting out to Leif's bike, I throw it into gear and fly across town to Val's house.

She has to be home. I have to warn her that the Snakes are about to be uncaged. After the conversation I just had with my dad, any protection he might have provided will be removed immediately. All he has to do is make one phone call.

I have to warn Val that she should be careful not to let them corner her. I've always suspected something is not right in Gabriel's head, and if he sets his aim on her, there is nothing he won't do to hurt her.

That Better Be Powdered Sugar

Val

"Sweetie? Can you come make the guacamole?" Mom calls from the kitchen, where hints of garlic and cumin tickle my nose. Dinner is tacos piled high with cheese and a dollop of sour cream. My mom stirs the meat with one hand, then turns to chopping tomatoes.

"How hot do we want it this time?" Pulling our avocado from the fruit basket, I get to work. Gathering the ingredients I'll need, I slice open the perfectly ripe avocado. A quick squeeze frees the pit. I yelp when it rolls off the counter.

Bending down to retrieve it, I freeze. A fine white powder spills out of the pit. Confused, I pick it up. Someone drilled a hole in it. I upend the pit over the counter and white flakes float out.

"Uh, Mom? I think I accidentally bought some crack."

My mom turns, her amused smile dying at the sight of a small mound of white powder. I give the avocado a jiggle to demonstrate where the substance is coming from. More white flakes trickle out of the fruit's green-smeared pit.

She snatches the seed from my hand, lifting it just high enough to smell the chemical stink without inhaling any. Her eyes bulge in disgust as they whip to me. "Where did you get this?"

The fruit kid must have sold it to me by accident. Even without knowing the current street value of a couple hits of cocaine, I know it goes for more than the $.99 I paid. It had to have been a mistake. A fruit plucked from the wrong sack. "A guy was standing on the street outside school, selling them. I don't usually buy from those guys, but we needed an avo for dinner so. . ."

"Don't taste it!" My mom screeches, slapping my white-dusted finger away from my open mouth.

"Just making sure it isn't powdered sugar." My mom is not amused by my attempt to lighten the suddenly grim mood.

She sighs raggedly. "I'll call the sheriff. He'll want me to take it down there, so let's eat before I have to go." Mom deposits the pit into a plastic bag, and we both scrub our hands up to the elbows at the sink, using palms full of soap.

Our taco dinner is pensive. Chewing a tasty bite of fried-tortilla and spicy seasoned ground beef gives me a second to think. This time of the evening, it's about shift change time at the department. Since I was the one who bought the fruit in the first place, it makes sense for me to update the sheriff myself. I can give him a description of the guy who was selling the fruits on the corner, assuming no one else has found a drug avocado this evening and reported it. "I'll take the avocado to the station. It's your night off, so you shouldn't have to go down there again. Plus, Destin was riding along with Jonesie today, and I want to see how it went."

"You sure?" Mom pauses eating her taco to watch me over its shell. Tacos without guacamole aren't nearly as good, so I only eat two instead of three.

"I'm sure. Why don't you get the next movie on our list queued up while I'm gone? I won't be long."

Mom's eyes are heavy on me as she thinks it over. "If you're sure."

I assure her I am. She puts the leftovers away while I sweep and mop the kitchen floor. I don't want Rosie finding traces of white powder and getting sick. It's a good thing the kitten was occupied with her own dinner in the laundry room, or she would have come to investigate. That saying about curiosity killing cats might as well have been written for her. When I stick my head in the laundry room to check on my kitten, her bowl is licked clean and she is zonked out in her cute little cloud-shaped bed.

Shrugging on my bomber jacket, I jog out to the Corvette. Finding a drug avocado has left a taint on the day, and there's an uneasy sloshing low in my gut.

It might be the eerily quiet streets as I drive through town to the station. It's a Wednesday and not even late, but no one is out and about. Or maybe it's the storm clouds gathering on the horizon. Either way, something is poking at my peace, slithering under my skin. I have worries I can't quell. Or even pin down long enough to figure out where they're coming from.

Usually, driving helps, but not tonight. Graffiti keeps cropping up where it isn't wanted. Ugly words carved into the sides of businesses. Streetlights smashed and unusable, waiting to be fixed. I come way too close to getting T-boned when some idiot runs a red light. By the time I pull into the department lot, my heart booms like a toddler harassing a bass drum.

Jonesie exits the building, jacket zipped up to his chin.

A gust of wind cuts through my body, and I wrap my arms around myself for warmth. My feet eat up the distance to the door, seeking warmth and shelter. Coming within high-fiving distance of the deputy, I slow. "How was your farmer's market date with Kelley?"

Jonesie winks, his cheeks taking on a blush.

"That good, huh? Is Destin still inside?"

"Yes, indeedy." Jonesie resumes walking, turning backward to finish our conversation. "He'll make a good officer one day."

I should be happy for Destin, that he has found a calling to pursue. A noble way to serve and protect. But I'd be lying if I denied being afraid for him, too. My dad died on the job, for fudge sake. "I'll tell him you said so. Don't wait too long before you call her."

The wind delivers the deputy's sly answer. "Call who?"

Despite the biting wind, I want to stand here on the sidewalk and rib Jonesie a little more. Because it's a distraction from the drug-stuffed fruit in my bag. No innocent bystander finds a drugged-up avocado in real life. It's the kind of thing that happens on TV. But here I am walking into the department with a tainted avocado in a baggie. This never would have happened in Hacienda a year ago, before Dino Agani and Angus Hill were put away. The upheaval among the Snakes is affecting everyone in town, and I hate that for us. What I wouldn't give to go back to a few weeks ago, when drug avocados were inconceivable, and Mom and I were visiting the department to deliver jugs of spiced apple cider for Christmas.

Leander isn't at the front counter tonight, but Destin is. He grins at me, face flushed with excitement. "Val! You should have seen it. Some tweaker was getting ready to break into the pharmacy, but Jonesie pulled up and stopped him. It was so cool."

"Sounds awesome. That'll be you someday." My hand freezes in my bag as Destin visibly deflates. Now is not the time for drug avocados.

"I just have to figure out how to tell my mom." His head droops as he shuffles to hold open the gate in the counter so I can round to his side. My heart goes out to him. Being a police officer is one of the hardest jobs there is. Between the inherent danger in each shift and the fact that the few bad cops have made it incredibly difficult for all the good ones, I don't envy Destin's chosen path. I admire him for it. His tender heart and athletic build will make him a good cop. Caring and capable. I could definitely see him pairing well with a canine unit, too, if his closeness with Bert is any indication.

Being short is an advantage with Destin, because I don't have to stoop to meet his sad eyes. Lightly flicking his nose brings his face up. "She'll get used to it. She just wants you to be safe."

He slips a hand around my neck. "Maybe. Noogie time."

Screeching, I use a hold break I learned in kickboxing to get him off me. Laughing, I escape beyond arms' reach. "How many times do I have to say this? No more noogies."

Destin holds up a hand in promise, but his other is suspiciously behind his back. "What brings you in? Did you come just to check on me? Or to see Leander? He isn't here, by the way."

"I brought a present for the sheriff." Lifting the clear bag out of my backpack so Destin can see, I wait for him to absorb the full picture.

"Holy crap."

My smile is flat. "Yeah. So this happened."

"What happened?" Sheriff McCandles stands in the center of the bull pen. I proffer the clear bag, and his eyebrows shoot up. Boots clomp over the floor as he approaches, gently taking the pouch from my outstretched hand. The lawman holds it up to his eyes and scrutinizes its contents. Puffs out his cheeks. Turns to me. "That's a hell of a thing. Where did you get this?"

"Outside school after class." I tell him as much as I can remember about the guy I bought the avocado from, as well as the bags of fruit he had for sale. It's a short story. I have no doubt the guy is long gone, hours having passed since school let out and I made my surprisingly illicit purchase.

Sheriff McCandles taps one hand on his belt buckle. "I've heard about some of the cartels smuggling their product inside lots of different objects, but this is a first. Wouldn't surprise me if a few of them have taken over some of the avocado farms. It would make this kind of operation far simpler, and more lucrative. Once we're done here, I'll report it."

Destin loosens the collar of his button up shirt. "No wonder avocados have gotten scarce."

I knew the sheriff would be reporting my find, the second my eyes fell on the tampered avocado. "If they want to speak to me. . ."

The sheriff nods, already halfway to his office. "I'll let you know. Thanks for bringing this in so quickly."

Destin shuffles his feet, wading toward the front door without actually going anywhere. He doesn't want to go home yet. I sink down onto one of the counter stools and pat the one next to me. He takes it gratefully. Letting my mom know I'll be a little while is easy. She sends a smiley face back.

"How're you?" Destin asks, rotating back and forth on the swiveling stool. "Leander told me you almost got trampled at that party last weekend."

"Short people problems. Hey, question. What's the protocol for that, anyway? You and I are friends, and you and him are friends, but I'm not a go-between, right? And you aren't either." I had almost texted Leander to ask him to keep the fight to himself but hadn't gotten to it. As days passed, I hoped Destin wouldn't find out about my close brush with being smashed by drunken party-goers. He's had enough to worry about in the past year, and I don't want to pile on.

His knee buts against mine as he pivots. "We talked about this, remember? You promised to tell me what's going on with you. Sharing the hard stuff is part of being friends. We both tend to clam up when we're upset, but that doesn't work for us."

I do a full 360 spin on the stool, coming back to face him. "I thought friendship mostly consisted of sharing cafeteria brownies."

A laugh curls Destin's mouth. "I'm not Rock. I don't share my brownies."

"Selfish."

He snorts, but he doesn't let me get away with changing the subject. "I care about you, Val. And I want to know if you're hurting, or hurt, or anything. You can tell me."

Something loosens inside me at his reassurance. He's right. We've been friends forever, but I have never been good at communicating about the hard stuff. Or asking him to share his feelings with me. Most of the time, I'd rather pretend drama doesn't exist. The problem is, that made me a bad friend in the past. When Destin's girlfriend was murdered, I assumed he felt like I did. That he didn't want to talk about it either. Making that assumption almost cost me Destin. As much as I'd rather dodge this conversation, I won't. He deserves my attention. My... vulnerability. I wish that didn't feel like a curse word on my tongue. I lick my lips, and dive in. "I almost got trampled at the party. One of the Snakes tried to murder me, but Rock was there. He saved me."

Destin's eyebrows rise. "Wow, okay. Leander definitely didn't share that little nugget."

I shrug. "He probably missed that part. We got separated, and Leander didn't find me until it was all over. Also, I might have been a little tipsy."

My friend laughs. "I heard. I'm sorry I missed it. I want to try the famous pink drink."

Remembering the aching head and stomach I woke up with the next morning, I grimace. "Infamous pink drink. Stick to milkshakes. Pink drink might go down easy, but it has a nasty after taste."

We chat for a little while. I show Destin some photos from the helmet artist I saw at the farmer's market, and he gets amped up. Turns out, he's familiar with the girl's work and is saving up to have a helmet customized with a portrait of Bert.

In a conversation lull, I nudge Destin with my elbow. "You could bring a date. I saw you talking to Shelby at school the other day."

A cornered look enters his eyes. "She was talking to me. I was just trying to use the water fountain."

His reticence isn't a surprise. If I found out that my new girlfriend had murdered my old girlfriend, I wouldn't be eager to date again either. "No pressure. Just checking in."

Destin's floppy blond hair skims his forehead as he gives a shudder. "Seriously. Hard pass. To be honest, I don't know when I'll be ready."

Our conversation tapers, and Destin turns pensive. Sensing his need for quiet, I say my goodbyes. Sliding out into the wintery night, I fire up the Corvette. One of dad's favorite songs plays on the radio. It's been months, but I still have it tuned in to his favorite classic rock station. I don't know when or if I'll change it. Driving in his car, listening to his music, it's almost as if he's still here with me. If I focus straight ahead, I can almost picture him sitting in the passenger seat, his hair flapping in the wind from a rolled down window. But when I look over, the only passenger in the seat is my backpack.

The grocery store is on the way, so I stop in for an avocado that hasn't been meddled with. Tomorrow's lunch tacos will have guac, so help me.

Nope, they won't. I frown at an empty avocado display. There is not a single one anywhere in the store.

Only a few cars remain in the lot when I step outside with a disappointing tub of pre-made guacamole spread dangling from one hand. The Corvette waits in the middle of the lot, wreathed in deepening night. Which is weird because I parked directly under a lamp post.

That portentous tingle in my gut gets stronger. It's foreboding, and I am not a fan.

My feet slow as I walk between a couple of cars to get to mine. The light I parked under has been smashed. Shards of glass glitter under the sliver of moon, prickly confetti sprinkled over my car.

I halt between two cars, squinting into the dark.

Two, no three hooded figures take form in the shadows lurking around the Corvette.

I stare, heart in my throat, praying they haven't seen me.

One of the shadows turns their head slowly to survey the parking lot. Quick as I can, I tuck my body into the darkest depths between the cars. Hidden eyes pass over me without stopping. The figure nods to their companions.

Holding my muscles tight to keep steady, I turn my head

just enough to see the store entrance. It's almost a straight shot from my hiding place. If I run, I'd make it there before any of the shadows could reach me. But I can't move. I'm fused to the concrete by the dread surging and thickening behind my knees.

Nefarious shadows circle around the Corvette. My dad's beloved car, bequeathed to me in his in-case-of-death letter.

Metal glints in the dark, snaring my eyes. Is that…?

A vice tightens around my ribcage, rendering my lungs worthless. The shadows brandish tools that can be used to build or to break. An oversized hammer. The world's largest wrench. A tire iron.

My feet move before my brain registers the signal. They won't lay a finger on my dad's car; I'll make sure of it. Shaking fingers wrap around the can of pepper spray I keep handy. If this isn't enough to stop them, well… It has to be enough.

An angry shout is quenched in my throat when thick arms slam around my waist, dragging me behind a parked minivan and pinning me against a solid body.

"Do it," a gruff voice commands.

With a loud crack, metal meets glass. A window shatters.

Car Bashing

GLASS SPLINTERS THE SUFFOCATING QUIET. Clawing against the arms at my waist is pointless. My cropped fingernails are useless against leather and denim.

The shadows goad each other, and another tool makes contact. Glass crackles like thunder tearing a black sky.

Panic and desperation put my back up. Sweat breaks out on my temples. I have to get free. I have to stop them from wrecking my Corvette beyond repair. My dad loved that car. I love that car.

Bracing one foot, I aim a bruising kick out behind me. My foot glances off my attacker's leg. He fumbles an attempt to widen his stance, falling against me. Pinning me between him and a stranger's minivan. Cold metal presses against the side of my face. He could hurt me in a staggering number of ways with me trapped like this.

I can't breathe. Wriggling for air, I gasp like a fish drowning on dry land.

Immediately, his weight releases me. "Shit. I'm not trying to hurt you. Stop struggling."

No one hears my pain-filled scream for help under the keening screech of metal dragging against metal.

A sweaty palm tasting of salt and leather wraps around my mouth. I bite down hard. Rock's hand tightens, his growl rumbling in my ear. He encroaches with his larger, heavier body against my back, forcing me to the ground. Grit and rocks cut through my jeans, digging into the tight skin over my knees.

Metal clangs against metal. One punishing blow after another. More glass shattering. Angry words and jeers grow louder, emboldened by the utter absence of resistance.

Pain fills my chest as my own heart shatters. "Let me go!" I snap, throwing my head back against Rock's shoulder.

He barely stifles a hiss of pain. "No deal. Soon as I let go, you'll do something stupid."

My jaw clenched, I struggle and tug against his arms banded around my waist and my collar bones. Ineffectually. Knowing that Rock is the one bringing me to the ground has taken the fight out of me. From the soles of my feet to the roots of my hair, he would never hurt me.

Yanking an arm free, I pinch his forearm. Hard. He may not hurt me, but I'm still pissed at him for jumping me in a dark parking lot. Even if he was doing it to keep me from getting my skull bashed in by rabid Snakes.

"Ouch. That hurts." The bite has left his voice, but one arm remains snug around my waist. Anchoring me to him.

My car groans as feet stomp and pound. Its frame rocks, creaking under the onslaught.

"Let me go," I whimper, yanking halfheartedly at Rock's looser hold.

"You know I can't do that, Val. Your life, your heart, your

skin and bones are worth infinitely more than that car."

Shuddering and giving in, I slump to the ground. I lean my back against Rock's chest. His legs come around mine, cocooning me safely away from the tornado of hate and destruction swirling a stone's throw away.

Sniffing does nothing to quench the burn in my chest. I need a distraction. "You said you wanted to get your hands on that car, but here you are. Can't take your mitts off me, can you?"

Rock's laugh is warm against my hair. "Not yet, I can't. One can of pepper spray won't be enough to stop them, and I won't see you hurt."

Glass and metal groan and break, filling my ears with desolation.

"They're destroying it," I whisper through a sob.

"Nothing that can't be fixed or replaced." *Unlike you*, he doesn't say. But we both hear it.

The low rumble of a bigger vehicle encroaches on our position, backed up against a dusty minivan. The screeching cries of damage stop. I expect running feet, but no one moves. My lungs go still. At my back, Rock's chest rises and falls as he pants.

A car door opens and slams. Boots crunch on asphalt. "What is going on here?"

Help has arrived.

I give a subtle nudge at Rock's arm, and he releases me. Scrambling to my feet, I peer through the minivan's windows. Sykes is there. His hands are propped on his waist, but he's not in uniform. There is no telltale bump at the back of his shirt where a concealed firearm rests waiting to be called to duty. He's unarmed. But he's trained. He'll be fine.

The passenger door swings open, and a second person emerges from Sykes's personal truck. My stomach plummets into my shoes as Destin rounds the vehicle. He takes up position next to the deputy, glaring at the three shadows. Ill-used tools still gripped in their hands.

I allow myself a breath to skim over the Corvette, and the jagged edges of my damaged heart curl and blacken. Every window is shattered. The tires are slashed. Livid scratches run along the near side of the car, splitting the paint. A stab of relief at the untouched interior is short-lived.

"Drop your weapons," Sykes orders, hand extended toward the Snakes. "Des, get back in the truck. Call this in."

Destin clucks his disagreement, crossing his arms over his chest and glaring at the three men who beat my car to a dented pulp.

"Now."

My bestie doesn't flinch. His composure is complete. If his mom could see him right now, she'd be worried, but I think she'd also be proud. I am.

None of the three belly-crawlers moves. Tools remain in clawed hands. The tallest, probably the leader, bares his teeth in a malevolent smile. "No, thanks. I'm partial to this particular wrench. Useful too, don't you think?" Holding Sykes's eye contact, he swings the wrench. It dings off a broken headlight.

My frown tightens into a sneer. He's going to pay for that.

Sykes isn't stupid. He doesn't for even a split second take his eyes off the three gang members. "Destin," he growls.

"Yes, sir." He stomps around the truck and throws himself inside. Through the window, he jabs at his phone, making a call. Glaring out the windshield at the Snakes the whole time. The department is only a couple of blocks away, so backup will be here in a couple of minutes.

Sykes speaks again as he advances toward the gang members, confident and in control. Luring their attention away from Destin in the truck. Coming even with the Corvette, he doesn't spare it a look. "I don't want to ask again. Drop the tools, fellas."

The tallest of the shadows jeers. "Again, no, thanks."

"Officer," another snickers.

My teeth clench. Worried for Sykes. Worried for Destin. Not able to come up with a way to help diffuse the tension crackling through the air. My clothes stick to my sweaty skin.

Fury sears through me as my eyes linger on my car. It's completely racked and ruined. I have some money saved up, but not nearly enough to rebuild the Corvette's entire body. My shoulders shudder and my eyes fall closed. I'll have to sell it for scrap. The last and greatest gift from my father.

Turning to Rock, I find his soul-deep eyes already on me. "Can you do anything?"

Pained, he shakes his head. He taps his chest with a finger. "They'd kill me as soon as look at me. I'm a traitor, remember?"

Grimacing, I watch the deputy. I know he won't—Sykes is a by-the-book officer—but a darker part of me wants him to hurt them. Make them bleed. Immediately ashamed of that impulse, I fight it down and lock it into a box deep inside, away from the light.

There is a ripple in the shadow under the truck. It looks like—did Destin sneak out somehow? No. Des is right there, inside the window, talking on his cell. His eyes are trained on Sykes and the men facing off against him. Clearly upset, Destin slams a hand down on the dashboard.

The tallest shadow tilts his head. "How do you feel about jump scares, officer?"

Sykes ignores the question. "For the last time. Drop your weapons. This isn't a game."

I gasp. Someone is under the truck, inching closer through the shadows toward Sykes. Everything inside me tightens as fear ambles along my spine, curling up at the nape of my neck. Every hair on my head stands on end as I put it together. There's a fourth Snake under that vehicle, and Sykes doesn't see him.

My scream splits the tension, and our fragile truce breaks. "Sykes, at your feet!"

Sykes turns toward the truck just as the shadow scrambles from underneath it. He grapples with the deputy's legs and bears him down. The deputy is already fighting when his knees hit the ground. A brutal kick snaps the shadow's nose. Blood gushes onto the asphalt.

Yelling in surprise and anger, the other three Snakes lunge, swinging heavy metal tools at Sykes's head.

Blows connect with his raised arms, but Sykes doesn't stop swinging. Doesn't even slow down. He's fighting back on pure adrenaline. Years of experience and training kick in, and he subdues one of the gangsters with a few well-placed blows.

The guy goes down, leaving two more to grapple with.

Hammer gleaming in the air, a gang member brings it down on the deputy's shoulder. The man yells in pain.

Heart thudding, I look around. Frantic for help. There is no one.

As a civilian I shouldn't get involved, but I can't stand here doing nothing. That's not me.

An abandoned cart is parked half in the dirt-planter nearby. My feet slap the pavement, blood slamming in my ears. Yanking the cart out over the concrete barrier, I swing it around and take aim. Screaming my fury, I run. Push every ounce of muscle and energy and fear and anger through my hands into the cart's careening wheels.

Rock rushes past me, flinging himself into the fight. Cocking his muscled arm like a battering ram, he throws a brutal punch into one guy's stomach.

A third gang member wrestles with Sykes on the ground. The fourth has left his back unprotected. Big mistake.

Muscles straining with fury, I drive the cart into his back and run roughshod over him. The Snake falls to the ground, an arm crunching under the cart's wheel. Whipping the metal cart around, I aim to do it again so the guy stays down.

Through the buzzing in my ears, I hear a shout. "Stop!"

Sensing that they're talking to me, I ignore them.

Despite a dangling arm, the Snake tries to stand. I won't allow it. Not while Sykes is still fighting. Shoving the cart forward, I lunge.

"Val, don't!" Pounding feet rush toward me.

The Snake's eyes meet their mirror image in mine. A concoction of pain and anger. My hands tighten on the cart's rim. Knuckles white against the red plastic grip. The same red as the blood trickling from a cut in the Snake's forehead.

I pin him against another car. "Don't move, or I'll run you over again."

Tension mounts between us. We're two acrobats facing off on a tightrope strung between two towering buildings. If I flinch, I die. If he flinches, he loses a kidney.

Thick, sturdy arms come around me, gentle even as they pry my fingers away from the cart handle. Bloody knuckles brush over mine, rubbing the tension out of my arms as they smooth up to my shoulders. "You okay? Not hurt?"

Sirens wail, coming closer. Destin called for the cavalry, and it's almost here.

As if someone cut my strings, the fight goes out of me. Stumbling against Rock, I sob into his flannel shirt. His arms wrap around me, holding me tightly against him.

"Wait," I mumble. "Wait. Sykes."

"He's going to be okay," Rock soothes, his chin tucked on

top of my head.

"I need to see." Without letting go, Rock pivots us on the asphalt so Sykes is in my view. He leans back against his truck, hands bloodied. He cradles one arm against his chest—the one that took the hammer to the shoulder. At his feet lay three Snakes. The fourth one slinks out of my line of vision. I rattle the shopping cart with one foot, and he goes still.

Dustin kneels beside Sykes, checking him over. The deputy looks up at Rock and me. He shakes his head. Rubs at his eyes. "Why are there four of you?"

Destin looks from him to us, confused.

My hands twist in the front of Rock's shirt.

A patrol car rushes into the lot, sliding to a sudden stop just as Sykes's body crumples to the asphalt.

Ty's Stupid Theory on Love

Janice bursts into the front door of my house, her super cute boots thumping as she crosses the entryway and poses in the living room doorway. Ty stands beside her. "Who wants a smoothie?" she sings.

"That door was locked. How'd you get in?" I ask, incredulous. I was positive I had locked that door.

Her eyebrow arches. "What, like you're the only one who can look up lock picking on the internet?"

I splutter, shooting a look at Destin. "That was privileged information."

Janice's sharp grin makes me burrow down into my turtleneck. "He didn't tell you, did he?"

"No, but you just did. I got a new jacket. How do I look?"

Her new coat is yellow with brass buttons and perfectly tailored to her pear-shaped self. I swear this girl can wear any color and look impeccable. I stick to neutrals because color makes me look like a Muppet. Janice puts an elbow on my shoulder. "It's yellow."

"Goldenrod."

"Whatever. It's super bright. Makes you look like the sun."

Janice smiles beatifically at me as she twirls in the new designer coat. "If you're saying the entire world should revolve around me in this jacket, I agree."

Destin greets them, giving Ty a fist bump.

The smoothie guy holds up a cardboard drink container, but I'm distracted by his socks. They're baby blue with cocktails all over them. Seeing the direction of my gaze, he gives a bemused smile. "They didn't have smoothie socks, so my grandma got me these for Christmas."

"They work."

"Thanks, man." Destin takes the purple smoothie Ty offers.

I get my usual peach mango, thanking Ty after a long, scrumptious slurp. Eyeing Janice, I chew on my straw. "What happened to the red coat? And seriously, how did you get in here?"

She gives a one-shouldered shrug. "Got tired of it, so I sold it and bought this one. Don't you love it?"

"I love it."

"You hate it because it's not black. Or burgundy." She's dodging my question without breaking a sweat, which makes me want the answer even worse.

"I don't hate the jacket, but my opinion doesn't matter because you clearly love it. But Jan, seriously, how did you get inside my house?"

She beams, taking in my monochrome lounging outfit. "I totally love it. Why the sudden obsession with burgundy, anyway?"

Now I'm the one making evasive maneuvers. Holding up my drink, I cheers Ty. "This is the best smoothie you've ever made. What did you put in this? My avocado crack?"

Ty snickers. "That would be illegal. I bet I know why you're wearing burgundy all the sudden."

Sinking down into the couch and turtling in my shirt collar doesn't stop my face from heating. I have no idea why. "I just like the color, okay?"

Janice leans into my line of sight. "I see you trying to change the subject, my friend. Your conversation skills need work. Good thing you have me to learn from."

"Speaking of conversation skills, did you really pick the lock on my door?"

Tugging on her ponytail, Janice groans. "No. I did not pick your lock. God, you're like a dog with a bone. Mama Lamb gave me a key, okay?"

My jaw drops open. I did not see that coming. "Why would she do that?"

"Because we're besties now, obviously. And she wanted to let me know I'm welcome here any time. Apparently, she feels bad for what happened with Rock when you were kids, and frankly, she should. So last time I was here she pulled me aside, told me I had a safe place here whenever, and gave me a key. Do you want it back, or something?"

Janice has bravado in spades, but I'm getting better at reading her. The undercurrent of insecurity in her explanation is reassuring, somehow. That she isn't taking advantage of me for some nefarious plot I haven't sussed out yet. Maybe she really does want to be my friend. For some reason I will eventually figure out.

"See, there you go. You're overthinking it, which is why I didn't tell you. It's not a big deal, okay?" Janice's brown eyes shine with barely concealed worry. "I'm not asking you to let me move in here, or anything."

I distract myself by taking a long gulp of sweet peachy mango. "Not a big deal. Agreed."

Janice relaxes into the couch cushion like a puppy in a load of warm towels fresh from the dryer. "Now that that's out of the way, cute joggers/sweatshirt combo. The burgundy looks good on you."

"Thanks."

"Still curious why you suddenly wear burgundy, though."

I gesture toward the hall closet where she hung her coat. "My mom's bomber is burgundy and I've been wearing it for a couple years."

She twirls her straw. "True, but you got that new waffle Henley a couple weeks ago, and now this lounge set? I know it isn't the new color of the year. I would have heard about that."

Ty, who has sprawled out on the ottoman next to the couch and tucked his legs around Janice's, takes a loud slurp from his smoothie. "She's into burgundy because it reminds her of that Rock guy who drives a motorcycle and comes swooping in to rescue her whenever she gets herself in trouble."

"Which is a lot," Destin puts in.

I shoot an incredulous look at him. "Not helping, D. And I do not get myself in trouble a lot. Trouble finds me."

An O forms around Janice's mouth as she looks between me and Ty. To him, she says, "I knew there was something going on between you two at the diner."

Ty leans forward on his knees and presses a kiss to her shoulder. "Babe, you tell me everything, and it sounds like this Rock guy is obsessed with her. He's saved her like what, three times now?"

I can't sit still. Streaks of electricity snap through me, making me jump off the couch. "He's not obsessed with me. We're not even friends."

That's a giant lie. Rock kept me from throwing myself into the middle of a pile of angry Snakes when they attacked my car the other night. He didn't let go of me, even when I lashed out at him, heartbroken over my car.

If he didn't care about me at all, he wouldn't have sat there and taken it.

Ty watches me pace across the living room with a knowing look in his big, surprisingly insightful eyes. "That's not what it sounds like. He crashed your date with Leander that time, didn't he?"

I whirl on him. "No! I mean, yes, but only because I was blackmailing him. It wasn't my finest moment," I tack on when Destin gasps. "Sorry, I didn't tell you about that."

Janice scoots forward on the couch, running her fingers under the cuff of her opposite sleeve. "Seriously, though. Is the burgundy because of Rock?"

"No. Of course not. No. It's probably the color of the year, like you said, and I've seen it around everywhere enough to be brainwashed into buying it."

Sitting forward, Janice waits for me to stop pacing and meet her eyes. "Because if it was because of Rock, I wouldn't blame you. He's a great guy, and a good one to have in your corner."

The ice machine in our fridge rumbles. Janice waits for it to stop. "You'd tell me if there was something going on, right?"

Slumping against the wall, I pull my hair forward and grip it in both hands. "It's blatantly obvious to everyone in this room that I am crap at keeping secrets, so yes, I would tell you if there was something going on between Rock and me. There isn't. You know, he once told me that if a guy likes a girl, he'll do whatever it takes to let her know?"

Janice bites her lip. "He hasn't let you know."

Dropping back onto the couch between Janice and Des, I

pick up my empty smoothie cup and pump the straw in and out of it, wishing there was more in there to give me an excuse to end this conversation. I don't have a crush on Rock, or anything, but this line of questioning is making me squirm like an ant under a microscope on a 100 degree day. "I told you how fast he left after Sheriff McCandles got to the store lot the other night. He couldn't get away fast enough."

Easing closer, Destin bumps my knee with the outer rim of his hand. "But he made sure you were safe first."

"Yes." Rock stayed until he was sure I was safe, going so far as to personally buckle me into Deputy Kelley's car so she could drive me home.

The four of us go mercifully quiet. Soft music plays from the sound bar under the TV. I replay our conversation over in my head, wondering how on earth my friends came to the conclusion that Rock and I have something between us. It's ridiculous. Yes, Rock has come to my rescue a couple of times when I did something stupid and impulsive without having an exit strategy. I need to work on that, actually. But he hasn't sought me out. He was at the auto shop working when I blazed in there to demand the Corvette back. Same goes for the party. Those were rescues of opportunity.

I can't explain how he appeared in the grocery store parking lot just in time to keep me from getting my head bashed in by the pond scum who destroyed my car, but there has to be a reason. Maybe Granny Agani sent him to the store for milk and cereal. Or maybe he was driving past and the pop of a lamppost being broken caught his attention. There are a hundred reasons Rock showed up in that lot, and none of them have anything to do with fuzzy feelings inspired by me.

Janice shifts into my personal space, opening her mouth. I'm saved by my phone lighting up.

Scanning the text message, I read it over twice. "It's Jonesie. Sykes was discharged and just got home. The doctors kept him for monitoring since this is his first serious concussion, but they said he's going to be fine. A couple weeks of rest, and he can come back to work."

Destin wraps an arm around me. "Good news. He's way better to ride with than Jonesie or Kelley."

My laugh of relief is small, but it unravels some of the tension gathered at the base of my spine. "I get why Jonesie would be no fun to ride with given the amount of fast food he eats, but why Kelley?"

"She's too much of a stickler for rules. Doesn't let me do anything but observe."

Letting my head rest on his shoulder, I look up at his half smile. "Still haven't told your mom, huh?"

He shakes his head. "I'm trying to avoid that freakout for as long as possible."

"You should tell her," Janice says, "while you have the chance."

I nod in solidarity. Destin is lucky to have both of his parents, and keeping a huge secret like this from them could damage their strong relationship. Knowing Mr. and Mrs. Court, she's going to cry—and he'll try to dissuade Des from becoming a cop—but they'll support him no matter what he decides. In the past, whenever he's broken a bone, they fuss over him, but they've never tried to stop him from skateboarding or snowboarding or doing any of the other risky hobbies he enjoys. They're good parents, despite the puzzle obsession.

"Does Janice really tell you everything?" I ask Ty. The guy only smiles.

"So, about her fake ID guy…"

Ty mimes zipping his mouth shut and tossing away the key

to the soundtrack of Janice's gleeful cackling.

Competence and Cat Nip

"IF THAT WASN'T A NIGHT FROM HELL, MY MIDDLE NAME isn't Nancy." My mom's purse drops to the kitchen counter with a thump, and she makes a beeline for the fridge. Ice clunks into her glass, filled to the brim with water. She sinks into the chair across from me at the table, her throat bobbing as she glugs the entire glass.

"That bad, huh?" Soggy cereal bits float in my bowl. I poured it and sat down to eat, but then I couldn't stop thinking about all the teasing I took from Destin, Janice, and even Ty last night. We stayed up until 2 watching a mix of true crime episodes, skating videos, a skincare tutorial, and four episodes of *The Midnight Club*. Lifting my hair to my nose, I can still smell buttered popcorn.

Somewhere nearby, a siren wails. Now that I think about it, there have been a lot of those tonight.

Mom sets down her glass with a clink. Sighing, she rubs at her temples. "Scalp massage?"

Mornings after Mom's more emotionally draining shifts, she'd plop down at the table just like now, and Dad would know what she needed to wind down before going to sleep. I open the pantry and dig around inside. The spider-shaped head massager is buried behind a stack of cans. My mom's shoulders come loose the second the massager's rounded metal legs touch her head.

I work on her for a couple of minutes, her body sinking lower into the chair by the second. The organ in my chest warms seeing her unwind like this. At my ability to help her with something so simple.

With a pleased groan, my mom reaches up and takes my hand. Drawing me around to her side, she gives my fingers a squeeze. "Thanks, honey. That felt so nice. Want a turn?"

We swap spots, and my mom massages my head. It feels freaking amazing.

"To answer your question, yes, last night was rough." The massager caresses behind my ears, and I didn't know that was the spot, but that is the spot. No wonder she loves this thing so much. I almost kick my leg like a dog when you find its magic spot.

"Want to talk about it?" She won't. She doesn't talk about work with me, partly for privacy of the people she helps, and partly because she doesn't want to traumatize me. Those were her exact words last time I asked.

With a sigh, she talks. Explaining to me that everyone in the department is on edge since Sykes was attacked. The sheriff and all of the deputies are working overtime to make sure the town is in good hands, but with one man down it's a hefty job. On top of the extra long hours, they spend all of their time on the streets looking over their shoulders even more than normal. Even though they apprehended three of the four men who attacked Sykes, there are plenty more who would strike out at the department if the chance arose. They've seen a sharp uptake in people wearing snake bandanas and other clothing around town.

I hum, hearing everything she says while she works on my head. "It feels like we're turning a corner, and not a good one."

My mom squeezes my shoulder lightly with her free hand. "I agree. I don't know what's going to happen, but the balance has tipped, and I don't like it. I wish we could rewind time to ten years ago, when the town felt small and friendly, and your dad loved his job. He loved his job, Val. God, he… He just wanted everyone to be safe, and he worked so hard, and in the end. . ."

The spider massager hits the floor with a clang. My mom collapses into the chair next to me, face held in quaking hands.

Wrapping my arms around her, I lay my head on top of hers. Letting her know that I'm right here with her. That my chest is burning with an ache that still takes my breath away sometimes. Seeing Sykes collapse onto the asphalt lit my entire body on fire. Watching him fall was like watching my dad fall. Struck down by enemies he couldn't see even though they were standing right in front of him.

Squeezing my mom tighter, I hold on until her breathing settles and the sobs quiet. Tears trickle down my nose and drip onto her hair.

Rosie comes skittering into the room in a whir of gray fluff. With a super cute meow, she catapults herself into Mom's lap and starts scratching at her work pants with tiny, razor-sharp claws. The cuteness overload makes both of us laugh, cleaning ourselves up with paper napkins to our eyes and noses. "No making biscuits in Grandma's nice pants, okay little girl?"

Rosie does not agree to the terms. She pulls her tiny paws out of my mom's hands and leaps onto her shoulder, lifting both front paws to bat at my hair. Tucking the tiny terror into my arms, I rub her downy soft fur against my cheek.

"For someone who gave you a cat, I don't see Rock around much. Have you talked to him lately?" There is a wealth of unasked questions in my mom's eyes. Through her job, my mom has seen and heard about the growing numbers of Snakes in town. She knows a lot more about their movements and activities than I do. "He's keeping his head down. Janice told me his dad is pretty mad that he hasn't fallen in line. But Mom, he doesn't want to follow in Dino's footsteps. He never wanted that."

Mom hums. Opening the fridge, she takes out a jar of overnight oats and heats it in the microwave. "I imagine it's getting increasingly hard for Rock to stay out of it, given the way he was raised, and the pressure surrounding the Snakes right now. The sheriff thinks they still haven't chosen a new head, and that's leading to the increased incidents. They're building to something. He just hasn't figured out what it is yet."

"He will."

She gives me a knowing look. "For someone who isn't a fan of his, you sound pretty confident."

"Sheriff McCandles isn't so bad."

A loud clang out front makes us both jump. Eyes wide, we freeze.

Another loud clang of metal on metal.

My heart scrambles up my throat. I just had the Corvette towed home yesterday. It sat at the auto shop for a week while the owner totaled up what it would cost to fix it. Too much. Which is why it's sitting in the driveway like a stripped whale carcass washed up on shore. I curse loudly, swiping a frying pan off the stove and making for the front door. "If they came to finish the job, I'm gonna—"

"Stop right there, Valencia Pamela Lamb. I forbid you from going out there. I'm calling the sheriff."

My hands tighten on the pan handle, but my feet slow. "I won't go out there." But nothing is stopping me from going to the front window to witness the carnage.

A power tool roars to life, its shriek assailing my ears. It sounds like a saw or a drill or something of that ilk. If they're hacking at the Corvette, I'm going to—

"You stay inside, Valencia. I mean it!" My mom grips her phone in hand, talking to someone from the department about the noise and the suspected culprits. The sheer hubris of them showing up in broad daylight! But with the department down a body, they're stretched thin. Help could take a while to arrive.

I nearly drop the frying pan on my own foot when I catch a glimpse of the person standing in my driveway.

Yelping, I jump away from the falling pan. It thumps onto the carpet, but I'm already halfway to the front door.

"Don't you dare!" My mom shouts after me.

The front door flies open under my hand. The concrete walkway is frozen in the early morning, seeping through my socks and making me wish I'd stopped to put on shoes. "What are you doing here?" I rasp, rounding the Corvette toward the opened hood.

Rock straightens, meeting my eyes. In spite of the freezing cold winter morning, the sleeves on his denim overalls are already rolled up to his elbows. "Just wanted to take stock before I get started. See what parts I need to replace first."

Seeing my mouth gaping and eyes wide, he keeps going. "Whoever did this knew crap about cars, because they wrecked the body but didn't break many of her crucial parts. I can have her running again in a couple of weeks, assuming the parts aren't too hard to find. The body work, though… That'll take a while. Good thing they didn't rip into her seats, either, 'cause my reupholstering skills aren't great. That was always my dad's favorite part of a job, but he's…" Clearing his throat, Rock gestures to the air. "You know. Never mind. Morning, V."

I gape at him. Rock is going to rebuild my car? Why?

Rosie streaks out of the garage, and I yelp a warning. If she gets past Rock, I'll never catch her. She hasn't been outside, and the little devil is fast. "Stop her!"

The kitten must understand English better than she lets on, because she swerves between my legs. I swipe at her. Missed. Spinning on my bare feet, I lunge for her.

Rosie shoots up Rock's pant leg, scaling him like a professional free climber, and perches on his shoulder. He pets her chin with a knuckle. "Nice to see you, too," he croons to her.

Between showing up early before I've had time to put my armor on, and the offer to fix my Corvette, and cuddling with my kitten that he gave me, Rock is making me one hell of a ball of confused feelings.

There's nothing left to do. He's giving me no choice.

Flinging myself at Rock, I wrap my arms around his waist and hold on tight.

Rock's arms go around me ever so gently, hesitating. I burrow in deeper. On a sigh, his hands lock behind my back. His voice takes on a wry lilt. "I knew you were crushing on me."

"You're the one crushing me." Leaning back against the band his arms form across my lower back and meeting resistance proves my point. Rock doesn't let go. Not even an inch.

"Say the word, and I'll let you go."

Tightening my grip on him, I step out onto the limb, hoping he won't leave me dangling in the air alone. Following the impulse, I relax my cheek against the worn-soft Henley stretched across his torso. His head dips once, twice, and settles on top of my head like it was made to fit there. "Don't let go," I whisper.

"I'm never letting go." Rock's voice is a rasp in my ear.

Rosie makes a nest in my hair, pulling a laugh out of the tightness in my chest. "Thank you. For all of this. And for being so great, even after all the crap."

His arms loosen, but mine constrict. I'm not ready to let him go.

"Don't thank me yet," he whispers against my hair. "Maybe I'm not so great. Maybe your dad was right."

"He wasn't," Finally, I loosen my death grip on him.

Disentangling himself from my arms, Rock runs a hand over his growing curls. "You have a lot of faith in me, V. Don't know what I did to deserve it."

You know what I hate even more than the confusing barrage of feelings Rock inspires in my chest? The confusing flame of flickering emotions in his dark eyes, and the fact that my dad helped put it there.

Rock may not know what he did to deserve my trust, but I will never forget. He's saved my butt so many times it could be considered a habit. Me getting into trouble and him getting me out. And he does it with a combination of ferocity and gentleness that hits me square in the chest every time.

Turn around is fair play. I don't know how, but next time Rock is in trouble, I'm going to get him out of it. No matter what it takes.

New Friends and Old Jackets

Rock threatened to drive the Corvette into the aqueduct if he wasn't left alone to work. Is it my fault watching him work on my car is so fascinating?

Janice, Destin, and I simply wanted to hang out in the garage while he began repairs on the Corvette. But no. Apparently, having the three of us watching him work on the car was "distracting." That's a direct quote.

The three of us skulked inside and lined up in the front window to watch him in peace. We're perfecting our peeping skills. At this point, looking out to keep track of Rock's progress is more consuming than a weekend job. Which I am going to be late for if I don't leave in the next ten minutes. But I don't want to miss anything.

All week during school, Rock has been distant and withdrawn. The only time we spoke was when he texted to let me know he'd put together the tools he'll need to keep working on the Corvette. Today is Saturday, the day I usually enjoy sleeping in. Not today. Rock began much earlier in the morning than I would have liked, but beggars can't be choosers.

"You hugged him." Janice taps a fingernail against the window, pointing at the guy pacing between the sad, bent shell of my car and his tool bag sat on my dad's old work stool. Rock glares over his shoulder at us, and instinctively we duck out of sight.

Leaning back against the wall below the window, Janice swivels her head to catch my gaze. "I still can't believe you hugged him."

Pulling my hair off my face, I sit forward enough to work it into my usual Dutch braid. "Are you surprised I hugged him, or that he let me? Because I was a little surprised he didn't run away when I tried. But I think he liked it, even. Possibly."

She kicks my foot with her own socked one. "You. I'm surprised you, who is deathly allergic to any kind of physical affection, initiated a hug. You're the one who practically ran away the last time I tried to hug you."

"Untrue. I let you hug me. Twice." Finishing off the braid, I swipe a hair tie off my wrist and secure it.

"Under duress. You're like a toddler who giggles and runs away any time her mom asks for a hug." A power tool turning on makes our heads snap toward the window. From the determined set of Rock's shoulders and the confidence of his movements, he knows exactly what he's doing. That kind of competence is hard to look away from.

Imagine what he could do if he was still working at Agani Auto, with all of those professional tools and supplies. I asked him about it earlier this morning, and he pointedly refused to answer. I'm guessing he's still persona non grata over there, thanks to me. Realizing Janice and Destin are staring at me while I stare at Rock, I become very interested in tying the laces of my boots.

"I don't giggle. I panic." Destin makes a choking noise that sounds suspiciously like laughter.

"Ah ha! Point proven. You hate physical touch." Janice throws up her hands.

"I don't hate it. It just… doesn't come naturally to me." My laces end up a tangled mess, and I have to undo it and begin again.

Janice leans down into my line of sight. "Your mom is a toucher. How are you the way you are?"

"She's my mother. Of course, I hug her. Seriously, your hyperbole knows no bounds. I'm not anti-touching, right Des?"

My traitorous best friend shares a loaded look with Janice. Sucks his bottom lip into his mouth between his teeth. Clearly avoids answering my nudge.

"Oh, come on! Not you too. We've been best friends since we were four. We cuddle all the time."

He shakes his head. Gently, he lifts a hand to my shoulder and perches it there. What, is he afraid I'll bite him or something? "We've cuddled a couple of times, after traumatic experiences. Why do you think I give you noogies all the time?"

I hold still, trying not to duck out from under his hand and prove him right. "Because you know I hate it?"

Destin grins. "Because secretly, you love it. And because it's the only way to break the touch barrier without freaking you out."

Rolling my eyes, I stand up. "I have to go. I'm gonna be late."

Janice hands me my bag. "There you go. Freaking out."

"Objection. I am not."

Destin follows me to the front door. "Just so you know, it's okay not to be a physically affectionate person. If you honestly don't like it, we respect that. But if you resist because you're afraid to let us in, or because you think it means you're not independent and capable, you should know that's a lie. You can be independent and capable and also be a cuddler."

I give him a grateful smile. "Thanks. See you later."

Janice excuses herself to the bathroom, promising to meet me outside since she's my ride to work, and disappears down the hall.

"Wait!" Destin follows me out to the front porch. "Portia wrote me a letter this week. I kept deleting her emails, so maybe she thought it would be harder for me to ignore if it came in the mail. I don't know, but yeah. I wanted to tell you."

The conflict in his eyes makes my heart squeeze. "Thanks. For telling me. Do you… want to write her back? Because if you do, you can. I won't judge you for wanting to understand."

His head shakes, jaw adamant. "I'm not interested in understanding a murderer. Honestly, I had to stop reading her emails because they got really awkward. She's not… she sounds unstable, maybe? She needs help. That much is obvious."

"Agreed. Is it weird I wish someone was so into me they'd send me sonnets though? Because I could get into that."

A heavy tool falls to the ground with a metallic thunk. Rock bends down to pick up a socket wrench and pointedly doesn't look at us as he ducks under the Corvette's hood.

Destin toes the walkway. "I could slip Leander a few pointers if you want. Not as a middle man. Just, I don't know, as a friendly spirit. If you want. Would you? Want that?"

I chew on the inside of my cheek, watching Rock work on the car, wearing one of his burgundy tees. A shiver rolls over his shoulders. Is he cold? I don't think he brought a jacket. When he rolled up on his bike, he had a flannel shirt over his tee. A flannel shirt that ripped in two when it got caught on a jagged chunk of the Corvette an hour ago.

The weather app on my phone has icicles hanging from the temperature reading. It's freezing cold outside.

Destin nudges my shoulder with his elbow. "Val? Should I talk to Leander?"

"No, that's okay. I'll be right back." Janice comes to the door when I step inside, but I brush past her. Jackets and sweaters fill the coat closet, all mine and my mom's. None of them will fit Rock's broader frame. I go through each one, looking for something to lend the guy working on my car despite the chilly early February temps outside, and come up with nothing. There has to be something he can wear. Maybe one of my dad's old jackets.

Pushing to the very back, my fingers brush leather. A zap runs up my arm and sets my heart skipping. Before I unearth the jacket, I know what I've found. Maroon leather in a fitted men's coat. The same shade as the bomber I wear constantly. Years ago, my grandparents gave my mom and dad matching leather jackets one Christmas.

Sliding the jacket off the hanger, its weight is deceptive in my hands. Lighter than it looks. Lighter than I assumed it would be. Memories flood my mind. Dad wearing this coat while driving the Corvette. Dad one fall when my mom insisted we have family photos taken in a nearby orchard. Dad conditioning the leather of both coats, spreading them out on newspaper on the dining table to dry.

Janice appears at my shoulder, looking from the coat to me. "Are you crying?"

My fingertips dig into the coat's shoulder seams. Blinking dries the moisture gathering in the corners of my eyes. "No."

Her lips bunch as she watches me for a couple seconds. Returns her focus to the leather. "If you say so. Nice jacket. Your dad's?"

I nod, knowing if I try to talk, I actually will cry.

"Drive safe," Destin says, opening the front door for me. Janice follows me out.

Detouring toward the driveway, I shove the jacket at Rock. "Here."

Straightening over the car's hood, he wipes his grimy hands on a rag. "What's this for?"

"You're cold."

His shoulders roll. "I'm fine."

"Take the jacket, Rock."

Rock's jaw tics. "That was your dad's. I can't take it."

I roll my eyes, not to keep them from watering. Just to register my annoyance at his stubbornness. "You can, and you will. Or you can get your hands off my car."

His sigh puffs in the cold. "That isn't cool, V. You know how long I've dreamed of getting my hands on this car. Not under this condition, mind you."

"And here I thought it was me you dreamed about." One corner of my mouth lifts in a smirk. He walked right into that. I couldn't resist.

Rock's eyes fasten on my face. "You have no idea."

Janice rolls down the car window. "You're late, V. Get moving."

I don't budge. Don't look away from Rock's eyes clashing with mine. "Take the coat, or leave the car. Your choice."

His focus is heady as he weighs the determination I'm telegraphing for him. "Fine. Okay. I'll wear it, but I'm not keeping it."

Taking the jacket from my outstretched hand, Rock shrugs it on. Pushes up the sleeves.

My heart bottoms out, seeing my dad's jacket on Rock's

solid, sturdy frame. It fits like it was made for him. Watching him work on the Corvette made me feel so cared for. So seen. Hopefully knowing I don't want him to freeze to death will mean something like that to Rock. Rock hugs his arms over his chest, then holds them wide. "Huh, feels good. Thanks."

"You're welcome." I hurry into Janice's car. The Sheriff is not going to be impressed at my lateness. Hopefully I'll get lucky and he won't be in his office when I tiptoe into the department.

Leaning into my seatbelt, my head rests on the window on the drive through town.

"What are thinking about?" Janice asks as she pulls into the lot.

"Not much."

She hums in disbelief but doesn't press.

I wouldn't know what to tell her if she did. Because despite my dad's successful ploy to keep Rock and I apart, I can't help but think he'd approve of Rock now. Approve of his gentleness and care, with the Corvette, and with me. That he'd understand why I couldn't leave until Rock accepted the jacket.

Even if I don't understand it myself.

Taking the Bait

Standing on the desk chair, I crow. "Done! I win. Eat that, Leander."

A mountain of newly scanned files slides across my desk, plummeting toward the ground. The chair careens away as I dive off, arms scrambling to catch the files before they spill over the scuffed linoleum floor.

Leander guffaw of laughter rings out as he crouches at my side to help pick up the shambled papers. "Look at that. Pride really does come before the fall."

"Yeah, yeah." Amusement draws laughter out of me. Laughter tickles my ribs, making any attempt to collect the papers futile. Contagion sweeps through Leander, gripping him in a chuckle fit.

"Look, paper angel." White sheets slide across the floor as Leander flops onto his back and swans his arms and legs through the mess.

"No! You're making it worse." Jumping over him, I scoop

up as many papers as I can before he drags them further apart.

One of his hands wraps around my ankle, taking me by surprise. Falling back, I elbow him in the side on the way down. He groans. "Oof. Wait until I have padding next time before you throw those pointy little elbows."

"Whose fault was that? Come on, get up." He takes my hand, rolling onto his side. Brown sugar eyes meet mine, and suddenly being on the ground amidst a pile of disheveled papers isn't funny anymore. All of the silliness is vacuumed out of the air, leaving a sticky molasses gumming up my thoughts in its stead. Up close, Leander is stupid handsome. Honey blond eyebrows over those soft eyes. Cherry-flavored lip balm tickles my nose.

He inhales, moving a tiny bit closer. Those eyes bob downward from mine. Did he just look at my mouth?

Hopping up, I brush off my jeans with brisk pats. "Right. No more snow angels, mmkay? It's gonna take me the rest of my shift to put everything back where it goes."

Leander gets to his feet, scooping up papers and perching them on my desk. "It'll go faster if I help."

I politely decline. The pulsing organ in my chest is pushing for distance from Leander, and I obey. Whether my hesitance to get close to him again is due to how we broke up the first time, or if it's because of something… or someone… else, I can't say. All I know is that I don't want Leander looking at me like he was a minute ago. Like he wanted to kiss me.

The sheriff's office door flies open, and the man himself rushes through the bull pen toward the front door. "I thought I told you to stay home, Deputy," he growls.

Sykes fills the doorway, cutting a striking figure in his uniform. Mustache pristinely groomed, bruises and cuts faded, he looks good. Healthy. Several of the knots in my chest unravel from around my heart. Sykes looks miles better than he did when my mom and I dropped off some Thai food for his family one night last week.

"The doc said I could start back to work, Sheriff. I came in to get some paperwork done." He shuffles past the sheriff toward his desk.

Sheriff McCandles is already shaking his head. "Not on my watch. You need to take a couple more days, at least. I want you completely healed and ready to work when you come back. Heaven knows I need everyone sharp as I can get 'em with this place in the shape it's in."

My eyebrows draw inward in confusion. Yes, tension around town is high, but it's been like that for a couple months. Why would the sheriff be bringing that up again today?

"Someone threw a homemade Molotov cocktail at Jonesie's front lawn on fire last night." Leander's whispered words hit my ear, and I go still.

"What?" I hiss. "Did they catch anyone?"

Leander gives a slight head shake. "He wasn't home. He was at Kelley's."

My lungs take in a relieved breath. "The plot thickens. Glad they're both okay."

"Good thing Jonesie's neighbor—you ever met Mrs. Gibbons? She saw the whole thing and called it in. Didn't get a license plate or even a good look at the car, though."

I pinch at my neck, processing this. It's not good if the Snakes have begun threatening the deputies in their homes. A frisson of fear goes through me, thinking of how Jonesie must feel. How I felt when I got home from snowboarding with friends and found my own front yard burned and my house painted with insults.

Sykes glares at the sheriff. "Now, look, Sir. I've got a wife and baby girl to protect. I want to be back at work, helping clean up this town so it's safe for them. I've rested for a full week, and I'm ready to come back."

The sheriff grunts. "No can do. I'm not putting you out on the street for another week, at least. I won't risk having any of my people out there in less than peak condition."

Sykes rests both hands on his belt, jaw squared. "I'm telling you, I'm fit and ready."

McCandles crosses his arms, mouth in a firm line. "Answer's no."

Neither Lender nor me can take our focus off the sheriff and his deputy arguing at the other end of the room. The two men go back and forth about head injuries and doctors for a few minutes before Sykes's shoulders curve inward in frustration. "I'm coming back with a note from the doc."

"You do that." Front door swinging shut, the sheriff takes his hat off and runs a hand through graying hair. Breathing hard, he goes back into his office and closes the door.

I whistle low and long, sinking into the desk chair I retrieved from where it slid along the back wall. "On the one hand, yay for Jonesie and Kelley. On the other hand, yikes. Good thing Mrs. Gibbons is such a busybody. It could have been so much worse."

Leander's head bobs over his desk. The scanner beeps as he feeds sheets through the machine's slow mouth. "My mom is worried our house will be next."

My gut churns at what an attack might mean for Leander and his mom. It deeply sucks to be afraid in your own home. The primary place where a person should always feel loved, warm, and safe. "She know how to defend herself?"

His eye catches mine over the stacks of papers. "First thing she learned after my dad went into law enforcement was how to shoot the handgun he gave her. But still."

I agree, chewing on the problem while I work. My mom knows how to shoot too. It's practically a requirement for LEO spouses, and the tumult the Snakes are causing is one of the main reasons why.

"Whoa." Astonishment makes Leander's voice thin. "Look at this."

"What?" Rounding my desk, I make for his. "What is it?"

He looks from the phone out on his desk, to me. "Fake ID guy finally texted me back."

"Seriously? It's been over a week. What'd he say?"

Color me surprised. I've been trying to write the article Janice asked me to, about my experience as a sheriff's daughter in our small town, but I can't get a handle on how to start it. What to include. What to hold back. Basically, I have a serious case of overwhelm. I haven't written a word. Instead, I've been fixating on ways to catch the fake ID guy and write a story about that. Last week, under a surge of motivation, I'd asked Bri to tell me everything she knew about the guy. Again. She didn't give me anything I didn't already know, so I asked Leander to pretend to be a customer. He never heard back, so I put the article idea out of my head.

Leander's fingers tap on the desktop by his phone once, twice. "See for yourself."

I peer at the message from the fake ID guy. Inside are instructions for where and when to drop off his info so the guy can craft the false identification cards for him. Along with a hefty amount of cash.

It's not what I was expecting. No farmer's market. No produce stall. He switched it up on us.

Referencing the calendar on the desk, my eyebrows rise even higher. "That's tomorrow."

I don't realize how I'm encroaching on Leander's space until he slides his arm out from between us and inches it around my waist. His hand is a gentle weight on my side. "Looks like I need to hit the bank on the way home tonight."

I hold still, not sure how to respond to his casual touch. It feels friendly, but also maybe more. "Nope. I'm the one who had you do this. I'll pay for it."

Leander's eyes slide up to mine, fingertips pressing just a touch harder against my side. As if to make sure I've noticed he's touching me. Noticed and chosen not to pull away. "You have that kind of cash?"

I ease out of his reach. Paper corners crinkle under my butt as I lean against the desk's edge. "Haven't spent my Christmas money yet. And I just got a paycheck."

His hands drop into his lap. Eyes, too. "I can't let you use your Christmas money."

My toe taps the linoleum floor to get his attention. "Yes you can. This was my idea. It's for my story, so I'll do it."

Sighing, he raises his gaze to mine. "You're not going to let this go, are you?"

My lopsided grin says it all.

Slowly, resigned, he smiles back. "Fine. You can pay. But I'm doing the drop off. Don't argue. They're expecting a guy. It has to be me."

"I agree."

"That was surprisingly easy."

"I have conditions."

Corrupting My Friends One at a Time

THE DIVE BAR TREMBLES UNDER A GUSTING WIND. Its brown-painted siding is riddled with cracks and dents. The front door doesn't square in its frame. Filmy windows sit like loose teeth in receding frames. Propped in one is a decades-old, half-lit sign of a waitress serving bubbling brews. The thing is so sun bleached the woman's edges are blurry, much like the building itself.

Leander whistles low. "Now I know why I didn't remember this place. It's basically a shack."

My seat belt comes undone with a click. "I preferred the farmer's market."

"Doesn't matter, because you're not going inside, right?"

"Right. I'm not going in." I give him an exaggerated wink.

Leander's hand flexes on the door handle. "I'm serious, Val. You can't go in there. They'll take one look at you in that outfit, and they'll start a brawl. The roof will cave in on our heads, and I'm not risking another concussion. Please, just let me go in without you there as a distraction. Deal?"

This is the second time in a few days I've been referred to as a distraction. No power on earth can stop the pleased smile that takes over my face. "That might be the most flattering thing anyone has ever said to me, so thanks for that. But if I'm that good of a distraction, I'm going. It'll give you an opening to make the drop without anyone noticing."

Leander shakes his head. Slowly, he leans over me—and oh fudge he's close—snaring my seatbelt and buckling it. I hold my breath, pressed back against the seat to minimize contact.

Leander's eyes flit up to mine. "Please stay in the car."

"You're no fun." I lift my hands in the air and away from my buckle.

Wind whips through the cab when he opens the door, slicing through me. Hissing at the cold, I hunker down in the seat.

With a backward glance, probably to make sure I'm still in his truck, Leander ducks into the grimy building.

Fake ID guy's instructions were simple. All Leander has to do is tape his info and payment to the back of the far left toilet in the women's' bathroom, and leave. The forger will contact Leander when the goods are ready to arrange a pick up.

Cars slink past in the dimming light. One still has a Santa hat dangling from the toe hitch even though Christmas was six weeks ago. Across town, a siren cries. I hope whoever is responding is safe.

I drum my fingers on my knees, scoping out the bar. Leander hasn't been gone for more than a fistful of minutes, but I'm already antsy. It shouldn't take this long to tape an envelope to the back of a toilet. Unless he had to wait for someone to finish using it so he could go inside.

Something slams into the crooked blinds in one of the windows, making the wall shiver. Are people fighting inside? Easing open the truck door, I listen through the winter breeze.

Shouted words escape through the bar's thin walls. Loud, muddled words that make me squirm in the seat. What if the bar's patrons took one look at Leander and decided to break his pretty face, just because he's the sheriff's son?

Closing the door, I trap my hands between my knees.

I'm projecting; I know it. Leander has never gotten guff like I got, because Sheriff McCandles has never been suspected of being a predator turned murderer. That journalist's offer pops into my head. Partnering up to tell the real story of the double murders of Gracia and my dad is still a possibility. Not only would working with her allow me to get everything that happened off my chest and on public record, the advance would pay for the first couple years of community college.

The window shutters rattle again. What is going on in there?

My knees jiggle as I tap my feet on the floorboard. Itchy fingers run along my seatbelt and rest on the release button. I never promised to stay in the truck. Leander inferred it.

Leander is probably inside telling football stories. That makes total sense. It's plausible. He'll wrap it up and come out. Any second now.

The bar door remains shut no matter how hard I stare at it.

Far away, a rumble catches my ear as it approaches. Closer. Louder.

Around the corner comes a pack of muscle cars and motorcycles, their engines revving so loud my brain pulses inside my skull.

Flashy vehicles pour into the bar parking lot, filling the world with their roar. I sink low in the truck seat so they can't see me. For once, the darkness is a help instead of a hindrance.

Icy sweat breaks out on my back when a familiar figure dismounts from an oversized motorcycle with skulls painted on the sides. Of course, Rotten Egg Breath would drive a hyper macho bike. I sink down in the seat far enough that I can just see over the dashboard. Snake tattoos flash on arms and necks and calves as the guys secure their bikes and cars and stow their gear. More than a few of these dudes haven't even bothered to conceal the guns and knives they have strapped to their bodies. That amount of firepower means trouble. Inside my chest, my ribs pull tight, making it difficult to breathe.

I stare at the bar door. Now I'm willing Leander to stay inside. Nothing good can come of him running into a swarm of Snakes on his way out of the building. So far, they haven't threatened him due to his being the new sheriff's son, but I wouldn't put it past them. If Leander walks right into the middle of a writhing mass of Snakes, there's no telling what they'll do to him.

My hand digs into my purse, fingers curling mercilessly around my can of pepper spray. I roped Leander into this, and I won't let them hurt him on account of me.

Wrapping my fingers around the door handle and gripping tight, I tease apart my options. I should call the sheriff. And I will, but by the time someone from the department would get here, Leander might be in the middle of a weaponized brawl, getting more than the concussion he's hoping to avoid.

All while I sit in the truck doing nothing.

Protective ire flares in my gut. Leander is in that bar because of me, and they won't hurt him. I won't allow it. I just need a plan.

Jonesie picks up when I call the department. I spit out the bar's address in a rush.

"Val? That you?"

"Yes, it's me. Listen, Jonesie. Did you get that address? Because I need backup like, now."

He says something to someone in the background, muffled. Probably covering the phone with his palm. Then, "I hear you, but why do you need someone to come out to the Corner Bar? You're not inside are you?"

More muffled conversation. "Kelley says she still doesn't want to give you your first ticket."

My eyes pop as the gang streams into the bar. From the rough looks on their faces, they have more than a couple beers in mind. Gruff hands push as they all fight to get inside at the same time. Jostling for a fight. There's no love lost between them.

I lean forward, both hoping for and dreading a glimpse of Leander through the wide open door. "I'm not drinking! But seriously, Jonesie, please. I need you to come to the bar. Hurry."

His tone hardens. "You in trouble? Is someone bothering you? Because I'll—"

"I'm fine. It's Leander. He's inside, and a bunch of Snakes just walked in."

Jonesie doesn't hesitate. "Be there in ten. Stay on with Kelley while I—"

I hang up. Ten minutes is nine too long.

My teeth clench. If Leander gets hurt because of me…

Palming my one miniscule can of pepper spray, I jump out of the truck. My hoodie drops low over my face as I ease the heavy wooden door open and step inside.

The bar extends across the back wall of the long room, open shelving overcrowded with glass bottles. They're so precariously stuffed onto the shelves, one strong wind could topple the entire setup, raining glass everywhere. Every barstool is taken. Several people slump forward in their seats, eyeing the empty glasses in front of them. The remaining stools and standing room are crowded with Snakes, each trying to get the bartender's attention long enough to order. Their shouted drink requests blend as they rise in volume. The bartender pours one drink after another.

A clink of pool balls yanks my attention to the left, where a line of three pool tables sits, each under a single overhead light that highlights the green top while concealing the players. The first table has been claimed by a group of women dressed for a night out.

No fights have broken out, which means the Snakes either haven't spotted Leander, or don't know who he is. Yet. But I have to hurry. Find Leander and get him out of this bar before someone recognizes either of us.

The amount of drooling some of the younger Snakes are doing over the ladies at the pool table makes me shake my head. With those women sashaying around the pool table every chance they get, no one bothers to look at me braced in the doorway.

It takes me a few seconds to find Leander, and once I do I move along the wall toward him. Leander is in the back of the room at the third pool table. A middle-aged guy, thankfully missing a Snake tattoo. He says something inaudible over the clamor. With a laugh, he claps Leander on the back.

Most of the tension coiled in my muscles eeks away. Leander is fine. None of the gang members are paying him any mind. Not when there are beautiful women to look at and tumblers of liquor to drink.

From the looks of it, Leander was waylaid on the way to the bathroom by a happy pool shark. Which is not great. But at least no one has thrown any punches.

Leander makes a deft jab with his pool cue, sinking a couple balls into the table's pockets. His opponent snorts in surprise, moving to the side when Leander slips past him to line up another shot. My partner in tonight's scheme has everything under control. I should go back to the truck and wait. Call Jonesie and let him know I won't need that backup.

But curiosity has always been my weakness. Has Leander had a chance to drop the ID info yet? Chewing on my lip, I slink past the first pool table, smothering in cloying perfume from the ladies. A Snake shifts away from the table, bumping my shoulder. The growl he aims at me is without heat, so I keep moving, making sure my face is hidden.

My heart beats a quick rhythm as I duck into the scuffed black hallway I'm assuming leads to the facilities. I'll just slip inside and check to see if Leander made the drop, and I'll leave. No one will notice I set foot inside the bar. I'll hear it from Jonesie next time I see him, but that I can handle.

At the far end, an exterior door opens. I missed it because the Exit sign is unlit. A figure all in black slinks inside.

I freeze.

One of the Snakes saw me come inside, after all, and went around the building to head me off. It's more creative than I would have expected from one of the knuckle draggers that joined the gang, but it isn't the first time I've underestimated one of them.

The figure is heading straight for me, pinning me to the wall.

I'm backed into a corner. The air is too thin, leaving me lightheaded.

This bar is a powder keg, one bruising punch away from erupting into flames and chaos. And it looks like I'll be the one on the receiving end of that curled fist.

The Human Under the Hoodie

MY HEAD AND MY LUNGS ARE ON FIRE, GASPING FOR AIR that isn't there.

It takes me a couple seconds to realize that the hooded guy isn't attacking. No one is. I open my eyes to see the figure slinking toward the women's' room.

They're not here for me.

Pressing myself against the wall, I take slow breaths. My clothes stick to the grimy surface as the figure slips into the ladies'.

I don't move a muscle. Waiting for sounds of someone using the facilities. Waiting for my body to calm the heck down.

Out in the front room, Leander's voice filters through the din. He's telling the story of the football team's championship game. A game I missed because I was recuperating from my dunk in the aqueduct. Pool balls clink as they ricochet off each other.

The Snakes still haven't figured out that they've got a

sheriff's kid in the middle of them. I give myself two minutes to get myself together, and then Leander and I have to go.

The restroom door opens and the figure steps out. A flash of white sticks out of his pocket, making my eyes widen. The envelope. It's him. Fake ID guy.

He leaves the way he came, moving quickly without looking back. Shoving off the wall, I power walk after him. I have to get a glimpse of this guy. See what kind of car he drives. Maybe get the plate so I can run it and figure out who he is without a confrontation. Last time I went head to head with a member of the Snakes, he threatened to kill me slowly. An experience I'm loathe to relive.

Gripping the pepper spray tighter, I step out into the lot behind the bar. It's empty aside from one car. The hooded figure is making for a newish Civic, which is odd because that's the same kind of car Janice drives.

My eyes snap back to the hooded figure. That confident walk, the way the hips move. I know that walk.

A suspicion rears in my mind. I know him. Or her, I should say. Picking up my pace, I yell, "Hey. Janice?"

The figure flinches. And bolts for the car.

I'm right on the money.

"Janice! Wait." I lunge after her. When she said she knew a guy, she was talking about herself. Sneaky witch. *There are some expectations I'm not meeting, okay?* I'm impressed that she fooled me, and a little sick to my stomach that her dad expects her to engage in a bunch of illegal crap to keep her place in the family. Forging ID cards is probably the least bad thing she could think of to do to keep her dad happy.

I call out again, but Janice doesn't stop. She doesn't look over a shoulder as I chase her across the cracked parking lot. She knows I'm the one after her. She knows I know why she's at the bar. I have to give it to her for being committed to eluding me. Girl can move.

Pumping my legs with everything I've got, I jump. My arms wrap around her hips, and we tumble to the asphalt.

The hard ground scrapes and tears at my knuckles, making me yowl. I'm tangled around her, my face smothered in the back of her sweatshirt.

"Ouch. Get off me!" She shrieks, kicking and bucking.

"Quit kicking and I will." I yank at my hands, but they're pinned underneath her. The backs of my hands are going to be shredded after this.

"Valencia?" Janice wriggles around in my arms, her face white when her green eyes meet mine. She scurries up to a seat, freeing my hands.

"Yeah. Didn't you hear me yelling at you?" Folding in my arms, I get a good look at my cut and bleeding hands. A hiss parts my teeth as the pain hits my nerves.

Janice scowls at me, her annoyance clear. "No, I did not hear you yelling at me. I heard a crazy person yelling at me, which is why I ran. What were you doing in there anyway? Isn't this place a little rough for you, miss pal of the sheriff?"

I fake laugh. "Pretty sure we've already established I'm not a shrinking violet."

Janice stands up, stretching out her legs and arms and wincing. "Can you not tackle me next time?"

My attention snags on the envelope on the ground at her feet. The one with Leander's photo and fake information inside. Along with a crap ton of my money. "No promises. Now, let's talk about how you're the fake ID guy."

She swoops on the envelope, picking it up and tucking it into the front pocket on her hoodie. "I have no idea what you're talking about. I just came in to play some pool. But instead, I got accosted in the hallway and decided to beat it."

Gingerly, I cross my arms. "Is that so? How'd you find the envelope on the back of the toilet, then?"

Now that I think about it, Janice always has money, unlike me. I get an allowance from my mom and a paycheck from the department, but it isn't enough to buy premium ski resort passes or gorgeous new coats, or the expensive manicure supplies Janice uses to keep her nails looking sleek and trendy. She must be using some of the profit from forging IDs to pamper herself. How much of it does is she required to tithe to the Snakes?

Janice's hands plant on her hips. Aloof denial brackets her mouth. "It was on the floor. I picked it up."

Dusting off my jeans with my less torn hand, I shoot her a skeptical look. "Oh, okay. You're not a forger, but you're willing to take someone's money if you find it, is that right?"

She frowns, eyebrows pushed together and her mouth chewing on irritated words. It's obvious she was not expecting to be caught, especially by me. Looking me over, she eyes her car in the corner of her vision. Her explanation is half-hearted. "Finders keepers."

Even though her dad is a high-ranking member of the Snakes, and even though she has been very clear she has to maintain her usefulness to them, Janice doesn't like getting her hands dirty. It was her who pushed me so hard after Gracia was murdered that I vowed to solve the murder.

Janice might talk a big game, but she has a strong sense of justice that happens to line up with mine pretty nicely. Couple that with a strong sense of self-preservation. Nobody would have thought the gang member's daughter and the sheriff's daughter had that kind of commonality. It could be a country song.

She rises onto the balls of her feet, ready to bounce.

I hold out my hands, palms out. "Jan, come on. We're friends, right?"

Her shrug is barely there. "I thought so, until you tackled me."

Stifling a laugh, I wait. Use one of my dad's tactics to see if she'll fill the silence with information I need. Either Janice admits to being a thief or a forger, and I've got all the time in the world. Either way, there won't ever be an article about what I learned tonight.

Resignation wraps around her shoulders. "Here. Take it."

Janice offers the envelope, and I wrap my fingers around it, stuffing it into my coat pocket.

"Janice Hill and Valencia Lamb. When Jonesie let me know I needed to come down here, I did not expect to see you two together."

My stomach drops into my boots. Janice and I both swivel to look at Sheriff McCandles, standing at the corner of the bar. Like he'd heard a commotion and made his way toward it, determined to break it up and bring peace.

The smile I put on is faker than a healthy tan in February. "Hello, Sheriff. Nice night, don't you think?"

The lawman eyes us, then the bar. "Why do I get the feeling you're up to something?"

"Occupational hazard?"

Sheriff McCandles's eyes narrow. How much of our conversation did he overhear?

I gulp, forcing myself to stand straight and project confidence. I have a perfectly good reason for being here, and I'm going to come up with it. Any second now.

Sheriff McCandles's grim expression pins me to the blacktop. My brain ping-pongs through possible explanations for being behind this smudge on the face of humanity. Drug deal is out. So is dumpster diving. I'm not that desperate.

"Where is my son?"

My face flushes as I remember Leander. Who is still inside with a bunch of Snakes. I point at the bar, and the sheriff braces himself. Makes for the back door with one hand hovering over his service weapon.

Yelling rises inside the bar, making my insides plummet. I got so carried away with Janice that I forgot about Leander. Guilt crests in my throat.

The back door bursts open and Leander barrels out, frantic energy crackling around him. He almost rams into his dad. "Dad? What are you— Where is she?" Leander's eyes fall on me. The anxiety melts off him as he makes for me. Grips my shoulders. "There you are. You promised to stay in the truck."

"If you recall, I made no promises." It's hard to talk with my face mushed against his chest.

Leander pulls back enough to meet my eyes. His mouth opens, then snaps shut. I've got him there.

"You, don't move. We're going to have a conversation once I make sure Miss Hill and Miss Lamb are off safely." Sheriff McCandles points a commanding finger at his son.

Hunching to make himself shorter without moving his feet, Leander keeps eyes on his dad while whispering in my ear. "Did you see anything? And what's Janice doing here?"

The sheriff clears his throat, pulling us around to look at him. "I'd also like to know if you saw anything, Valencia. And I'd like to remind both of you that it is not your job to go chasing after forgers, or murderers, or any other criminals. That's my job."

Janice inches toward her car, stopping when I hit her with a look. I'm not done talking to her yet. I just have to get clear of the sheriff first. "While I agree that it is your job, I am a journalist, and if I don't come up with good article ideas, Janice assigns me boring ones. The onramp construction. Friends of the library sale. Mrs. Caruthers's lawn gnomes. Between you and me, I hate lawn gnomes. They give me the creeps. So if it's all the same to you, I'll keep looking for more interesting news to report."

Sheriff McCandles pinches his nose. "Now I know what your dad meant when he kept complaining about the Thomas twins. Gonna get a damn ulcer at this rate. Listen good, Valencia. It isn't all the same to me. I can't sleep at night knowing you're probably somewhere you shouldn't be, getting into trouble. You've already been manhandled and almost drowned twice. Can you please stay home where you're safe? Even for a week?"

I smile at the lawman, oddly flattered. "Aww Sheriff. I had no idea you were so concerned for my well-being. I'm touched."

Is that a smile around the corners of his eyes? I think it is. "You and your mom are part of the family. And you're residents of my town, don't forget."

My grin widens. "I won't."

"Now about this forger you're trying to find…"

I bust up laughing at the lawman's obvious maneuvering of the conversation. He may want me to stay home and out of trouble, but right now? I'm useful to him, and by the grudging way he's looking at me, it's annoying him to high heaven.

Behind me, Janice goes rigid. Because Leander is watching me, he doesn't miss my responding twitch. His eyes flick between Janice and me, questions forming behind them.

I start talking before he can voice any of them. "Sorry, Sheriff. Janice showed up to play some pool, but when we walked inside, all the tables were taken. So we came back out here to hang out while Leander waited inside for the forger. I didn't see anyone else the whole time. Then a bunch of Snakes showed up, and I had enough of a sense of self-preservation to call Jonesie and stay the hell away."

McCandles runs a hand down his lariat. "Let me get this straight. You two taped an envelope full of money to the back of a toilet, hoping to catch a forger, and the envelope is now missing. Neither of you saw anyone go into or out of the bathrooms, and therefore have no clue who could have taken the bait."

I glance at Leander. Of course, he told his dad what we were up to tonight. And then I called Jonesie for backup, which alerted the sheriff that we were in over our heads and needed help. Yay.

Leander nods, looking sheepish. I feel bad for him, but when I meet Janice's eye, loyalty to her rears up, taking my breath away. I am not ratting her out to make Leander and me look less like idiots.

Janice? She needs me to shield her right now. I'm going to come through for her. "No clue. Which is why, as you've emphasized, investigating is your job and not mine. Sorry, Sheriff."

The man huffs, looking between the three of us. "All right then. You will let me know if you hear from the forger again. Is that clear?"

We agree, our heads nodding out of sync.

He aims an authoritative look at Leander. "Son, go on home. Your mom is waiting up. And you two? Do I need to escort you, or can I trust you to go straight home?"

I do the scout's honor gesture. "You can trust us."

Janice clears her throat. "I was, um, thinking of going to the diner for a milkshake. You in, Val?"

"Yep. Sounds good."

McCandles eyes us warily. "Go, then. I'll wait."

It isn't until Janice parks in the diner lot and kills the engine that she collapses against her seat. "Oh my god. I thought for sure you'd tattle on me back there! Why didn't you? I thought you wanted to stay on his good side."

I grip my chin. "You know what? You're right. I'll just call him real quick…"

She snatches at my phone in hand, but I keep it away from her. "Seriously, Janice. I'm not telling him. Don't ask me why because I can't explain it. Now, I believe I was promised a milkshake, and I'm thirsty."

The diner is almost empty this late at night. We slide into a booth and a bored waitress takes our orders.

Janice relapses into quiet. An old country music song filters through the speakers.

I wait, giving Janice space to gather her thoughts. To say whatever's on her mind. "Thank you."

Pulling a couple paper napkins from the holder, I set them on the tabletop in front of us. "You're welcome. I was a little surprised, myself."

She laughs. "If you want, I could make you an ID. I'm good at it."

"You must be with the price you charge. Speaking of, I have questions. How did you get into forging? Isn't that kind of a niche area of expertise?"

Janice frowns, sliding the salt shaker back and forth between her hands. Back and forth, back and forth like a metronome. My eyes follow its progress.

"Growing up, I had no idea that most kids didn't watch cartoons in the same room as their dad counting piles of drug money. I didn't know that my parents yelling and fighting constantly wasn't normal or healthy. I thought everyone's dad had weird friends over at all hours of the night. Some nights, my mom would bring me into her bed and lock the door. That was my normal. When I got older and I began to understand who my dad was and what his job meant, I... This is gonna sound so stupid, but he's my dad, okay? I wanted to prove to him I was worth his time, like his guys in the gang. So I tried to find something to do for him that didn't involve drugs or guns or anything else more repellant. That left hiding paper trails. He had a guy who did all of that for him, so I asked questions. I watched videos online, and I practiced. A couple years ago, Dad's forger got killed in a raid, and my dad turned to me. He didn't say, but I got the feeling he'd been waiting for me to prove my usefulness. Forging is my way of doing it without turning my soul black. You understand?"

I take in everything she's said, and everything she hasn't said. Like what her dad might have done to her if she hadn't found a way to be useful without getting her hands dirty. Like turning her into a monster like Leif Agani or Rotten Egg Breath.

"Yeah, I do."

The waitress comes back with our milkshakes and curly fries, and we dig in, changing topics to my favorite reality TV show, the books we're reading, and how she always gets her manicures to look so perfect.

As we talk, a new article idea takes shape in my head. Writing it will be a challenge, since the people I'm thinking of featuring won't cooperate. Janice has had to adapt to fit into the life her parents have built for her. And Rock? Rock has been almost completely consumed by his father's thirst for power and violence. Janice has found ways to be valuable without compromising herself. But Rock? My stomach churns at the types of things he would have been forced into doing if he'd been crowned an heir of the Snakes alongside his brother.

By writing my article, it'll get Janice off my back. Maybe it'll encourage Rock to keep resisting, to keep striving to forge his own path. One that doesn't require him to pay a toll with his own blood.

One Man's Junk

Rows and rows of classic cars—most with large rust spots or twisted frames—line the wide dirt field. "I was expecting big, scary dogs, and a greasy-bellied dude named Lester. Not this."

Rock chuckles. "Sorry to disappoint. My buddy Darren told me about this place. Looks like they might have some parts we can use."

I take another sweep of the place, noticing this time that many of the cars are incomplete. A hood here, a door there. Several of the broken-down cars are little more than a rusted frame overgrown with weeds.

"Come on." Rock's hand wraps around the zippered front of my bomber jacket and he tows me toward the opening in the wood-slat fence. A tan mobile home sits just inside the fence, door facing the road. A middle-aged guy emerges from the trailer.

"Welcome to Danny's Vintage Car Yard. I'm Danny. What

can I do you for?" They shake hands. Pulling a list of parts we need out of a pocket, Rock goes over it with the owner. Danny's excitement rises when he hears that Rock is essentially rebuilding the Corvette. They go on for a few minutes about tool choices and body tweaks. I zone out because it all gets more technical than my limited car knowledge.

Looking out over the rows of decaying cars, their bodies in shades of orange, red, yellow, and green, my eyes flick to Rock. He and Danny are talking animatedly about the project. My heart squeezes with an emotion I can't quite name. It's a mess of feelings and impulses all tied up in Rock's determination to fix my dad's car for me. Nothing is obligating him to do the work. I never would have considered holding him accountable for the extensive damage those Snake jackholes wrought on my car, but here he is, talking to a junkyard guy to find the parts he needs for the restoration.

The yard owner nods a few times, rubbing his hands together. Probably sensing a big sale. "I've got just what you need. Follow me."

And that's another thing. I don't have the money to pay for the parts or Rock's time put in working on the Corvette. When I tried to tell him as much, he waved me off. He insisted he wouldn't have let me pay anyway. Then where is he getting the money for all of this?

The yard owner leads Rock off down one of the rows, having him push a wheelbarrow.

Danny calls back over his shoulder, a teasing note in his voice. "If you're hoping to impress your girl, maybe stick with chocolates and flowers next time. Doesn't look like she's too impressed with my collection."

Rock chuckles, glancing at me over his shoulder. "Val is her own person. She's not mine. But if I was trying to impress her,

I'd do it with cheesy carbs and a true crime documentary. Maybe a bouquet of roses. Seem to remember she likes the red ones."

Cheesy carbs and a documentary would work. And the roses? My heart squeezes again. Rock is having that effect on me more than is probably healthy. I kind of like it. But Rock isn't trying to impress me.

We return to the front of the yard an hour later, the wheelbarrow piled high with parts for the Corvette. Rock whispered to me as he hunted and gathered, assuring me that these were good parts. That he'd have it up and running in just a few weeks. It meant a lot to me, his explanation of what he would be doing to my car. I have no doubt a mechanic would have talked down to me, but Rock would never.

Danny totals up the cost of the parts we're taking, and I gasp when I hear it. "That much, for all this?"

The owner looks apologetically at me. "You'd be surprised how tricky it is to find good parts like these for fifty-year-old cars. I guarantee you won't get a better deal anywhere else."

"Thanks, but no thanks. Come on, Rock. Let's go."

Rock looks between Danny's relaxed posture and my body, which seems to want to curl up in a protective ball and roll away. Gently, he hooks a finger in the belt loops at each side of my waist, pulling me closer to him. "What's going through that pretty head right now?"

I suck in a breath, eyes fastened to the collar of his tee. "Why are you doing this?"

He gives a gentle tug on my belt loops. "This car important to you?"

"Dumb questions get dumb answers."

"V." He lifts my chin with his fingers and looks me in the eye.

I let him see in my eyes how much that car means to me.

"More than almost anything."

"That's all I need to know. Hey, why do you look like you're about to cry?" His fingers are firm on my jawline.

I feel unmoored and vulnerable, so I burrow my hands into the front pockets of his leather jacket. Further tying us together. "People keep asking me that, and I don't know where it's coming from. I almost never cry."

Rock's eyes are warm and knowing. He's one of the only people who've seen me cry, and the last time was when we were kids. Wisely, he doesn't comment. "I thought we agreed you were going to let me restore your Corvette, so why are you fighting it? This guy's right. I looked all over online for parts, and everyone else was charging way more."

Blowing out a breath pushes some of the loose strands of hair out of my face. "Then let's just forget it. The car was great. I loved it while it lasted, but this is too much."

"You love that car."

"I do love the car, but it's not worth it. Where are you getting the money for all the parts and time anyway? Last time I asked, you pretended you didn't hear me."

His hands skim to my elbows, pressing not enough to hurt, but enough to let me know he doesn't want to answer the question.

"Does it have something to do with the fact that you haven't been riding Leif's motorcycle around? Wait, did you sell it? Are you using the money to pay for all this?"

The firm tilt to his mouth is answer enough.

"Seriously? Why would you do that? My dad's Corvette isn't worth it."

Rock's hands skim up to my shoulders. "Do you want to let it go? Say the word, and I'll drop it. But I don't buy that's what you want. Give me the truth, V."

I am crying now. "What if it's too broken to fix?"

Slowly, his head dips. His forehead presses against mine. "It isn't too broken to fix. I can do it, no problem. Let me do this for you."

Heat from his skin seeps into mine, welding together some of the jagged parts of my battered soul. Somehow, I got it in my head that I was broken and beaten, just like the Corvette. That it couldn't be fixed, and maybe neither could I. Worse, after how awful everyone in town treated me over the past year, I internalized the idea that I wasn't worth the effort Rock is putting in now. Wasn't worth Janice's pestering friendship. Or Leander's playfulness when we're working at the department. The confidences Destin shares with me when he's feeling unsure about his chosen career path. The town treated me like crap, and maybe that was what I came to expect. What I thought I deserved.

Standing in the middle of an antique car yard with Rock, I'm kind of a mess.

Rock's thumbs sweep the base of my throat, pulling me out of the mental pit I've fallen into. Coaxing my attention back to him. "Please. I can't fix everything, but I can fix this. Let me fix it."

Chest heaving, I open my eyes and meet his.

Rock must intuit that I need some quiet to put myself back together, because he doesn't speak the entire drive back to my house. He pulls my mom's car onto the driveway next to the Corvette's bones. The engine falls quiet, but neither of us moves.

Rock's hands grip the steering wheel. "You remember when we were kids, and some people would bring their parents to school to talk about their jobs? Remember how one dad was a firefighter. One mom was a lawyer. One owned a coffee shop. Your dad even came in to talk about being sheriff a couple times, right? I never asked my dad to come talk about the auto shop, because even as a little guy, I knew that wasn't his real job.

"Back when we were kids and he still lived at Granny's, he'd lock us in the back bedroom when he had someone coming over for a meeting. We weren't even allowed to use the bathroom. A couple times, one of my younger cousins ended up peeing in a toy bucket while we were locked in there. We'd pretend it was normal to be locked in for hours while my dad talked to whoever out in the front room.

"When Leif was around nine, my dad started keeping him in the front room during his meetings. I don't know what he saw, my brother would never tell me, but that's when he turned hard. Got meaner. Sometimes, there was yelling. It scared the crap out of me, knowing my brother was out there, but my dad wouldn't let him come into the back anymore. I was lucky he didn't make me sit through those meetings, too, but Granny insisted she needed me in the back. I don't know why, but he let her keep me with her. I did my best to look tough, so the cousins wouldn't be scared.

"This one time, the yelling didn't stop. Then there were a couple gunshots. Maybe four or five. One came right through the wall into that back room. If we hadn't been on the floor playing a board game, someone could have been hurt. Or worse. My cousins were crying, and Granny was trying to comfort them, but none of us knew what had happened. I knew I had to do something, so I picked up a metal toy truck. I remember creeping along the hallway to the front room, and seeing a guy laying in a puddle of blood. There was so much of it, I almost threw up. And there's my dad, standing over the body with his gun still smoking in his hand. Leif was up against the wall covering his ears. One of my dad's guys came up, and my dad told him to take the body and take care of it. He told the guy where to go, and I heard it all. My dad caught sight of me, and I ran back to the back. I was afraid he'd kill me too, for overhearing. But he didn't say anything.

"That night, Granny and my dad had a huge fight. He moved to the apartment above the garage the next day. I guess what I'm saying is, your dad knew about everything wrong that went on at my house. He was right to keep you away from my place. It sucked. I didn't understand it, but I do now. There are memories in my head I wish I could erase, but I'll carry them for the rest of my life. Your dad was saving you from living through something like that, because he loved you. You were worth it to him.

"And your car? It's worth it to you because it was part of him. All of this? It's the reason I'm going to fix your car. You're going to drive it around for the next fifty years, if you want to. Right out of this town into whatever kind of life you want."

He slides out of the car without giving me time to respond. Even if he had, I don't know what I would say. I'm so pissed at his dad for putting them all in danger like he did. For caring more about his precious gang than about his mom, his sons. His nieces and nephews.

My dad was right about keeping me away from the Agani house, but that doesn't make the ache in my chest for Rock and his family hurt any less. Getting out of the car, I help him unload the parts from the trunk. We're both carrying panels into the garage when I speak up. "I'm sorry you had to go through all that. I wish you could have just moved in with us."

"I wouldn't have. Someone had to keep Granny and the littles safe."

"That wasn't your job. You were a kid too."

"I was the only one there for them. I had to.

We work unloading the car parts and organizing them on and around the workbench in the garage. There's a piece of his story that sticks like a splinter in my brain, burrowing deeper in until I have to ask. "The place where your dad had that guy take the body. Was it the same place as where Gracia was left?"

Rock's throat bobs as he deposits a large panel of metal next to the Corvette. "No. Leif wouldn't have taken her there. He wouldn't have risked anyone finding the other skeletons in my dad's closet. He's still loyal to him, my dad."

I push my hair out of my face. Do I dare ask the question that sits on the tip of my tongue? "Where is it? Where are the bodies buried?"

His eyes are bright when they meet mine. "You really wanna know? I'll tell you. If you ask, I'll tell, V."

My throat goes dry and I can't swallow. I'm not sure I do want to know. The thread of conviction in his words underscores Rock's vow. If I ask, he'll give me the ugly, unpainted truth. "Tell me."

He does, and the rush of it, knowing Rock meant it when he said he'd tell me anything, makes my skin tingle. Here is someone who proves with every word and every action that I mean something to him.

I can hear Rosie caterwauling inside, so I rescue her from the laundry room and deposit her inside the Corvette. Tools cranking and clanging don't bother her anymore. Dragging the stool closer, I hand Rock tools as he needs them.

"Thank you, for telling me."

Our eyes meet for less than a breath, but I hope it's enough.

For him to see that he means a lot to me too. More than I can say.

"Hand me that wrench?" I do, and he uses it with deft hands.

"How does it feel? Working at a different garage? I bet you're glad to be out of the mess at Agani. Since it's basically Snake HQ now?"

Rock's jaw clenches. He loosens a bolt and it drops into the tray with a ping.

A car rounds the corner. Vintage but in pristine condition.

The hairs on the back of my neck stand up. My eyes narrow as the car picks up speed.

Something is wrong.

"Get down!" Rock's arms come around me, and he flings us to the ground.

Gunshots rip through the air, pinging off the back of my mom's car. The rear window shatters.

The concrete is hard and cold under my back as Rock's body weight pins me to the ground. One of his large hands covers the crown of my head, keeping me pressed underneath him.

The car screeches away down the road just as my front door slams open. My mom comes running out with her handgun poised to go, just like my dad taught her. She doesn't fire a single shot. Instead, she chants the license plate number of the car. A car whose driver just tried to end Rock and me.

Mom's slippered feet thunder toward us, trampling on a strand of my hair as she halts standing over us. Protecting us. She bends at the waist, pawing at us with one hand between repetitions of the license plate. Adrenaline must be running so high in her system there's no room for fear, because her tone is capable and measured. Then it hits me that she deals with people in crisis every day. She probably has her emotions locked down tight. "You two okay?" she demands.

Rock's eyes met mine. Our hearts beat in tandem, our chests pressed together. His hands curl into my hair, keeping me still while I work up the voice to answer.

"I'm okay," I rasp, eyes locked on Rock's. "You?"

His chest shudders up and down, up and down. A hard object in his pocket digs into my hip.

"Is that your wallet in your pocket, or are you happy to see me?"

My bad joke breaks through the haze in his expression, and he huffs. Rolls of me and flops to the concrete at my side. His hand brushes my side, tangling our fingers together. Like he's not quite ready to break contact. "My wallet, and you know I'm always happy to see you. Just not right now. Like this."

I squeeze his hand with my fingers. "We're okay."

With a firm nod, my mom stands up. Calls the sheriff. His protective commands are audible coming through the phone, even from down on the ground.

Rock's fingers tighten around mine, his eyes fastened to the dusky sky. "Before, when you asked how I feel about being out of the mess at Agani? That's the thing, V. I'll never be out."

Running Out of Time

Rock

DARREN IS WAITING IN HIS GARAGE WHEN I JUMP THE CURB with the bicycle I borrowed from a cousin and coast up the driveway. Leaping off it, the metal clangs to the cement. I don't care. I stalk toward a man I thought was my friend, the scowl on my face starting the conversation before my mouth can.

His hand not wound around a beer can comes up between us in a whoa gesture.

It doesn't stop me. I'm too fired up as I enter the garage. "What the hell, man? You were supposed to let me know if Gabriel was trying to start shit. And yet here you are, drinking in your garage without a care in the world."

Darren plunks the can down on his well-organized

workbench and swivels on the stool to square with me. "I wasn't anywhere near the shop or the bar today. Bonnie has me repainting the kitchen cabinets, so I didn't hear about Gabe's idea to pay a visit to the Lambs until they were already on their way. At that point, I thought about calling you, but I didn't want to distract you. You've got good instincts. Always have. Which is why you should've—"

"Don't start that with me right now. I am not in the mood for that lecture again. She could have died. Just like that." Desperation morphs my fingers into claws that yank and tear at my hair. It's just about long enough to need a haircut to reshape it into the style I prefer.

The old timer sighs. "She okay?"

"Someone tried to shoot her! No she is absolutely not okay. As soon as it hit her what could have happened, she hurled all over the driveway. I had to carry her inside, she was shaking so bad. I have never seen her so messed up like that, and I never want to see that much fear on her face ever again. Luckily, I was there and sensed it coming. If I hadn't been there…"

The last time I threw up was the night my father shot someone dead on Granny's living room floor. I took one look at all of that blood and lost the cold pizza my cousins and I shared, hiding in that back bedroom. My dad's cutting disapproval forced me to stand up straight and bury the revulsion deep down where it didn't show.

Seeing Val like that colored over my world with angry red. The Snakes are going to regret going after her like that. Because I have no doubt she was their target. Those bullets were a message for me, delivered via Valencia. My father knows me well enough to realize that hurting her will get to me. That thought digs sharp, ugly claws in my chest and tugs hard.

Darren taps his temple. "Like I said. Good instincts. Which

is why you should have agreed to step into the top spot like Dino asked you to. If you had, you wouldn't have to worry about peeling your girlfriend off the sidewalk."

Images of Valencia bleeding out on the concrete assault my senses. Her gorgeous dark brown hair falling out of that braid. Her eyes glazed, reaching for the clouds. A metallic tang fills my nostrils. Thunder builds in my throat, and I lash out in anger. The toe of my boot crashes into the side of a sealed paint bucket, sending it clanging against the wall. I had no idea I was capable of making the anguished roar that tears from my throat.

Chest heaving, my fists clench and flex at my sides.

When Leif and I were younger, my dad trained us to settle fights with our fists. If we argued about dumb crap like what to watch on TV, he'd kick us into the backyard and lock the door. Neither of us was allowed in until we'd fought and resolved our differences. Usually, that meant trading punches until one or both of us had a black eye or a split lip.

Standing in Darren's garage, anger charging my blood, I ache for a fight. To punch the lights out of something until my knuckles are cracked and bleeding. But the only one here is Darren, and even though I'm pissed at him, he doesn't deserve that. No one does, except that boxer stain Gabriel. "Where is that buttwipe now?"

Lifting his beer off the workbench, Darren holds it up to his mouth, answering me before taking a long glug. "Probably at the bar with everyone else, getting drunk and hoping you'll do something stupid. You want my advice? Don't do anything stupid."

"Sounds familiar," I grumble under my breath. I am not the one given to impulsive decisions that get her in trouble. In spite of the turmoil in my chest, my mouth twitches like it wants to smile. Valencia's middle name should be "Impulsive." One of these days, her penchant for firing off without thinking it through will get her into trouble she can't talk or pepper spray her way out of.

Again, the image of her dead body tortures me. Darren might as well have tossed a bucket of ice water over my head. That's how fast a chill slices through me.

Clenching my teeth, I force every muscle in my body to uncoil. To relax so I don't look like a predator ready to strike. To coil and squeeze. Like my dad.

Lowering myself onto the free stool next to my only friend in the Snakes, I grip the seat with claw-like fingers.

Unlike Valencia, I can't go marching into the bar and demand the Snakes leave her alone. My father has stated that he won't protect me anymore. Today's drive-by nailed that coffin closed. I'm standing on the opposite side of the line from where my dad wants me, and he's lifted the ban on gunning for me. Snakes like Gabriel won't hesitate to take shots at me if it gets them closer to heading the gang while my father and brother are behind bars.

As much as my dad's angry voice in my head orders to take the gun strapped to my waist and light up the bar, I have no doubt I'd end up dead by daybreak.

Valencia won't take this lying down. She'll do something reckless. Put herself in danger.

I can't be around her right now. I'm too pissed off. Wound too tight, and the last thing I want is to hurt her by venting my anger, or giving head to my fear. But I have to make sure she doesn't get it into her head to retaliate.

My fingers fly as I send a text to Janice. She agrees to go to Val's and make sure she stays there. It's weird knowing that my ex and the girl who makes my heart a complicated mess are friends, but today it's a relief.

Reaching into the cooler under the workbench, Darren lifts out a beer and hands it to me.

"What will you do?"

I take a long drink, giving myself another second to think. Wipe my mouth with the back of my hand. My expression is grim when I meet his eyes. "Give me a couple weeks. I have to finish fixing Val's car first."

Darren's somber nod is a gut punch. He and I both know what I'm agreeing to do, and once I go through with it, there will be no going back. Dino Agani will finally have succeeded in making me the monster he has tried to shape me into since long before I should have been using my fists or holding a gun.

Hissing at the sour taste of the beer, I set the can down. "You need any help painting?"

"Grab that paint can and follow me."

Taking it up, I trudge after Darren into the house.

My words to Valencia earlier today haunt me.

I'll never be out.

Even as those fatal words passed my lips, I had no idea how true they were.

A Truckload of Trouble

Val

Single Awareness Day is next week. Excuse me, Valentine's Day. Members of the student body council are going from room to room fundraising by selling Valentine's roses made with red cellophane and chocolate kisses. In the past, Portia used to buy one for Destin and me, but she won't be buying anything from jail.

Destin hasn't mentioned her in a while, which I take to mean he hasn't changed his mind about reading her emails. If she has tried to contact me, I'm unaware, because I blocked her butt the second I climbed out of the aqueduct she and Gus tried to drown me in.

The student body treasurer traipses over when I wave.

"I'll take three." I give her the names and tap my phone against the payment device. She thanks me and moves on to her next fundraiser victim.

"Did you just buy me a rose?" Janice asks, leaning a hip against my desk.

I spin to look up at her. "I don't know what you're talking about."

"You did. That's so sweet. I'll get you one too."

"No, seriously. It's fine. I just thought—"

"Thought you preferred the real thing, V." Rock props an elbow on Janice's shoulder, rubbing his thumb under his chin. There's a twinkle in his eyes. The turd is having fun teasing me. His ribbing doesn't distract me from the purple shadows under his eyes, or his sallow cheeks.

Tucking the concern away to be dissected later, I sniff primly. "My preferences are none of your business."

He quirks an eyebrow. "I was going to get you a rose, seeing as how I owe you one, but if you're sure you don't want one…"

This pact the two of them have to gang up on me? Not a fan. But tell that to my grinning mouth.

I purse my lips, fighting it. I am not admitting to Rock that I'd be more than mildly pleased if I got one from him. Not with Janice watching is with growing awareness.

"I ordered a bouquet of them for my mom. She loves 'em. I'm hoping they'll soften her up. Think it'll work?" Destin slides into his desk next to mine.

"It's worth a try."

The rest of my morning goes smoothly. It's unremarkable, which is becoming increasingly rare in my life. It's a relief. At lunch, Janice and I team up to steal Rock's cafeteria brownie and split it while he makes empty threats to fill our lockers with nuts and bolts or sneak into the *Herald* office and tamper with the next week's newspaper layout.

After school, I take my time weaving through the rows and slide into my mom's car.

"No way," I breathe.

On the corner outside the school is the scrawny kid I bought the drug-filled avocado from. He's back, selling the fruits for two bucks a pop. There are two partially filled produce crates at his feet. I watch as he sells to passersby. Some buyers get fruit from one crate, and some from the other, but there isn't any rhyme or reason to it.

At least, there wouldn't be if I didn't know exactly what he's doing. One of the crates is filled with extra special avocados.

I'll never be out, V.

My teeth grit together. Rock might think he's trapped with the Snakes, but not if I can help him.

Pulling into the grocery store parking lot across from the school, I park in the sunshine. And wait.

The Snake recruit sells avocados to lots of people as they leave the school, until the stream of students slows to a trickle. Several teachers stop at the light to buy from him as well, and they all get fruit from the crate on one side. Must be the drug-free side.

Immediately after the guy sells his final avocado, a vintage car parked farther down the row from me roars to life. The vehicle pauses just long enough to scoop up the scrawny kid.

That's my cue.

I follow the vintage car as it weaves through afternoon traffic. Stay a couple of cars behind. Don't make any sudden moves. Don't gain on them too quickly. I repeat the pointers my dad gave me once when I begged him to show me how he tails someone he's keeping an eye on. At the time, it was a fun game to play while riding through town in Dad's SUV. I didn't have any skin in that game.

This isn't a game. If I can find out where the Snakes are keeping their drug-laced avocado monopoly, I can hand the information to Sheriff McCandles. He can bust their operation wide open and dismantle the Snakes.

Rock will be free.

There will be consequences, but I'll deal with them.

Hands tightening on the steering wheel, I follow the vintage car to an older neighborhood on the edge of town. The car turns into a court, and I glide past. I can't follow them onto the short dead-end street without being seen.

I park around the corner, pull my hood up over my head, zip up my leather bomber, and slink closer, hiding behind cars as I go.

The house at the apex of the court has a wider lot than the rest, and a plain white diesel trailer is parked to one side.

Scrawny guy and two more Snakes climb out of the vintage car and go inside the house.

From where I'm crouched behind a car, I can't see the inside of the trailer to confirm if that's where they're getting their product. It's likely, but I need proof before I call the sheriff and bring him down on their heads.

February has been hella cold from the start, which is a lucky break for me. Not a single person moves on the street. Everyone is tucked into their warm houses, sheltering from the frigid weather. Alone, I move toward the trailer. A narrow gap between the fence and the side of the trailer allows me to squeeze through.

My blood is pumping through my body at a fast clip as I inch along the side of the big white container. All I have to do is get eyes on those tainted avocados. Then I can call the sheriff. The way he'll crush the Snakes with the weight of the law will be Biblical. Justice will be served. Rock will no longer have to live under his dad's cruel expectations.

Nearby, a door opens. A man's voice hollers that he'll be right back. Footsteps grow louder as they approach.

I freeze, pressing my back against the side of the trailer. If this guy looks underneath it, he'll see my jeans-clad legs. I stifle a shudder. I have no misconceptions about what the Snakes will do to me if they find me snooping around one of their hideouts.

One of the vintage car's doors opens and shuts. The footsteps return to the house.

My body relaxes against the trailer, even while blood roars in my ears. That was too close.

An individual with more self-preservation instincts would turn and run after a close call like that.

That's not me. I have to see this through, because it might be my best and only chance to help Rock. To pay him back for saving my life multiple times.

This might be my only chance to save him right back.

Bracing myself, I fling my body around the back of the trailer.

These Snakes are even stupider than they look. The trailer is halfway open, and it is stacked floor to ceiling with crates of avocados.

A smug grin spreads across my face. Gotcha, you pack of freeze-dried sea monkeys.

Climbing into the trailer, I swipe a handful of avocados from different crates. Crouching on the ground, I gouge into them with my mom's car keys. I find one drug-filled avocado. Two. Five.

Time to go.

Bundling the avocados into my arms, I step off the trailer, feet dropping toward the ground.

The front door opens in the same heartbeat as my soles hit

the ground with a smack.

"Shut up," a male voice yells. "Did you hear that?"

An avocado drops from the pile in my arms and rolls under the trailer.

My entire body seizes. I might as well be frozen into a small human-sized popsicle, because I can't move an inch.

Rotten Egg Breath growls something too low to hear. His footsteps are almost silent as he prowls toward the trailer. If he lays his punishing hands on me, there won't be anyone here to pry him off. I remember how it felt when his hand squeezed around my throat.

I can't let him lay even a finger on me.

A Trap of My Own Making

MY GAZE JUMPS LEFT AND RIGHT. THERE IS NOWHERE for me to go. The entire backyard is a dirt patch with little landscaping flags pounded into the dry earth.

I sure as shooting can't stay where I am—frozen at the back of the trailer with my arms full of stolen fruit. But I can't run either. Rotten Egg Breath will hear me. If he catches me, he'll shoot me dead and have one of his peons dump me in Dino Agani's favored burial ground.

Trying to pile all of the avocados in my arms to one side without dropping them is the hardest thing I've ever done. My hands are shaking so hard it's a miracle I don't drop another one. Eyes locked on the avo I dropped, the one that rolled under the trailer, I hold my breath. Wait for the vicious Snake to come close in on me.

For some reason, he's stalled in front of the house. What is he waiting for?

What am I waiting for? An engraved invitation to my own

death?

Clutching the avocados against my chest, I manage to slide my phone out of a front pocket. Hit the messaging app, praying I can type silently one handed in case REB has dog-tier level hearing.

Pulling up the sheriff's number, I share my location. Type a single word.

The phone goes back into my pocket, and I inch along the side of the trailer. Maybe if I hide behind the wheel well, the Snake won't see me and I'll be able to slip away.

He shifts on the driveway, and I halt. The avocados shift in my arms, and I clutch them tighter. If I drop another one, I'm dead.

A minute ticks by, marked by heartbeat after ringing heartbeat.

Why won't he go back inside so I can get out of dodge?

The garage door opens with a rumble, and a second person joins my nemesis on the driveway. An older man speaks. "Told you there'd be enough room for the trailer, didn't I?"

"You can't blame me for being skeptical. You've always been one to sit back and watch instead of pitching in. It's about time you take steps to help out the gang, old man."

"I wait for the opportune time, boy. It takes skill to know when to make a move, and when to wait."

One of them grunts.

An avocado at the top of my pile wobbles, and my heart tries to leap out of my chest as I scramble to tuck it under my chin. My chest rises and falls in silent pants. I'm breathing so quick and shallow I'm feeling lightheaded.

"Speaking of the opportune time, how long is this trailer going to be parked here?"

"Already trying to weasel out of doing your part?"

"Don't put words in my mouth, Gabe. I just need to tell Bonnie something. My woman isn't happy about your guys coming and going and tracking dirty shoes through the house. It's not a bus station."

"The trailer will stay here until I say otherwise. That's all you need to know."

The two men move into the garage. REB snarls. "Knew he was staying with you. Old coward."

"Didn't know that was a crime," the other returns.

"Watch it, Darren. You're already on thin ice with me."

"You don't own the ice yet, Gabriel. Best not make enemies of the old timers like me."

Another grunt. Then a forced laugh. "You may be right. It's cold as my girl's feet out here. Let's go inside."

They move into the house.

As soon as the door closes, I bolt for the street. An avocado flies out of my arms and rolls down the sidewalk, leaving a trail of white powder.

Heart screaming between my ribs, I round the corner and lunge into my car. It wasn't the best idea to bring drug avocados into my mom's car, because now it will have to be detailed to get rid of the traces of coke. I'm gonna have to launder the crap out of my clothes. Dry clean my leather jacket.

The sheriff's vehicle comes tearing around the corner into the court, followed by two patrol cars. Sheriff McCandles, Sykes, and Kelley. Car doors slam, and I try to wrangle my heavy breathing.

Dumping the avocados in the passenger seat, I peer through the windshield. The sheriff and his deputies stand on the porch, talking to a middle-aged man. He shakes his head, but the lawman keeps talking. Probably asking him if he's seen a pint-sized brunette skulking around his yard.

Sykes walks backward from the conversation, strolling across the driveway toward the trailer. Just looking around. I wave a hand. The deputy's eyes widen. He moves closer to me, waiting until we're toe to toe before he speaks.

"Val, you okay? What's with the distress signal?"

"I found the reason for the avocado shortage." Leading him to my car, I fill him in on my after-school activity while I pile drug-stuffed avocados into his hands. Sykes looks from me, to the avocados, to the trailer. There's a pleasing shine of reverent incredulity in his smile. "You sure your middle name isn't Trouble?"

"I'm having it changed next week."

He chuckles. "Let's go show the sheriff what you found."

I rub my hands together, anticipating the look on REB's ugly face when he's arrested. I feel a little bad for whoever Bonnie is, but she kind of asked for it being involved with a Snake.

I'm one to talk. My best friend is their best forger.

Half an hour later, the entire house is crawling with law enforcement. I've watched several Snakes being marched out of the house in handcuffs and corralled into the back seats of patrol cars. They wait while Sheriff McCandles and his deputies inventory the trailer and any contraband they find in the house.

The front door opens. I perk up. REB is coming out that door in handcuffs, any minute. A middle-aged woman is escorted in handcuffs to a patrol car. She casts nervous glances at Sykes as he escorts her. A man about her age in another car starts hollering that she didn't have anything to do with it. This must be Bonnie.

Frowning, I turn back to the front door. My least favorite Snake was inside when the sheriff and his cavalry arrived, so where the hell is he?

Kelley comes to check on me, and I drill her about their search of the house. Insist that there's still at least one guy inside, and they have to find him. They must put him away.

The deputy looks over her shoulder at the house. "Sorry, I don't know what to tell you. There isn't anyone else inside, or the backyard, or the trailer. We've looked everywhere."

"He was there! I swear." REB was inside that house. They have to find and arrest him. As far as I can tell, he's been running the Snakes since Dino and Leif Agani were snatched from the picture. I don't have proof, but I'm almost positive he's the one who sent a car full of mouth breathers to shoot Rock and me at my house. I don't know for sure which of us was the target, but that doesn't matter.

Either way, REB is at the top of my list. They have to find him.

Setting my jaw, I look past Kelley toward the house. Maybe I can find him.

I try to pivot around Kelley and make for the house, but she catches me by the shoulders. "Nope. Not happening. Your ride is here."

I squawk. "I don't need a ride. I have my mom's car."

"Ah ah ah. You've proven you can't make the smart choice to stay away from the Snakes. They tried to shoot you. We, everyone in the department, we care about you and your mom. We aren't going to let anything happen to you if we can help it, but you've got to stop putting yourself in risky situations like this."

I groan in protest, even though Kelley is right.

She chucks me on the chin. "Promise me you'll stay safe, okay?"

"Does Jonesie know you're a big ole softie?"

"It's his favorite thing about me. Come on. Your ride's here.

I'll make sure your mom's car is detailed before it makes it home."

Kelley turns me around on the sidewalk and steers me toward the corner, where Leander's truck is parked.

What is This Feeling?

ONE WEEK HAS CRAWLED BY SINCE I HELPED SHERIFF McCandles blow up the Snakes drug avocado operation. No one has seen REB since. I've taken to double checking my mom's car before I drive anywhere to make sure he isn't lurking in the back like an urban legend. The security cameras installed around our house are hugely reassuring. No one knows where the slithering serpent is hiding. He hasn't shown his face.

The drive-by is constantly on my mind, too. Not knowing if they were coming for Rock or for me makes the dread low in my gut melt and puddle like molten candle wax. If they weren't coming for me, they will be now. And if they were coming for Rock, he's still in danger and I can't do anything about it. I hate it, thank you very much.

Taking into account how much REB must hate me, I had to be the intended victim. For some reason, assuming I was the target makes every day a little easier. I have the entire department at my back. My mom. My friends. They'll do everything they can to protect me.

But if Rock was the target? He doesn't have anyone in his corner making sure he isn't knocked down and dragged out. Permanently. The truth of it chills the acid in my stomach until the merest flick could shatter it.

Know what else I hate? My new, bone-deep understanding of the reason my dad always sat facing the door when we went out to restaurants, or the library, or Twinkle's Ice Cream Emporium. He wasn't paranoid. He was prescient. He was familiar with the sort of evil that could creep too close if he was caught unawares. After the drive-by assassination attempt, I do too.

Hate, hate, hate.

Janice has been clingy as heck. I don't hate that. Maybe the drive-by scared her as bad as it scared me, or maybe she's bored. No matter her reasons, which she won't tell me—I asked—Janice bursts through my door every chance she gets. She drives me home after school and stays until we're both falling asleep on the couch. When he isn't slinging smoothies, Ty hangs out too, which is great because he brings us smoothies. He also takes a weird amount of enjoyment out of waiting on Janice hand and foot. She revels in the attention, so I don't tease her about it. Too much.

Okay, her new nickname is Her Majesty, and Janice rolls her eyes every time I say it. It's way more entertaining than Bridge Troll. She agreed when Destin pointed it out. He's still avoiding his parents and the whole "I-want-to-be-a-cop" conversation that he knows won't go over well with his mom.

Having been on the receiving end of a bullet bouquet, I can't say I blame her. Being shot at is freaking terrifying.

Tonight, Janice and I got tired of sinking into butt-shaped indentations in the couch, so once we were done working on a couple of articles for the newspaper, we texted Ty and Destin to meet up at the diner. It's a weeknight and the place is packed. The waitresses hurry between tables, expertly taking orders and delivering milkshakes, piles of fries, and sizzling burgers. After all the scrutiny I was under since my dad disappeared, it felt strangely nice to walk into the diner without getting a bunch of dirty looks.

Janice and Ty are at one end of our corner booth, cuddling and feeding each other fried mozzarella sticks. "Here's your next bite, Your Majesty."

"Why thank you, good sir."

Oh, so she doesn't roll her eyes when Ty uses the nickname. Only me. Rude.

Destin is next to me, leaving plenty of space between us and the canoodlers. He and I are splitting a nacho mountain with extra jalapenos. "Needs more heat," Destin says, grabbing the hot sauce and dousing his half.

I shield my half of the nacho mountain with both hands. "Keep that stuff away from my chips."

He chuckles. "Can't stand the heat?"

"Your mom can't stand the heat."

My friend caps the hot sauce and puts it down. "Don't remind me."

I offer him one of my jalapenos, which he snags and plops on the chip poised at his mouth. He chews, head bobbing in enjoyment. "Apology accepted."

On my other side, Leander takes a large bite of his bacon burger. We joke about Sykes's return to patrolling. The raccoons that live behind Twinkle's scared the crap out of him on his first shift back on patrol. Just like old times.

"How was I supposed to know raccoons love bananas?" Leander mimics the deputy, making me giggle into my hot cocoa piled high with whipped cream and chocolate sprinkles. Don't mock until you try it. Hot cocoa pairs deliciously with nachos.

"That is scary accurate, bro." Destin and Leander bump fists over my head.

Getting my laughter under control, I crunch a nacho. Sweet, comforting cocoa warms my insides. Since February has been butt-cold, it's been impossible for Rock to work on the Corvette. I haven't seen him outside of school since the drive-by, and it irritates me how much I miss hanging out with him in the garage.

Missing Rock isn't the only reason I like having Janice around. For better or worse, she's becoming my best friend. My criminally bent, impeccably stylish, workhorse editor friend. I'm as surprised as anyone, but it's true. Speaking of which, I watched her pick up an ID order at the resort's smoothie hut yesterday. Girl was incredibly smooth. If I hadn't been watching her I wouldn't have seen her retrieve the envelope from underneath a western-themed slot machine near the food court. Her eyes had snagged on mine as she returned to the counter in front of Ty's workstation. We'll have to talk about it at some point, but right now we're both avoiding the topic.

Does keeping her secret make me a good friend? Or does it make me a good girl gone bad? It's a question I've avoided examining too closely.

A plate clatters to the floor across the diner. People clap and cheer.

Destin eats a nacho drowning in hot sauce, breathing through the heat as he chews. When he realizes his water cup is empty, he makes a play for mine. I slide it out of his reach. "Hey, I need that."

"You're the king of hot sauce. Are you sure you need water?"

Our waitress appears, offering refills. He thanks her

profusely and chugs, ears red.

Leander props his cheek on a palm, leaning on the tabletop. "Did you hear about Jonesie and Kelley?"

"What about them?" I ask, leaning in to hear the juicy gossip about the deputies.

"Jonesie asked me to help him with some paperwork, so I sat next to his desk. He was digging through his drawers for an extra pen, and I saw a ring box in the top one. You know, small, black, velvet."

My palms slap the table. "Where was I when this happened?"

Destin leans into me, his chin bumping my temple as he reaches for an extra fork. "Yeah, where were you?"

"Gotta say," Leander adds. "It's been boring at the department without you. I don't have anyone to beat at paper scanning."

My finger runs around the rim of my cup lid. "You wish. And I don't know. Maybe my mom will let me go back to work later this week. She was pretty scared after what happened—"

"—With good reason—"

"—And she wanted me close to home."

"You'd be safe with me, at the department," Leander says, close to my ear.

My spine goes rigid at his nearness. Wormy discomfort niggles in my belly. Ignoring the jiggling, I zero in on the pile of mozzarella sticks in front of Janice and Ty. "Hey Jan, I thought you ordered those for the table. I'd like one before you and Ty feed them to each other like those two cartoon dogs."

Janice uncurls from around Ty long enough to slide the appetizer basket down the table. It comes to a stop right in front of me, the heavenly scent of greasy cheese making my mouth water. Thanking her, I gobble up a few. "Sykes is wrong. These are the best thing the diner makes."

"I see your mozzarella and raise you nachos." Destin and I toast our snacks.

Leander fishes a couple of the soggiest nachos out from the bottom of the basket and devours them. "Hard agree. So good."

Janice's eyes gleam as she focuses on me.

Uh oh.

"Hey Val, how's your article coming?"

I nearly choke on my food. I shouldn't have poked the bear. "Which one? The one on the new heaters in the gym? Because I'm almost done with it. I'll get it to you tomorrow."

Janice shakes her head, which is unnecessary because I know which article she's asking about. The one about my life as the sheriff's daughter. The one I've tried to write a hundred times and deleted just as many. None of the words I put down are adequate to capture what it was like being the sheriff's daughter, or how gut-wrenching it was to go from the town's darling daughter to the spawn of an alleged pervert and murderer. Fun times.

I force my gaze to steady on her so I don't look like I'm avoiding the question. I absolutely am avoiding it. "Almost done with that one, too."

Janice eyes me with well-earned skepticism. "How long is it? How many words?"

I take another nacho, chewing them slowly to buy myself time. "Thousand words, give or take?"

Lies. All I've got is a blank page and a whole lot of survivor guilt.

"Send it to me. I want to read it. Maybe I can help you out with it. Don't argue, I know you're having a hard time with it. Let me help, okay?"

I mumble an agreement, not sure how I'm going to get out

of this. Honestly, I could use her help, but that would involve admitting that I haven't written anything good enough to keep, and Editor Janice is scary.

She gives me a quick nod and turns back to Ty. They're sharing a mint chip milkshake with two straws, and it's stinking adorable.

Leander's breath huffs against my hair. "You haven't even started, have you?"

Eyes wide, I press a finger to his mouth. "Shh, she'll hear you. She has spies everywhere."

He laughs again, not moving away. Puppy dog brown eyes catch mine.

It is incredibly awkward to be touching my ex-boyfriend's mouth. Yanking my hand away, I sit on it. Because that's totally something I do all the time. Totally cool. Cool, cool. Nope, sitting on my hands is uncomfortable. I pick up my cocoa instead. It's delicious, the perfect temperature to warm me up without burning my tongue. I already did that with the piping hot nacho cheese.

Leander's arm brushes mine. "I won't tell her."

The earnestness behind his tone makes me sigh into my mug. "I know, and thanks. I want to stay out of Janice's dog house as long as possible."

He hits me with his golden boy smile. "I can help you with the article, if you want. I know what it's like being a sheriff's kid. My experience isn't the same as yours, but still. Plus, I helped you look into Gracia's murder in the fall, right? Let me help you. Please."

That genuine please pulls on the threads of my resolve. Having help would be great. Maybe talking to Leander will give me some ideas for the article. He can help me balance being honest with being interesting to read, which is what I'm having trouble with. I have mixed feelings about my dad's career, because of how I was treated after his integrity was called into question. The public scrutiny and vitriol were brutal. I'm finding it impossible to write something that doesn't come out sounding bitter and hurt, because that's how I felt.

This town has gone through enough hurt to last us for a while, and I don't want to dredge it up. I've been working on forgiving them for shunning my mom and me, and letting the bitterness go. Because holding onto the ugly parts won't do anything to convince them they were wrong, but it will eat away at my heart, damaging me more deeply than any thoughtless words could.

Maybe talking it through with Leander can be part of my process. Maybe it'll encourage healing in my still tender spots. "I could use some help."

Leander doesn't see the hesitance in my eyes. His smile is way too big. "Excellent. I was thinking we could grab dinner sometime, maybe at Villipianio's? You like their food right? We could go out there and eat and talk about the article. Friday maybe. What do you say?"

Am I crazy, or does that sound like a date? The Italian place out by the airport is too fancy for an article brainstorming session. Usually, people from school only go out there with their serious significant others, or for pre-prom dinners.

Pink and red heart paper garlands are strung along the diner's windows and above the counter. A pink-cheeked Cupid with a loaded bow hangs from the ceiling, spinning gently in the draft from the building's heater.

Friday is Valentine's Day.

I start to suggest something more casual, but Leander plows on. "I can pick you up, if that would make your mom feel better. What do you think?"

That definitely sounds like a date. "Their lasagna is amazing. Seriously, top tier. I'll ask my mom. You know how she's been the last couple weeks."

My mom has told me multiple times that she doesn't mind being the bad guy. If I don't want to do something but don't want to upset a friend, she has given me permission to blame her for being an overprotective mom. I have an easy out and I won't have to hurt Leander's feelings. Whatever those are.

"Again, with good reason."

On second thought, maybe I should decline right now. "Hey, Leander…"

The hairs on my arms stand up, along with an army of goosebumps. My instincts flare awareness as I swivel to look toward the front of the diner. Rock stands in the doorway wearing the leather jacket I gave him. My mouth goes dry. Damn, does that jacket make him look good.

Rock's eyes are trained on our table. Not just our table. Leander and me.

A pungent wave of deja vu smacks me in the face. To another night in the diner, and another pissing contest.

Rock strides through the bustle, eyes boring into mine. The singular attention is heady. Swiping my napkin off the table, I wipe my face to make sure I don't have a nacho cheese beard.

As Rock approaches, I realize how close Leander and I are on the bench seat. Suddenly, putting space between us is paramount. I shove the nacho platter at Destin and wave at Leander to back off down the bench.

"What the— Oh." Leander rolls his eyes when he sees Rock approaching.

Janice's cat-eyeliner emphasizes her eyes that swing between my face and Rock's prowling approach.

My hand rises to pat at my cheek, making sure it's clean; it's warm. When did I start blushing like an idiot? Ignoring it, I cup both cheeks with my hands, feigning being tired rather than ramped up with nervous anticipation.

Rock stops at the edge of our booth, his knuckles tapping on the veneered wood tabletop. "My invitation get lost in the mail?"

"Didn't have your address," I say. "No hard feelings?"

The fake chuckle he gives me while he glares at Leander is telling. "Sure. No hard feelings."

Leander glares back until his phone buzzing interrupts. He glances between Rock and me, as if deciding something. Pursing his lips, he shows the screen to Destin. "Sykes is going to the shooting range. Wanna go?"

"As long as we can drop Bert home first." The dog is so quiet under the table I forgot he was with us. I drop a plain chip surreptitiously, and crunching sounds come from between my boots.

Destin gathers his dog and says his goodbyes, moving up the aisle. I expect Leander to follow, but instead he lingers. Gripping the lapels of his letterman jacket, his brown eyes search for mine. "Let me know if you're free for dinner, yeah?"

"I'll let you know."

He's all sweet smiles until he turns toward Rock. Roughly, he pushes past. "Agani."

"McCandles Junior." Rock gives him his back, claiming the empty bench seat next to me. Stretching his arm along the back of the seat, he orders a burger and fries from the waitress. Once she's gone, he levels a look at me.

"Think he'll bring you a whole bouquet of his mommy's roses for your date?"

I take a long sip of my cocoa, not sure what to do about the rippling hints of jealousy underscoring Rock's teasing. His hand brushes against my shoulder as he gets comfortable in the booth, sending warmth down my arm. "It's not a date. And even if it was, your posturing isn't necessary."

"You sure? Because you're leaning back against my arm like you belong there."

I snap forward, curling around the table edge. "I was not."

Mirth sparks in his dark eyes. "Don't worry, V. I won't tell Junior you like me better. He should hear it from you."

"You're insufferable."

"And yet here you are, not suffering." He plucks a nacho from my plate and eats it.

"Hey!"

Rock leans in close, gaze snaring mine. "Want me to give it back?"

I stare at him. I think I'm hallucinating, because Rock's eyes glint as they drop to my mouth.

Too slow, I lean away. "Ew, gross."

He grins.

Down the table, Janice is also grinning. That's concerning.

I need a conversation change, fast. Taking a loaded nacho chip, I nibble at it while Janice draws both Rock and Ty into a conversation about their thoughts on Valentine's Day. Ty is all for it because he's all about celebrating the love. The beaming smile he gets on his face whenever he looks at Janice tracks with that. Rock grumbles something about hating shopping for chocolates and flowers, to which Janice scoffs and tells him to be more original.

"Some girls like chocolates and flowers," I point out.

"You're saying if Leander showed up at your door with a heart-shaped box of chocolates and a bouquet, that would make you feel special?" Janice's eagle eyes are trained on my face, so she doesn't miss the instant frown I get picturing Leander making a romantic gesture on Valentine's Day.

"See?" she says, gesturing at me while looking at Rock. "Chocolates and flowers are boring. Even the golden boy can't pull Valencia with that cliche stuff."

Feeding into Janice's opinions almost always ends in her writing an op ed for the paper, and we get a lot of parent feedback whenever she publishes those. Parents in Hacienda have thoughts about Janice's opinions. Strong thoughts. Instead of contradicting her and sparking what would probably be a funny rant, I finish my cocoa. And try not to notice that there's only a pinky width between Rock's leg and mine on the bench seat.

"I meant what I said," I whisper out of the corner of my mouth. "I would have invited you if I knew how to get a hold of you. You haven't been answering my texts."

Rock's leg presses against mine. "Been busy."

"You never told me where you're staying. Isn't Granny Agani worried about you?" I don't mention that I know he was staying with Darren the Snake, and that since the bust, I once again have no idea where Rock has been laying his head at night.

"I'm crashing with a friend, okay? Don't worry about me so much."

Tossing my braid, I pluck an olive off a nacho and eat it. "Please. I'm not worried about you."

He boops me on the nose. "You're cute when you're in denial."

Glaring at him only makes him smirk. Idly, he takes another chip. "I finally heard from the junkyard guy. He has those parts we were waiting for. I can start working on the Corvette again tomorrow after school, if you want."

"Think you can check your ego at the sidewalk?"

His grin widens. "Not my fault you're obsessed with me. All

I did was save your life a couple times. No big deal."

I bury my forehead in my palm, thankful that Leander and Destin aren't here to see the full wattage of Rock's teasing. "Never mind. Drop off the parts and I'll figure it out myself. They have videos online I can watch. No need for your brand of helping."

Rock chuckles. "I have no doubt you could do it. But I don't mind helping, and you should let me." Drawing closer, he whispers in my ear. "You're leaning back against my arm again."

This time, I lean forward and smash back against the offending arm. "Not my fault you're dying to get me in your arms."

In retaliation, he plucks my cocoa off the table and takes a long drink. "It absolutely is your fault, V."

"If you finish that, you owe me another one."

"Should we leave you two alone?" Ty teases. "Because it looks like he's leaning."

Ignoring Ty's bait, I focus on what's left of the nacho mountain. More like a nacho molehill at this point, but still. I chew on a few, pointedly not looking at Rock. The table falls quiet.

After a couple minutes, I can't take it anymore.

"Do I want to know what leaning is besides encroaching on my personal space?" Not to mention, how awkward it was when Leander did it compared to how comfortable I am sitting in the booth with Rock.

Chuckling, Ty points between Rock and me. "Leaning means two people moving closer together. Sharing space. Leaning means wanting to get close, and the other person letting them. You two are definitely leaning."

"They totally are," Janice puts in.

Rock says, "Yes," at the same time I say, "Please no."

We look at each other and bust up. Rock's huffing laugh is becoming my favorite sound, probably because it's so rare.

Tension broken, we chat about nothing for a while. The waitress brings Rock's burger piled high with sizzling mushrooms and bacon so scrumptious I steal a piece right out from under the bun.

"Table tax. This stuff is delicious. Can I have another?"

He takes another piece out of his burger and hands it to me. I catch a hint of a smile as he focuses on his food. "Go ahead. I didn't order a bacon burger specifically because I wanted bacon, or anything."

I help myself to a fry. Or two. Okay, five.

Setting down his burger, Rock parts the golden-brown deliciousness into two piles, gesturing that I'm welcome to the smaller one. I dip them in nacho cheese and munch happily while people watching.

The waitress stops to ask if everything is okay, and Rock orders another hot cocoa. When she brings it back, he slides it in front of me. "Seriously, you going on another date with McCandles? I thought that was done."

"It's not a date." Yes, okay, I'm pretty sure Leander intends it to be a date. A giant ball of awkwardness coils inside my gut every time he hints that he's still interested. I... don't think I'm interested.

It's odd that there's no awkwardness between Rock and me even though his arm stretches behind my back. Hell, it's practically wrapped around my shoulders. If it were Leander, would I be able to relax against the bench seat like I am now? Deep in my gut, I know I wouldn't.

But Rock and Leander are not friends, and I don't want to expend energy defending one to the other tonight. Two boys, both alike in pride, holding ancient grudges bolstered by new conflict. The Snakes versus the sheriff's department. For my whole life, I was devoted to my dad's work and to everyone at the department, but these days? I have ties to the Snakes, too.

Does that make me the priest in this situation? I nearly choke on a fry.

Rock tosses a fry in his mouth and chews thoughtfully. "What would make it a date? A hot cocoa brought to your door?"

The intent way Rock is looking at me makes me keenly aware of how close we're sitting. The heat of his arm warms where it presses along the width of my shoulder blades, firm but gentle.

"I've brought her cocoa before," Janice says, "I vote not a date."

"She likes Shakespeare," Ty puts in helpfully.

I do like the bard's work. I fold my napkin a couple times. "How's the towing going?"

Rock shrugs one shoulder. "Pay is good. I need the cash to rebuild some girl's car."

"Just some girl, huh?" Immediately, I bite my tongue. What a stupid question to ask. It almost sounds like I'm fishing for compliments, and I absolutely am not.

He looks at me, really looks at me. I look away, focusing on the paper cupid spinning near the ceiling. I'm spinning in circles too, little guy.

Ty smiles, nudging Janice with his elbow. Janice watches Rock and me, her expression shrewd. She and I are going to be having a super fun conversation about this later.

If You Can't Take the Heat

It's been a couple of days since the diner, and I have successfully avoided the topic of Rock and me whenever Janice tries to bring it up. This morning I resorted to faking a bathroom emergency after first period, but desperate times.

A shift at work is a welcome distraction, and Sheriff McCandles sets me to work inventorying the office supply closet. As he was finishing explaining their ordering system, he got a call and ducked out, jaw set in a hard line.

I'm elbow deep in the supply cabinet when the department entrance opens. A fluttering in my stomach makes me turn from the closet, gravitating toward the front of the building. Maybe Rock had time to pick up the Corvette parts he needed and came by to let me know he's ready to resume working.

"Excuse me? I'm looking for Miss Goodie-Two-Shoes? Super short, dark braided hair, smart mouth?" Janice is here, which means my fake bowel emergency didn't scare her off. She's going to ask me about Rock, and I'm going to have to tell her I might possibly a little bit have mushy feelings for her ex-boyfriend. Fantastic.

She stands at the front counter with a pair of hot cocoa cups steaming in gloved hands. "What are you doing here? Did something happen?"

I let her behind the counter, and Janice plunks down in my desk chair. She takes a dainty sip of her cocoa.

I test mine, grinning when I scent peppermint. Peppermint cocoa is the supreme best of all the cocoas. My visitor toys with her cup, avoiding my eyes. Surprising. I lean on the desk at her shoulder. "Why does it look like you're about to ask me for a favor?"

Her chin rises, stubbornly set. "You're being paranoid. And besides, you don't have anything I want. Can't a girl bring her friend a treat without being interrogated?"

I stare her down, eyebrow raised. "No, because you've never brought me cocoa at the station for no reason."

She ignores my skepticism, completely nonchalant. "What does McCandles have you doing this evening?"

"The thrilling task of supply closet inventory. Want to help?"

"No, thanks."

"Fair enough, but I do need to get back to it."

"Then I'll make this quick."

"Aha! You are here with ulterior motives." I cross my arms, smirking at her. I've learned a lot about Janice in the last couple of months, and one of my favorite things about her is that she is not subtle. Although, to be fair, she never was. Back when she thought my dad had killed Gracia Cuoco, her attack was blunt-edged and relentless. I used to hate how easily she got under my skin, but I'm used to it. It's kind of endearing.

Janice sighs. Her gloved fingers tap the side of her cup.

Then she lays her eyes on me. "Lately, I've been noticing you get pretty fidgety and flushed around Rock, and I was wondering if there's something going on I should know about. As your new best friend, confidant, and style consultant. Those jeans you're wearing are perfection, by the way. Did you take them to the tailor I recommended?"

"I totally did. Thanks for the tip."

The clock on the wall ticks seconds away. Outside, a car horn blares. I take another sip of my cocoa. Janice blurts, "I want to know what's going on between you and Rock. Because Ty and I both agreed you looked pretty cozy at the diner the other night."

My stomach squirms as if there's a litter of wriggling kittens in there. "Nothing."

"Your face is red."

"The cocoa is hot." I blow on the cup before taking a drink even though it's already the perfect temperature.

"Val."

Setting the cup down on the desk, I shove my hands between my knees to keep from pressing them against my hot cheeks. The kittens in my stomach are chasing balls of yarn all over the place, the little twerps. "To be honest, I don't know what's going on with us."

Janice drops her empty cup in the trash can under the desk. "Do you like him?"

I shrug. "Maybe? I don't know."

"How can you not know?"

Running my hand down my braid, I tug on the end. "It's complicated, okay? Ever since Leander and I broke up, we've been working on being friends again. I thought we were in a good place, but then he dropped that dinner invite."

"For the Italian place out by the airport? Yeah, that didn't sound like a friendly outing to me either. Do you want it to be a date?"

I pull on my braid again. Remembering the awkwardness that filled me when Leander leaned into my personal space at the diner. I kept waiting for the excited buzz of infatuation, but all his nearness did was make me want to slide off the bench and run away. That reaction confirmed for me that I'm not interested in going on any more dates with Leander. He was my childhood crush and my first boyfriend, but I don't see me going down that path again. I'm mostly convinced he still likes me, but I'm also convinced I don't feel the same. Which sucks, because at some point I'm going to have to tell him. Joy.

I word vomit all of it to Janice, who nods along, her expression carefully placid. "And those kitties in your stomach. Do they make biscuits for Rock?"

"I think we're taking this metaphor too far."

She smirks.

I swallow, nervous. "Like I said, I don't know. But if I did, would that be okay? Because I don't want to step on your toes or anything. If you don't want me to date him—not that that will ever happen—I won't. Just say the word."

Janice rubs her gloved hand over her temple. "That's the thing. I talked it over with Ty, and I'm surprisingly okay with it. Rock and I were together for a long time, but we started dating in junior high. Basically, we held hands and ate lunch together sometimes. It doesn't even really count. As we got older, we stuck together because we both knew what it was like having parents in the Snakes, and having that commonality was comforting. Being with Rock felt safe."

"He makes me feel safe, too." It's the most straightforward and honest thing I've said to Janice tonight. Spending time with Rock makes me feel secure. Cared for and protected. It doesn't hurt that he's so solidly built either, and that sly grin of his. A shiver goes through me, and Janice laughs.

"What I'm trying to say is that I think he and I trauma bonded. There was so much crap going on in both our lives that it pushed us together. We were there for each other when we both needed someone to lean on, but it never would have lasted. We don't have that much in common, really. Not like you two."

I snort. "He and I are nothing alike."

She rolls her eyes. "That's crap, and you know it."

"Do tell."

Janice lists things off on her fingers. "You both know what it's like to lose the parent you were closest to. You both have a strong sense of right and wrong, although your morals and his don't completely line up. You're both fiercely protective of people you care about, and will do anything to protect them, even putting yourselves in danger. You both tend to make stupid decisions when it comes to that, actually, because you're both so busy trying to shield people from bad things that happen, although you tend to jump without thinking. He's more methodical. Impulsive! That's you. Rock is more calculated."

"I'm not impulsive."

She gives me a look, and my mouth forms half a smile. "All right, maybe I am. Occasionally."

"See? You two have a ton in common."

"I guess we do, but that doesn't mean there's anything going on with us."

"You're lying to yourself, and I as your friend am not going to let you. At the diner the other night, you and Rock—"

My phone goes off, and it's a great excuse to end this conversation. Speak of the devil. Rock is messaging to ask when he can come work on my Corvette some more. I answer, telling him that I'm not working tomorrow after school.

When I look up, Janice is grinning at me. "You're lit up like a Christmas tree. Who was that?"

"My mom."

She makes an angry buzzer sound. "Wrong."

"Okay, okay. Rock wanted to know if he could come over tomorrow to work on the car."

"I knew it. You like him. A lot. The question now is: what are you going to do about it?"

An excellent question, because Janice is right. If my reaction to Rock's message is any indication, I have a massive, inconvenient crush on Rock. Lots of warm fuzzy feelings. All the feelings. Seeing his name on my phone and reading that he wants to come over and work on my car sealed the deal.

Rock has a crap ton of other things to do: schoolwork, his own job, and who knows what else, but he still spends a huge chunk of hours rebuilding my car. That's got to mean something, right?

"I guess I—"

The front door slams open and Sheriff McCandles bursts inside. "Is Valencia still here? Val? Good."

He marches over to me, patting my head as if to make sure I'm really here. I look up at him, all rigid lines and grim-mouthed. Worry splinters the warm fuzzy feelings, turning them cold.

"Did something happen, Sheriff?"

"Jonesie will escort you home after your shift. Don't leave without him, got it?" The stormy expression in his eyes makes the kittens in my stomach yowl. Something bad must have happened while he was out to make him storm in like an angry tornado. No, not an angry tornado. A worried tornado.

Setting my shoulders, I meet his eyes. "Is there something you're not telling me? Something I should know?"

The lawman runs a hand down his lariat, looking from

Janice to me.

"Whatever you want to say, you can say in front of her. She won't tell her dad. They aren't speaking right now."

"She'll tell me anyway," Janice puts in. True.

Groaning, the sheriff kneels down in front of my chair. The position is oddly fatherly, and does strange things to the organ pumping blood in my chest. "Promise me you won't leave without Jonesie, and I'll tell you."

"You're scaring me, Sheriff. What happened? Is my mom okay? Is it Leander?"

His frown is deeper than the Grand Canyon. My lungs stutter. If he doesn't tell me what's going on right this second, they're liable to pop.

The sheriff's hands grip the chair's armrests, as if to shield me from the outside world. "We found someone trying to set fire to your house. We stopped them, and your house is fine. There wasn't much damage. A couple of the siding boards will need to be replaced, is all."

I go still, glued to my seat. I stare at the sheriff, dumbfounded. "Someone tried to burn down my house?"

Sheriff McCandles nods. "They had blocked off the doors, too."

Those seven words hit me like a battering ram to the gut. Someone tried to burn down my house, and they blocked the doors so whoever was inside couldn't get out. My mom was there alone. She could have died. I'm going to be sick. Shoving the nausea down, I nudge the sheriff's forearm. He lets me up.

"I have to see my mom."

"Understood. Jonesie?" The sheriff gestures to the deputy, who is poised at my shoulder.

"I'm ready, Sheriff. I can take you whenever you're ready, Val."

My entire body shakes with fear and anger. Someone tried to hurt me tonight, and instead put my mom in danger. They're going to pay for that. Clenching my fists, I meet the sheriff head on.

"Who was it?" Even before I ask, I know. It was the Snakes, likely sent by Rotten Egg Breath. Which means that they're still out to get me. "A couple of new Snake recruits. We sat them down for a talk, and they admitted that one of the higher-ups in the gang put a price on your head. If they get a chance, they'll kill you."

There it is. The confirmation I was both seeking and dreading.

Rock wasn't the target of the drive-by. I was.

The Snakes have a ransom out on my head. Hot flashes of fear and anger ripple through me.

My hands ball into fists in my pockets as I follow Jonesie out to his patrol car. Janice comes too, watching with sad eyes as I climb into the passenger seat.

The Snakes are going to regret targeting me. My mom. Rock. Everyone I care about.

They tried to strike me with scare tactics and sharp teeth, but they're about to find out how hard I bite back.

Singles Awareness Day

THE PAPER CUPIDS FROM THE DINER HAVE SPREAD, and now they hang from the ceiling in the school hallways, overseeing the festivities. Happy couples promenade down the corridor clutching stuffed animals and heart-shaped boxes of chocolates and love letters. Janice got all moon-eyed when a bouquet of wildflowers—her favorite—were delivered in the middle of second period, courtesy of Ty.

If I'm being honest, I might have wished for a certain someone to deliver me something too, but I knew he wouldn't.

By the time I got home, I was ready for some alone time. Luckily, my mom went out to dinner with some girlfriends. I could tell by her wavering between the front door and the living room that she was hesitant to go, but I insisted. I want her to go out and have fun, especially since she could have died if the Snake recruits had succeeded in setting our house on fire the other day.

As soon as my mom leaves, I run upstairs and change into

a cute but warm outfit and undo my braid so my hair lies in waves down my back.

Rock is coming over with those car parts he was waiting on, and I'm looking forward to a hot evening in the garage watching him work and trying not to drool. I ordered his favorite pizza and breadsticks. A quiet night with Rock sounds amazing after a long week of busting my butt at school and the *Herald*.

A chime on my phone makes me grin stupidly. It's our security system letting me know someone is at the front door. Rock is here. Running my fingers through my freshly blow-dried hair, I skip down the stairs.

The guy on our porch is not Rock.

It's a blondie with puppy dog eyes.

Leander dressed in a suit and carrying a bouquet of red roses.

My stomach kittens drop and play dead. Why would he be here today?

Oh, no. It's Valentine's Day, and Leander is on my front porch.

Crap.

I never did get back to him about the dinner date he asked me on, because I didn't know how to let him down easy. It turns out there's nothing easy about breaking someone's heart.

Leander has always been confident; I'll give him that. Remembering his touchdown victory dance still makes me smile. He must have decided to shoot his shot.

The doorbell rings. "Val? You in there?"

Blowing out a breath, I smooth out the glitzy sweater Janice insisted I looked fantastic in, and trudge to the front door. I don't want to hurt Leander's feelings, but it looks like I don't have a choice. And it needs to be quick, because Rock will be here any minute.

"Hey Val. I'm here to pick you up for…" Leander trails off when he gets a look at my cute outfit. "Wow, you look amazing."

"You look amazing," I parrot back. Leander preens.

"Are those flowers for me?"

He offers them up to me. "I bought them from the florist this time. I chose these ones because they smell great, like you."

Ugh, this is going to be harder than even I thought it would. Lifting the stunning roses, I inhale deeply of their gorgeous smell. "Thanks. They're beautiful."

"You ready to go? I'm craving lasagna something fierce."

I wet my lips, trying to figure out how to tell Leander that I'm not going out to dinner with him on Valentine's Day, or any other day, when a figure melts out of the shadows near the garage.

"Lasagna sounds delicious." My stomach drops as Leander turns to glare at Rock over his shoulder.

"What are you doing here?" Irritation is clear in the line of Leander's back.

Rock paces closer. He isn't in his usual tee and ripped jeans. The maroon leather jacket hugs his shoulders over a snug black tee, dark wash jeans, and black shoes. An earring glints in one ear. He's dressed up. Rock is dressed up, and he looks freaking good.

Did Rock dress up to spend Valentine's Day with me in my garage? I bite back a smile, running a hand along the hem of my sparkly sweater dress.

Leander looks from Rock to me, confusion between his brows. My smile drops. "Did I miss something? I thought we were going out to dinner tonight. At Villipiano's?"

Rock's thick eyebrow rises. His arms cross. But instead of speaking for me, instead of bragging to Leander that he's the one who made plans with me tonight, he stays quiet. Rock never tries to speak for me, instead giving me space to stand up for myself. My heart puffs up with the warm fuzzies.

Both guys stare at me, waiting for an explanation.

My frail smile vanishes. I don't want to do this. But I guess I must. Meeting Rock's eyes, I say, "Can you wait for me in the garage? I'll be there in a minute."

"You know it." Turning, he saunters toward the garage, opening it with the clicker I gave him.

Leander's puppy dog eyes are sad when I meet them. "I don't have a shot, do I?"

"I'm sorry, Leander. I—"

He shakes his head. "No, it's okay. I didn't hear from you, but I went ahead and assumed it was because you wanted to come out with me tonight. You know what they say about assuming."

"I should have texted to let you know."

His sigh is rough-edged. "Yeah, you should have, but I forgive you."

"That's big of you."

"What can I say? I'm a big person." He does part of his touchdown victory dance, halfheartedly, but it still brings a smile to my face.

He runs a hand over his gelled hair. "I knew it was Agani, but does it have to be? I hate that guy."

I'm keenly aware that Rock is right around the corner, listening to everything we say. "He's not so bad."

Leander's huff is skeptical, but good-natured. "If you say so. Just be careful with him, okay?"

I nod, touched that he cares so much.

Leander turns to go, but I stop him with a hand on his arm. I have to know. "Can I ask you something?"

"Anything."

"How did you know?"

He rubs at the back of his neck under the suit collar. His eyes find the first stars twinkling in the dusky sky. "You never looked at me the way you look at him. Like you're staring at the ocean, eyes wide, waiting to see what the next wave will wash ashore. He looks at you the same way. Like the other night in the diner. That's why I left."

Rock once told me that if a guy likes a girl, he does everything he can to make it happen. And here Rock is, standing my garage on Valentine's Day, ready to spend the evening with me working on the Corvette. And he dressed up, too. The kittens in my stomach start wiggling again. "For what it's worth, I love the roses."

"You're welcome. And for what it's worth, I'm here if you need me… Need anything. Just ask, okay?"

A smile graces my lips at his sincerity. "That means a lot. Thank you."

"See you around, Val." Leander gets halfway to his truck before he halts, pivoting toward the garage. I jog around the corner, bracing to break up a fight. Leander has a fistful of Rock's jacket sleeve, and Rock stands still as a marble column.

I wait, heart in my throat. Leander wouldn't pick a fight with Rock after saying something so sweet to me.

Leander's jaw twitches. He might.

The sheriff's son mumbles something to the gangster's son. Rock tilts his head sarcastically. Surprise sparks in my eyes as Leander chuckles. He says something else, and Rock bobs his chin.

As soon as Leander's truck leaves, I double back to lock the front door and go through the house to the garage. Rosie follows, batting at my ankles until I scoop her up and bring her outside cradled in the crook of my elbow. Rock leans against the workbench, his curly hair tousled as if he's run his hands through it a few times while he waited for me. The door clicks shut at my back, and Rock's eyes lock on mine. Lifting off the bench, he looks out at the street. "Want me to leave so you can go on your date with Junior?"

I shake my head, running a hand along Rosie's downy spine. "I already ordered us pizza. It'll be here in twenty."

Rock's relieved smile hits me square in the chest, and I can't breathe. "Let's get to work."

Is it stupid to work on a car in a nice outfit? Yes, it is. But the appreciation in Rock's eyes as he hands me a wrench makes it a hundred percent worth it.

He looks at you the same way.

Oh, I hope Leander was right.

Despite the chill in the air, the little standing heater in the corner keeps the garage comfortable. Rock shrugs off the leather jacket, draping it over the kitchen doorknob. I roll up my sleeves and lean in to tighten the bolt he pointed out.

We work together for a couple hours, talking easily as we make progress on the Corvette. Rock takes every opportunity to brush against my arm or my back as he shows me how to fit a new part and make adjustments until it's just right. My skin is flushed with pleasure as he bumps my shoulder with his. "Nice work, Val. You're good at this."

I wave him off but am not so secretly pleased. "If my career in journalism doesn't pan out, it's good to know I have a fallback option in car maintenance."

"Your break checks would bring all the guys to the yard."

Laughter colors my voice. "You did not just say that."

Rock leans back against the front bumper, eyes on me. "Have you returned that writer's email? About working with her on a book about Gracia and your dad?"

I shake my head, even though I've decided I want to work with her. My article for the Herald is a non-starter, despite Jan's pointers on my hot mess of a draft. And it would feel awkward asking Leander for help after tonight.

My lips roll between my teeth. "I'm still thinking about it."

"You should do it."

My surprise at his encouragement must show on my face, because Rock steps closer. "I know you're struggling with your article, and maybe working with that writer is the answer. She could help you tell your story. Everyone should hear your story, Val."

His support echoes everything I've been thinking. Maybe working with a professional is the way to go. I could tell my story on my terms, and she could craft it into something worth reading. It's a story that could reach people, inspire them to treat their neighbors better when they're going through challenging crap. Maybe add a little more grace to a graceless world. Literally, since telling my story would entail telling Gracia Cuoco's too. "Thanks for the encouragement."

Rock gives me a genuine smile. "Any time."

A loud bang makes us jump. My heart slams into my throat. Rock lunges for me. "Get down!"

Wrapping his arms around my body, he sweeps me behind the Corvette and pins me against the interior garage wall. Flipping the light switch with his elbow kills the light, shielding us in darkness.

Pressed together, chests heaving, we wait for the attack to begin.

Unrealistic Expectations

WITH MY HEART BEATING LOUD AGAINST HIS CHEST, I burrow deeper into his arms. My hand brushes over a familiar-shaped bulge in the back waistband of his jeans. A gun. Rock is carrying a gun. It should scare me, but it doesn't. Knowing how careful Rock is, I trust that he would know how to handle a firearm safely. And he would never do anything to hurt me.

There is no telling how much violence Rock has seen throughout his lifetime. Growing up around a street gang, it must have been unfathomable. It wouldn't surprise me if Dino made both of his sons learn how to handle guns at far too tender an age.

Tapping the grip with a fingertip, I whisper in his ear. "You know how to use this thing?"

Rock's arms brace on either side of me as a motorcycle speeds into the night.

Rosie meows from inside the Corvette. The space heater in the corner buzzes. We're not being targeted. Tipping my head forward, I rest it against Rock's collarbone.

Warm breath from his mouth brushes over my crown. "You know me. Would I ever do anything to put you in danger, including being an idiot with a deadly weapon?"

Clutching his sides tighter, my forehead rolls side to side. His chin brushes my hair.

Knowing that Rock is prepared, and that he's here with me helps my body relax. It took him less than a heartbeat after we heard that engine backfire to scoop me up and carry me to the back of the garage out of sight. He put his body between mine and the danger. He didn't even hesitate.

"It wasn't him." I exhale into Rock's shoulder, holding on tight.

"No." His hands glide up my back, moving around my shoulders to cup my neck. Guiding with gentle fingers, he nudges my face up toward his. His forehead presses against mine, firm and warm. "I've got you, Velvet."

His breath puffs against my skin. I lift my face, inching my mouth closer to his.

"Rock, I. . ."

Headlights blind me as my mom's car pulls into the driveway. I didn't realize how late it had gotten while Rock and I flirted over the open hood of the Corvette.

"Perfect timing." Rock chuckles. Reluctantly, we separate.

I flip on the garage light, blinking to adjust to its brightness. My mom enters the garage, calling our names.

"Hey Mom. We have a little pizza left. You hungry?""

Shaking her head, she laughs. "I stayed out so late. I haven't stayed up this late outside of work since… I can't remember. The karaoke place was packed, and Lydia made me do a duet with her. It was so much fun. I haven't done karaoke in years." She grins as she circles the Corvette, taking in the work Rock has done. "You two have been hard at work, I see. Car looks good. Daniel would be proud."

My mom pulls me into her side in a warm hug, extending her other arm to Rock. At first, he looks like he's indulging her by joining our three-way hug, but she tightens her arm around him and holds him close. His hand finds mine and gives it a squeeze. "Thanks, Mrs. Lamb. Glad you approve."

"I do. Mmhm." She pulls us in tighter, and we slot into each other. Maybe it should be a surprise how well we fit, but it isn't. Disentangling myself from my mom's octopus arms, I check my phone. It's after midnight. I have no idea where Rock has been staying since he's avoiding Granny's to keep her and his little cousins safe, and I'm not ready for him to leave yet. Spending all evening working so closely with him, flirting and making soft touches has made me feel like I'm riding a sugar high from diner milkshakes. I don't want it to end.

I clear my throat and try to sound casual. "It's pretty late, huh Mom? Can Rock stay here tonight?"

Rock's eyes jump to mine in surprise, but my mom doesn't skip a beat. Turning to examine Rock, she pats his shoulder. "You do look tired. I think that's a good idea. I'll get some blankets out of the closet, and Val can help you make up the couch."

He opens his mouth to say something, but she is already bustling inside. Warm eyes rest on mine, and he snickers. "Here I thought you were hard to get a word in edgewise."

"I used to think I got my stubborn streak from my dad, but she has one too. I was basically screwed from the get-go."

Rock hums. Together, we put the tools away and make sure both cars are secure in the garage before going inside. Heat hovers over my lower back as Rock escorts me in with a protective hand pressed low on my spine. I didn't know that was a thing I would like, but I do.

A quick survey of the downstairs confirms it's empty. Mom is upstairs in her room, but there's a stack of blankets and a couple extra pillows on the couch in the living room.

Rock follows me upstairs to brush our teeth. I shouldn't be self-conscious, because we used to do this all the time as kids. But we were kids, and we're not anymore. There is so much more on the table now besides shared popsicles and tickle fights.

Rock chuckles when he sees my face covered in green face wash, so I generously share it by smearing some along his cheekbones. His skin is warm and smooth. It's really not fair that he looks so good after hours of working over a car in a garage. Incredulous, he swipes at the green gel oozing down his chin. "That's how it is, huh?"

"Yep. What're you gonna do about it?"

Rinsing the green smears off his face and hands with a cloth, his eyes meet mine in the mirror. "Haven't decided yet."

Holy mackerel, we're definitely flirting now. Janice totally called it, that canny witch. Smiling to myself, I towel off my wet hands. "Meet you downstairs."

It takes me a few minutes to find and scurry into pajamas that are fit to be seen by anyone outside of my mom. By the time I get downstairs, the lights are off and Rock is stretched out on the couch, asleep. He must have been exhausted. Sighing, I circumvent the couch and pull the blankets up to his chin. My fingers ache to brush through his curls, but I won't. Not when Id don't know where he stands.

Instead, my butt sinks onto the coffee table and I sit in the shadows. I didn't realize how tired I was until I stopped moving. Plush carpet cushions my feet, and I toy with the idea of curling up in the oversized living room chair and sleeping. It's cozy, and so much closer than my bedroom upstairs.

Rock shifts in his sleep, drawing my eyes to his relaxed face. There's a lot I want to say to him, and maybe practicing while he's not listening will help me get the words out when he's awake in the morning. "Thanks for taking care of me tonight. Keeping me safe. I've been looking for a way to get you out of the Snakes, since I know you want one. I hoped that REB would get caught up in the avocado raid, and that would be that… But they still don't know where he's hiding. All that to say, I'm trying to get you out. Just hang in there for me, okay?"

His head shifts on the pillow, and his lips part on a slow exhale. "I want you to stay out of it, V. It's too dangerous. I can handle it, okay?"

Leaning forward, my hands weave together. "You have a tattoo that says, 'traitor' on your chest."

His breaths are even in and out. Flicking at his arm, I let my palm rest on his shoulder, daring to slide it across his chest to rest over where the Snakes left a permanent stain on his skin. I haven't seen it since that day he showed me, but I'll never forget the thick calligraphied letters that branded him guilty of betrayal.

"So, I got stabbed a little." His palm rests over mine, holding it there. He peeks one eye open, chuckling darkly at my dubious look. I'm mesmerized by the rhythmic beating of his heart under my palm.

Outside, crickets sing the song of their people. Upstairs, my mom's shower turns on.

"At least I don't have "golden boy" stamped on my forehead."

My fingertips dig into his skin. "He's not that bad. Why do you hate him so much?"

Rock's fingers brush my mouth, holding it closed. "Shh. I'm sleeping."

"No you're not. Come on. I want to know." I try to remove

my hand from his chest, but his fingers wrap loosely around my wrist. He feigns a snore. I poke him in the side with my free hand, halfheartedly. He doesn't flinch.

Eyes shut, a slow exhale parts his lips. "You wouldn't understand."

"Try me."

He groans. I wait, because right now, sitting in my living room in the dark with Rock, the words we're exchanging simmer with importance. We're standing over the pot waiting for a childhood comfort food to be ready. We're standing at the edge of a precipice, watching each other to see who will jump first. Whatever Rock says next will determine whether we soar together or retreat away from the cliff's edge. I don't move, caught in the hush before the plunge.

Rock is quiet, his breathing even and slow. He fell asleep. Disappointment stings as my teeth sink into the tip of my tongue, keeping me from nudging him awake. A good night of sleep will diminish the purple half-moons under his dark eyes.

Rising to my feet, I slip my hand out from under his. Rock's hand tightens around my wrist, holding me on the precipice. His eyes open and lock on mine. Swinging his legs off the couch, he sits up. Runs both hands through his hair and keeps them there, searching my eyes with his own. His Adams apple bobs. "You really want to know why I can't stand McCandles?"

"Yes." I sink back onto the coffee table, leaving little space to breathe between us. My heart pounds in my chest. For the first time, I don't push away the truth that flashes in my mind. Rock used to be my best friend as a kid, but now? He's the boy who helped me look into Gracia's death, even knowing it would lead me back to him. He saved my life at least twice. He stands up for the people he cares about in the hardest moments, when it matters most. He makes me feel safe and protected, and I never want to lose him again. I, Valencia Juliet Lamb, have mushy romantic feelings for Rock.

Some indication of my realization must show in my eyes, because Rock's gaze takes on a shine. "I hate him because everyone in this whole town loves him. I hate him because for a long time, you loved him. Don't deny it.

"People love him for his confidence and his football ability and his prominent family. And he knows it. He lives in this town knowing that his place is secure thanks to sports fans and a family legacy of service.

"You know what my family legacy is? Violence, murder, drugs, and stolen cars. I'll never have the kind of security Leander has, and it eats me up inside. My dad has poisoned everything he touches, including my brother and me. No matter what I do, I'm trapped in a situation that is very much not a game. It's my life. Our lives. Thanks to my dad, I can't live at home because I'm afraid of what Gabriel will do to Granny and my cousins. I can't live at the shop because it would be like begging them to kill me. I have no home and no family. I have nothing. Because of all the evil my dad and brother have done, I'm stuck playing the bad boy. Seven years ago your dad finally put his foot down and separated us. And I didn't fight it. Because deep down I knew he was making the right choice. Being around me was too dangerous for you. I wasn't good for you then, and I'm not good for you now."

"Rock," I croak. My heart cracks under the devastation in his every word. Standing up, I slap the switch to turn on the light. Suddenly it's imperative that we step out of the dark. Maybe by banishing the shadows, I can banish the lies that Rock has walled around himself.

My eyes adjust to find Rock still on the couch. His face is buried in the heels of his hands. "I will never be good enough for you, and as long as I'm in your life, people like Gabriel will think they can hurt you to get to me. I can't have that, V. You gotta let me go. Just let go."

This is a test. Whether Rock knows it or not, he's testing me. Sounding me out to see how I'll react to all the rotten stinking lies in his head. He's forgotten who he's talking to, but I haven't. I'm the girl who solved a murder and discovered what happened to my dad. I'm the girl who refuses to give up until all of the answers have been uncovered. I'm reckless and impulsive and as stubborn as Bert with a bone.

"You don't get to make that decision for me. I get to decide when something is too dangerous, and you're not it, Rock. I'm not letting you go just because your family is crap. You aren't them. And I'm not scared of REB. He's probably out of the country by now, since no one at the department has been able to find him. So no. I'm not letting you go that easy. I just got you back."

He groans, hands fisting in his curls. "Why you gotta be so stubborn?"

Snatching up an extra pillow from one of the plush chairs flanking the couch, I toss it at him. He catches it effortlessly, dropping it in his lap. "Get some sleep. We can talk about this tomorrow when exhaustion isn't making you say stupid things."

He doesn't try to stop me climbing the stairs.

Up in my room, an article idea sparks in my brain. I dive into researching like a girl possessed. By the time dawn seeps in the cracks between the window blinds, I have an article outlined and am itching to write. But first, breakfast.

The downstairs is silent. It's still a little early for my mom after her night out, and heaven knows Rock needs the sleep. I tiptoe down to the living room. Stacked on one end of the couch, the blankets are neatly folded. Pillows are fluffed and in their proper spots. The living room is empty.

I'll never let you go.

Rock is gone.

This feels an awful lot like letting go.

Leaving No Stone Unturned

Rock

ONE BENEFIT OF RIDING A BIKE THROUGH TOWN IN THE early morning is that it gave me even more time to replay my conversation with Val on repeat in my head.

I tried to tell her how scared I am that she'll be hurt even more than she already has. Being close to me has done nothing but put a giant, flaming target on her back. When we were kids, my brother made fun of her. My dad has always been wary of how much I cared for her. He watched us, his sharp eyes taking in the way I stood up for her when Leif was being a flaming turd. He knew then that I'd do anything for Val, and God help me, he knows it now.

It's the reason he let Gabriel off his leash. My dad hoped to force me into compliance by threatening the girl who means more to me than anyone else ever has or ever will. It's the reason I tried to tell her I wasn't any good for her. Because I'm not. Everything my dad touches goes bad, and that includes me. If Val gets involved with me, she'll be ruined too. So why can't I stay away from her?

The bike coasts over the sidewalk as sunlight seeps over the horizon. Ever since the police raided Darren and Bonnie's house, it's been deserted. Darren is locked up, waiting to go to trial, and Bonnie packed a suitcase and went to stay with her sister. Police tape drapes across the front door, untouched. The garage is closed, and the windows are shuttered and locked. I wheel the bike into the side yard and enter the back door.

Inside the house is a mess. Kitchen cabinets and drawers hang open after the deputies' search. Closets gape and blankets spill out into the hall. The hatch door in the ceiling leading to the attic is a gaping black square. Darren had me up there a few weeks ago, fastening extra insulation between the boards because Bonnie complained about drafts keeping the heater from being efficient.

Dragging a hand down my face, I trudge into the kitchen. Since the raid, the Snakes haven't met up as far as I know. Most of the long-term members are either in jail or in the wind. The only man unaccounted for is also the one I'm most concerned about. Gabriel has always been unstable, which is why he and Leif got along so well. Both of them crave power and violence. With Leif in prison, Gabriel has gotten increasingly difficult for anyone to control.

And that was before my dad let him loose.

Last night at Val's house, I lay awake hating myself for my inability to stay away from her. Early this morning, I gave up on sleeping and left to cruise around town on the bike I'm still borrowing from my little cousin.

One by one, I checked every hidey hole I could think of. There was no trace of Gabriel anywhere. Maybe he has fled the country like Val suggested. Wouldn't that be easier for everyone.

Hauling a water bottle out of the fridge, I unscrew the lid and guzzle it down. Here's hoping Val is right that Gabriel fled the state. Never setting eyes on him again would be the best possible outcome. Without him here to manipulate the new recruits into committing all of the dangerous stunts they've been pulling, the Snakes will fall apart.

I drop onto the couch, crackling the bottle in one hand. For the first time in my life, freedom from my dad's grasping hands is more than a pipe dream. He and many of the Snakes will be in jail for years to come. With Gabriel gone… I bring the bottle to my mouth and drain it. I kick off my shoes.

I have never met someone as headstrong and willful as Valencia Lamb. She drives me absolutely insane with her refusal to do the smart thing. If she had any sense of self-preservation, she'd cut me loose and spend the rest of her life pretending she and I never meant anything to each other. It would be so much safer for her. Cutting ties with me would get most of the Snakes off her back. If my dad can't use her as leverage to get me in line, she'll be out of their sights.

But if Gabriel is gone…

I could claim her as my own and keep her with me, like I've wanted to since I was a kid and she was still convinced I had cooties. She hasn't mentioned college in a while, but I could follow her wherever she wants to go. Auto shops always need skilled workers, and I could work while she studies. We could find out who we are together outside Hacienda. Away from the sheriff's department and the Snakes and the expectations that have pitted us against each other for our whole lives.

With that thought lingering in my head, I crash on the couch.

I don't hear the low thud of someone dropping from the attic access.

God, I wish I'd heard it.

Facing the Music

Val

My mom and I haven't had dinner at Destin's house in a
long time. I forgot how fun it is to get together with him and his
family. As soon as Destin ushers us in the front door, the mouth-
watering smell of homemade chicken and dumplings makes me
groan with hunger. Bert circles our feet, licking our ankles and
wagging his tail.

Destin chuckles, letting me know the food will be ready in
ten minutes.

My mom joins Mrs. Court in the kitchen, and they give each
other a big hug. Mrs. Court waves me in for a hug, too. I've
always liked Destin's mom despite her helicopter parent
tendencies. I extricate myself from the mom hug, and the two of

them fall into gabbing, catching up on work and their troublesome kids and everything in between.

Destin snags my hand, pulling me up the stairs to his room. Bert plunks his furry behind down on my feet. Shutting the door, Destin leans against it. "I was expecting you fifteen minutes ago. You have to be a buffer. My mom is obsessed with college applications, and I keep putting her off because I don't know how to tell her about the whole studying criminal justice and becoming a cop thing. You have to help me. How do I tell my parents?"

Plopping down onto the edge of my friend's bed, I lean back on my hands. "She seems like she's in a great mood, so just rip the Band-Aid off and tell them. Your mom can't murder you while my mom and I are sitting across the table."

"Ha. Ha. Very funny. She is in a good mood though. She finished up a big project at work today that she's been stressing over."

"There you go. Tonight's the night."

Destin nods firmly. "Tonight's the night."

Dinner is delicious. The chicken and dumplings and roasted veggies are so tasty all of us devour it. Mr. Court brings out a box of cookies he picked up at a local bakery on the way home, and everyone enjoys dunking them in milk before eating them with relish.

I'm almost done with my third cookie when Destin catches my eye. His eyebrow lifts in a question. *Should I do it now?* Under the table, I take his hand in mine and give it an encouraging squeeze. He squeezes back and clears his throat. "Uh, Mom? Dad? I have something to tell you."

His face is a little green, but Destin gets it all out: his plan to study criminal justice and apply to the sheriff's department once he's done. Sensing his boy's unease, Bert leans his furry body against Destin's leg.

Everyone around the table is speechless. My mom looks from Destin to me and back, her expression shrewd. She knows I knew about Destin's plan.

Destin's face turns a deeper green, like he's going to be sick.

Mrs. Court turns from her son to her husband. He nods in agreement. Slowly, her fingers uncurl from the stem of her wine glass. I have no clue what is happening right now.

"You're sure this is what you want to do?" Mr. Court wipes his hands on a napkin and drops it to his plate. His visage is utterly calm and void of emotion. I can't figure out if he's hiding anger or shock or both.

"Yes," Destin says, licking his lips. "I've known for a while, but I didn't know how to tell you."

Destin's dad rests his hands on the table's edge. "We knew, son, and we're proud of you. If you're sure this is what you want to do, we'll support you."

A tear falls down Mrs. Court's cheek. "That's right, sweetie. We love you, and we'll be with you no matter what you decide to do. Even if it's terrifying."

Mr. Court chuckles. "It was obvious after your first ride-along that you loved it."

My friend's eyes bulge. "You knew?"

"As you know, your mother is very good at keeping tabs on you."

"Come here and give me a hug, sweetie." Destin complies, rounding the table and kneeling down so she can wrap him in a rib-crushing hug. "We love you so much," she vows against his cheek.

Mom doesn't say anything about dinner until we're driving home. "If there's anything you want to tell me about your future career, I'm all ears."

Laughing, I grin. "No plans yet, but you'll be the first to know."

"Still thinking community college first?"

I tell her I am. I'm not sure what I want to do for a job after high school, so community college makes sense. Attending a two-year school close by will allow me to take general ed classes while living at home. With luck, a specific class or area of study will catch my fancy.

Mom pulls in the garage looks at me. Reaching over, she gives my leg a love pat. "You know I'm proud of you too, right?"

Since my mom works tonight, we had dinner with Destin and his family early. We agreed that she would drop me off after and head in to work.

"Yeah, Mom. I know. And thanks."

"I love you, Valencia."

"Love you too." Wishing her a goodnight, I toddle inside. My belly is stuffed full of delicious food and too many cookies. My mom waits until I'm in the house before driving away.

I lock the door and make my way to the kitchen to whip up hot cocoa to chase down the cookies. A quiet night of digesting under a blanket in front of the TV is everything my full stomach is ordering.

Rounding the corner into the kitchen, a cold chill cuts through my clothes. I go still. It's odd. There shouldn't be drafts in the house that are strong enough to transform me into a human popsicle in the middle of the kitchen.

The breath in my lungs ices over. The back door is wide open.

I go deadly still, eyes glued to the gaping door. The door Mom made sure was locked before we left the house earlier this evening.

Dread whips through me. Is Rosie all right?

Turning in a slow circle reveals no hint of the tiny gray ball of fluff who has stolen my heart with her tiny biscuit-making paws. If she was loose, she'd have scampered for me as soon as I entered the front door. She must be safely closed in the laundry room.

Breathing against the pins and needles in my lungs, I strain to hear any wrong sounds inside the house. Not a one hits my ears, but a tingling up my spine screams that I'm not alone.

Someone is in the house with me.

Pivoting on silent feet, my eyes fix on the door to my dad's former office. We keep it open these days. If I can get inside before whoever is lurking gets to me, I might be okay.

Sucking in a breath, I tiptoe in that direction. My entire body aches with anticipation. Every movement is painstaking. The lurker could jump out from behind the wall into the family room.

He could be crouched behind the dining table.

He could be lying in wait down the hallway, ready to pounce the second I step into the open.

Locking my knees to keep from bolting like a spooked jackrabbit, my head is on a swivel. Unnatural quiet hums in my ears.

Rotten Egg Breath could be an arms' length away, come to make good on his threats to end me for interfering with the Snakes' plans. The malevolence in his eyes during our previous encounters draws fearful shivers along my skin. He'll hurt me if he gets the chance, and he'll enjoy it.

I'm almost to the office door, reaching out with a hand to hold the door as I skim past.

A creaking floorboard in the living room breaks the silence like the crack of a gunshot.

Leaping into the office, I bolt for the desk. Tear open the bottom drawer. My heart throttles my ribs as I yank the small gun safe out and drop to the rug. Crouching behind the desk in the dark, I run my hands frantically over the metal surface, searching for the keypad.

Another floorboard creaks. Closer this time.

I'm running out of time. Motherclucker, where is that keypad?

My shaking fingertips brush over the small rubber keys. I fumble to punch the code in the dark. This right here is the reason my dad made me practice this, impressing the code on me during intruder drills.

Step one: unlock the gun safe.

Step two: retrieve and assemble the gun.

Step three: load the gun.

Step four: keep the gun pointed at the ground until I'm ready to fire. Until I'm ready to take a life in exchange for mine.

My hands wrap around the metal of the handgun, and I take a slow breath. I can do this. My dad trained me for this. Logically, I know what I have to do to stay alive.

Sweat breaks out along my spine, and my breath comes in short pants. Oh, crap. Can I do this? If REB steps out of the shadows, evil gleaming in his eyes? Adjusting my grip on the gun, I stand up.

Whoever is approaching is in for a rude awakening. I'm armed and I know how to defend myself. This pancake-brained Snake should have known I wouldn't go down easy. I'm Sheriff Daniel Lamb's daughter, and he taught me well.

All that training didn't inoculate me against the way my blood hiccups in my veins. My brain blanks. Lungs seize.

A dark figure stands in the doorway. Time to find out what I'm really made of. A trial by gunfire.

This Is Not a Drill

The sensation of fear raising the hairs along my arms is way too close to how I felt the night Leif cornered me in Ms. Wayne's classroom and ended up almost drowning me in the gym pool. Like that night, I won't go down without a fight. I may be small, but I've learned in my kickboxing classes how to land a punch or a kick to make an opening to escape.

Subdue the opponent, take them to the ground, and run.

The metal of the handgun warms in my sweaty palms. Or shoot the guy and run. Either way.

I hold the weapon poised in both hands. Aimed at the floor beyond my feet. Fighting to slow the uneven rise and fall of my chest, I fix my gaze on the shadowy figure. "I'm armed, and I know how to shoot. Leave now, or I'll shoot you."

My words stutter through the dark. Disbelief rings in my ears. I cannot believe I just said that. I just promised to shoot someone.

Calm down, Val. This is not a friendly visit. This is a

vindictive gangster. He came into my house with the intent to hurt me. He snuck in and lay in wait until I got home alone, stepping into the dark where he laid a trap and waited for it to spring. He's here tonight with the express purpose to kill me.

If he gets ahold of me, he won't show me any mercy. If I want to live through this, I can't afford to show him any either.

It's him or me, and I'm not ready to die.

The figure takes a halting step into the room, groaning as his body sways unevenly. Through the fear, awareness scrapes my insides. That groan is all wrong for Rotten Egg Breath.

My hands tighten on the grip, finger sliding toward the trigger. Don't touch the trigger unless you intend to shoot, my dad taught me. "I'm serious. Leave now, or I'll shoot."

Another groan sounds as the figure takes another step. It's not a growl of fury. It's a cry of pain.

"Mighty. . . Mouse." Rock's plea wheezes through the air. He crumples to the ground.

I don't remember stowing the gun or turning on the lights or where I found the strength to carry Rock from the office to the couch, but here I am. Standing over Rock with horror written across my face.

He looks even more forbidding with the lights on.

Blood crusts on his temple from a nasty cut near one eyebrow. Both eyes are ringed in purple and black and swollen almost completely shut. His lip is split, and dried blood trails down his chin. Ripped tatters are all that's left of his maroon tee. My eyes water at the exposed, ugly bruising criss-crossing his ribs. Someone beat Rock to a bloody pulp. It's a wonder they didn't kill him. From the extent of his injuries, I'd guess that was the intent behind this attack. To end Rock's life.

Righteous anger scorches up my spine. Someone tried to take Rock from me tonight.

There's only one person I can think of who has the physical power and the hatred to do this. REB is still out there, and he's gunning for death.

This is a challenge leveled right at my heart. All of our previous encounters were nothing compared to this. I'm going to blow up that cretin sky high. When I'm done with him, he'll wish he was dead.

He's going to pay for this, but first things first.

Quickly, I search the house, gun held at the ready. Flipping on each light as I go through the rooms, I find nothing. There is no one else inside, and there's no evidence the bloody fight that nearly stole Rock away happened in or around my house.

I breathe a sigh of relief upon opening the laundry room door and finding Rosie curled up in her bed, asleep.

With efficiency my dad would have been proud of, I secure the gun in its safe and put it away. Wash my hands and grit my teeth.

Rock hasn't moved a muscle when I return to him. Gingerly, I pick up one of his hands and examine the knuckles. They're red and raw. Bruises run up and down his arms. He didn't go down without a brutal fight.

In the morning, I'll take Rock down to the station. He'll press charges, and REB will go away for a long, long time. He won't be able to hurt Rock, or anyone else, anymore. Then Rock will be out of the Snakes, who have got to be running out of potential psycho leaders by this point. With the drug raid and tonight's fight taking down the older members of the gang, Rock will be free. He has to be.

A groan splits his lips. He's awake. His hand twitches in mine, and I loosen my squeezing grip on his damaged hand. Rock's eyes open, eyelashes fluttering before his gaze lands on mine. A breath shudders out of his chest. "Val."

All of the feelings rioting around my insides fall still at that look. "It's me. You're safe."

He tries to sit up. Breath hitching, wincing, he sags onto the couch cushions.

"Don't move. I'll get you cleaned up."

Rock groans again. "Don't think I could, even if I wanted to."

"Stay," I order. Running upstairs, I get the first aid kit and a pile of washcloths. Dampening them in the kitchen sink, I nuke them in the microwave so they're pleasantly warm.

Rock lies still as I clean the blood off his bronzed skin, hesitant when I draw close to his wounds. "Go ahead," he breathes through clenched teeth. "I can take it."

His fists grip the couch cushions as I swipe the blood and grit away from his eyebrow and then his mouth. He hisses through cracked lips when I dab on ointment.

Exhausted, he goes limp.

I wipe my hands on a clean cloth and drop it onto the pile of Band-Aid wrappers on the coffee table.

"Who did this to you?" I demand, even though I already know the answer. As soon as I'm done tending to Rock, I'm going to make him tell me where that flaming excuse for a human is, and I'm going to sic the entire department on him.

Rock's mouth shuts in a firm line.

I wheedle him as I examine his clean wounds, but his resolve is unbreakable. I know the fugitive Snake did this, and he knows I know. But he won't admit it outright. And he has the nerve to say I'm the stubborn one.

Gritting my teeth, I finish cleaning the blood off his neck.

"Sit up and take this off," I order, plucking at the shreds of his shirt.

A flicker of light returns to Rock's eyes. "Desperate to get me shirtless, huh?"

"I want you. I need you. Oh baby, oh baby."

"Sheesh, no need to beg." Rock tries to lift it over his head, groaning in pain. His hands drop to his lap, and his eyes find mine. "Help," he mouths.

Frown deepening, I pluck the tiny bandage scissors out of the kit and cut away the blood-stained fabric. The bruising around his ribcage is even worse.

Hissing, I skim my hands over his bruise-mottled ribcage. "You need a doctor. Your ribs might be broken."

"They're not broken," He murmurs.

"You don't know that."

"Do too. Didn't hear a crack, and I'm not swollen enough for that."

"That's ridiculous. You need x-rays. I can't just kiss it and make it all better."

"Won't know until you try it."

My breath hitches. Did he just. . . ? Pulse fluttering like a hummingbird in my throat, I meet his eyes. They're clear and warm on mine.

"Try it, Val."

Oh. Crap on a cracker, he's serious. Do I want to kiss Rock and make him better? Yes, yes I do. Licking my lips, I lean toward him. So help me, I want to kiss Rock.

"Where does it hurt? Show me."

Eyes locked on mine, Rock points at the red cuts along the knuckles of one hand. With boldness I usually only use for doing something stupid, I lift his hand and kiss his knuckles. He sucks in a breath, taking the air from my lungs along with it.

He points at the knuckles on his other hand, and I kiss those too.

Craning toward me, he points to his split eyebrow.

Swallowing hard, I lean in and press a gentle kiss against his warm skin. He smells like antiseptic ointment and warm leather.

Rock's curled finger skims down his temple to a dark purple bruise on his jaw line. My ears go hot as I press a gentle kiss to his skin. I'm pretty sure my skin is sparkling. I'm aching to press my mouth to his.

If he asked, I'd do it.

Rock's fingertip brushes his swollen mouth. His eyes are locked on mine, daring me to close the distance and kiss him. I suck my own lips between my teeth, knowing I'll have to be gentle. It's got to hurt to take a fist to the teeth. Repeatedly, from the looks of him.

I hesitate. "Do you still have all your teeth?"

"Velvet." His nickname for me is almost a physical caress as his breath puffs over my cheek. He's asking, and I can't refuse. I don't want to refuse.

Hovering closer, I brace my body with a hand on the couch beside his knee and brush my lips over his. His palm rises to cup my cheek, holding me in place as he returns the caress, pressing his mouth over mine once, then twice.

Groaning, he falls back against the couch and squeezes his eyes shut. "You have no idea how long I've wanted to do that, but my mouth freaking hurts."

Fury at the Snakes burns away the sparkles dancing over my skin. My hands curl into fists in my lap. "Tell me where he is, and I'll make sure he can't hurt anyone ever again. Or let me drive you to the station. You can tell the sheriff. He'd be happy to take Gabriel off the street."

Rock's eyes open. Latch onto mine. "I'm not telling you where he is, Val. And I'm not going to the station. Don't ask me to, because I won't."

I bristle, the desire to push for answers holding me by the

throat. The sheriff and I haven't always seen eye to eye, but he'd agree with me on this. The sooner REB is locked away, the better for everyone in town. I start to say so, but Rock gets there first.

"I'm trying to protect you, Val. You gotta let me do this. Please."

"I'm trying to protect you, you numbskull. You gotta let *me*."

He doesn't budge. "You've done enough. And I appreciate all of it, but I'll take it from here."

Realization hits me hard. Even though Rock hasn't said, I know it was REB who clashed with him tonight. And if Rock is this bad, it was a brutal fight. For the first time I wonder the kind of condition REB is in if Rock is here. Rock escaped with his life. What does that say about his attacker? Is he in the hospital, spouting lies about how he's innocent and how Rock brutalized him for no reason? If he does, the hospital staff have to report it. The sheriff and his staff have to look into it. Will they find evidence that will force them to act against Rock?

Anger and disgust bubble up in my chest. I hope Rock hurt REB enough to put him in the hospital. That belly crawling, dust-eating Snake deserves it for all of the ugliness he has poured into our little corner of the world. If he tries to blame Rock, we'll figure out how to get out of it.

I won't let that happen. If there's something I can do to keep Rock here, free and clear, I'll do it. Legal or not.

Instantly, I understand down to my bones why my dad made some of the choices he did as sheriff.

My hand curls around Rock's bicep. "Where is he, Rock?"

Rock's eyes are hard on mine. His mouth tugs tight. He's not going to tell me.

I stand up, too full of burning energy. I have to do something, even if it's tidy up the first-aid kit I upended over the coffee table.

Rock's hand finds mine, and his fingers squeeze gently. "Stay with me."

"Please let me take you to the station. They can help you."

He gives one clipped shake of his head. "I'm already on their radar. Don't need to draw any more attention."

If I take Rock down there like this, they'll ask all kinds of questions. I'm assuming Rock was attacked and fought back in self-defense, but he hasn't confirmed it. He's frustratingly tight-lipped about the events that landed him on my couch.

"If you tell me what happened, I can help. We can figure out how to get you out of the Snakes for good. Together. But you have to tell me what happened."

His brown eyes are soft on mine. Tender. Aggravating. "Can't do that, Mighty Mouse. The less you know, the better."

"You don't get to decide for me."

"I'm deciding for me."

Frowning, I look away. Everything in me is pushing to take action. But what action? What can I do tonight to help Rock? To protect him?

Rock huffs, giving a light tug on my arm. "Sit. That's all you have to do tonight."

He's trying to protect me, and himself. I can't argue with that. Oh, I want to, but the extent of his injuries keeps me from trying to rile him into telling me what I want to know. Giving in, I sink onto the couch beside him. He closes his eyes but doesn't let go of my hand.

Releasing the tension swimming through my veins, I collapse against the cushions. Tuck my feet under me awkwardly since Rock still has possession of my hand. We sit quietly as the night ages, our breathing slowing and syncing up. Pulling a blanket off the back of the couch, I pull it over us and snuggle down into its warmth.

"Granny Agani used to sing me to sleep when I was sick," he murmurs.

"I'm not singing." But as Rock's eyes remain closed and his body gives in to weariness, I sing anyway.

Raising the White Flag

My mom found Rock and me passed out on the couch when she got home from the dispatch office. It would have been embarrassing, seeing as how Rock was shirtless and pressed along my back, but the bruising over his body was even uglier in the morning sunlight.

My mom fusses over Rock, checking him over and asking fifteen times if he wanted to go to urgent care. He declines politely each time, so she sends him upstairs with some of my dad's old clothes for a shower. Once he's gone, she asks me what happened. I tell her about finding him in our house, beaten and struggling to walk.

Her throat tightens as she swallows down the emotion welling in her eyes. "It sounds like he could use a good breakfast. Help me?"

We make pancakes and plate them up in high stacks with lots of syrup. Rock comes down a few minutes later looking and smelling so much better, and we tuck into our breakfast. The entire time we eat, Mom keeps checking to make sure Rock is eating and drinking okay. I try to distract her by asking about her shift, and if the gang violence around town has abated. It has.

Mom gives me a tight goodbye hug and a cider-filled thermos for the road.

Rock walks me out to my car, waiting while I open it and get it running to warm it up. "If you change your mind, I'll go talk to McCandles with you."

He leans into the car and lifts a hand to caress my cheek. "Not gonna change my mind, but thanks, V. For everything."

"I'm in your corner, whatever you need. We can win this."

Rock's mouth pulls down in a frown, and he withdraws. "We were always gonna lose, V."

Pain scrawls across my heart at the finality, the resignation in his tone. "Don't say that."

His Adam's apple bobs. "Have fun at work. Say high to Junior for me."

Town is strangely empty as I drive to the station. It's on the early side of Saturday morning, so I wasn't expecting bumper to bumper traffic, but it's more than that. There is no one out yet. It's weird.

Destin careens into the station minutes after I arrive. Grinning ear to ear, he skips over to where I'm manning the front desk. Sailing around the counter to my side, he leans on one elbow.

My eyebrows rise in amusement. "Someone's in a good mood this morning."

"Who, me?"

"You're grinning like a kid on Christmas morning."

"Christmas was two months ago. And besides, wouldn't you be this happy if you were me, after last night?"

My mind stutters. Last night? As in Rock, beaten to a pulp?

As in the veiled allusions he made to ensuring Rotten Egg Breath won't be sniffing around me anymore? "I don't know—"

"Dinner? Telling my parents I want to be a cop? You were there. It couldn't have gone better. This morning my mom got me donuts with maple frosting and fondant sheriff badges on them. I have no idea where she got them, but they were delicious."

I smile weakly, stumbling onto my friend's wavelength. "Yeah. Dinner. That's awesome, Des. I bet it's a relief to have that out in the open, right? And to know your parents are cool with it? Proud of you, dude."

He beams wider. "Thanks. I couldn't have done it without you."

"You would have told them eventually."

Destin laughs. "Eventually. See you in a bit. I have to change for my ride along. You seen Kelley yet this morning? She's taking me out today."

I shake my head, and Destin makes for the locker rooms. In the doorway, he pivots. "Was it weirdly empty in town this morning, or what?"

"Or what."

He disappears down the back hallway.

Everyone who comes into the department the entire day comments on how empty town is today. The streets are empty. The diner has an unusually slow day for a Saturday. Even the non-emergency line is quiet.

I'm not one to borrow trouble, but the silence is ominous, The calm before the storm hits with a vengeance.

We were always a losing game, V.

Rock's statement eats at me. I don't know what he did to remove the threat, and I refuse to speculate. What really gets me is this: if he's so confident the psycho Snake is no longer going to be a problem, why did he tell me we're a losing game? If REB has left town with his tail between his legs, wouldn't that mean we've won? Without their most sadistic member, the Snakes don't have anyone left to lead them. Their organization has more holes in it than a used paper target in the shooting range.

And then he kissed me.

It doesn't make any sense.

I text Rock, but he doesn't answer. I need answers, so I message my mom. She tells me Rock left in the late morning after he spent an hour or so playing with Rosie in the living room floor. The picture she sends of Rock's bruised face peering down at Rosie with her mouse toy is almost enough to send me into a cuteness coma.

During the never-ending lull, I sneak through the back hallway to the dispatch office. One of my mom's long-time co-workers waves. I make my way over to her desk.

It's quieter than the morgue today, and she isn't on a call.

I sink down into the chair in the station next to hers. Tap my fingers on the desktop. "You came in this morning, right? Did you hear about how last night's shift went?"

She shrugs. "Nothing unusual. Pretty quiet today, though."

"You noticed that, huh?"

"It's strange. I've never had so few calls on a shift. It's like everyone just decided to stay home and choose peace today."

"Wish that were every day."

"No kidding."

"About last night. No bar brawls or gang fights or anything?"

The dispatcher laughs. "Not that I heard. Is there any particular reason you're curious? Is there something I should know?"

The open curiosity in her eyes pulls me up short. I'm doing

exactly what Rock asked me not to do. I'm pushing for information when he practically begged me to steer clear. If I keep on this track, will I uncover something that gets him in more trouble?

"I could check the logs," my mom's co-worker says helpfully. "They're public record."

My curiosity is eating at me, but Rock's words weigh more. He didn't want me looking into this for a reason. I won't do anything that causes him harm. No matter what happened to Rock last night, I won't be the one to draw attention to it. He's trying to protect me, and I'm doing the same for him.

Excusing myself, I leave the dispatch office and hurry back to the front desk.

Janice is standing in the doorway when I enter the bull pen. Her hands are tangled in front of her, and her face is white as a sheet of paper.

Stomach dipping, I try not to run to her, since we have an audience. Deputy Kelley is at her desk, showing Destin how to fill out a form. Leave it to Kelley to make him practice doing paperwork before she takes him out in her squad car.

My heart is pounding as I reach the counter. Silently, Janice points at the stool beside mine, asking if she can come behind the desk. I let her through, and she sinks down onto the stool, breath whooshing out of her. She looks completely, utterly defeated.

"Jan, what happened? You're scaring me."

Her eyes are wide and filled with fear when they meet mine. "That's because I'm terrified."

My gut turns over. I have never seen Janice this scared. Whatever is going on, it's bad. My mind fills with worst case scenarios. Rock isn't answering my texts because he's been arrested. Or because he's in a hospital somewhere fighting for his life after collapsing from internal injuries. I knew I should have dragged him to the hospital. Or maybe Ty got hurt somehow? A rogue blender at the smoothie hut electrocuted him or something?

Taking her hand in mine, I hold on tight. "Make it quick."

Janice's breath is shaky as she swallows. "I got a text this morning from one of the Snakes. He's my usual contact, so I don't have to report to Leif or Gabriel or anyone. I usually get my forging assignments from this guy, he's cool. But this morning… Oh god, it's bad. He said we have a new leader as of last night. Apparently, there was a huge fight, and a bunch of people were pretty seriously hurt, Rock included. In the end, the new leader won the fight, and he called a meeting for tonight. Everyone in the gang has to come.

"I'm so scared, Val. What if it's Gabriel? If he's the new leader, there's no telling what he'll make me do. He has never liked me, that greasy-smiled creep. And if he gets his hands on Rock… And you! He has it out for you, too. What are we going to do if it's him? I think I'm going to be sick."

My chest is heaving at the onslaught of Janice's word vomit. "It's not Gabriel."

Janice's eyes are shiny with unshed tears. "How do you know?"

I brace myself for more questions I can't answer. "Rock told me."

Her breath hitches in surprise, so I keep going. "He showed up at my door after the fight, and I patched him up."

Janice's eyebrows rise.

"Don't get any ideas. It was the least romantic night ever." I don't tell her about cuddling with Rock on the couch. Or the kissing. Or that the way Rock looked at me made me feel like I was sparkling like a diamond.

Worry leaves no room for all of the girly squealing I'd like to do. If the Snakes have a new leader, one who was strong enough to win a fight between him and Rock and REB and who knows who else, he must be big. Strong. Brutal and ruthless. A guy like that taking charge of the Snakes will be nothing but trouble for my friends, for the sheriff's department, and for the entire town.

He won't be bothering you anymore.

We were always a losing game.

Suddenly I know deep down in my soul that Rock said those things because he knew who had won that fight. He knew who had become the new leader of the Snakes, and it's not my former attacker, which is a small relief. But that relief pales next to Janice's panic. Next to Rock's assertion that we were always going to lose this game we've been cornered into playing.

Whoever the new leader of the Snakes is, he's worse than REB could ever be. Rock doesn't see a way out from under this new leader's thumb.

That doesn't work for me. There has to be a way to protect my friends, to free them once and for all.

Wrapping my arms around Janice, I hold her tight. She sinks deeper into me, trying to get ahold of her breathing. After a couple minutes, her chest stops shuddering with every inhale. "I have to admit, I never saw this coming," she mutters.

"Someone new taking over the Snakes?" My mind whirls.

"You and me hugging. Mud wrestling maybe. Hugging, no."

"Me either. But I don't hate it."

Janice hugs me tighter. "I don't hate it either. Val, what am I going to do? I don't want to do any more for the Snakes, but what if I don't have a choice?"

"I have a plan. Do you trust me?"

"I never thought I'd say this, but yes."

"Whatever you're going to do, we're coming too," a familiar voice says.

"Yep, count us in."

Janice and I spin to find Destin and Leander watching us, arms crossed and faces in twin expressions of firm resolve. Destin and Deputy Kelley went out back to her squad car a few minutes ago. I thought he was gone, and I didn't know Leander was on the schedule for today.

From the grim lines of their mouths, I'm guessing they're not going to budge until I tell them what I'm thinking.

The old me would have lied through my teeth to keep them out of the mess I'm about to make. I was used to doing everything by myself since it's so damn hard to admit I need help, and even harder to ask for it. The old me wasn't a very good friend.

It's been a tough slog, but here I sit. On a stool in the department with three people I trust to have my back. Three people I will do anything to protect. The fourth is currently being annoyingly stubborn and tight-lipped, but I'll crack him. After tonight he won't have any more reasons to shut me out.

Leander and Destin huddle closer.

Janice links her pinky finger with mine.

I open my mouth and tell them everything.

This Isn't Over

I never thought I'd be prepared to bring the department down the burrow into the Snakes' den right when they're trying to crown a new leader. But that's my plan.

The Snakes and their reign of chaos are going down tonight.

If I have anything to say about it, Janice and Rock won't have to worry about their ties to the gang ever again. After tonight there won't be anyone left to head the organization. To force my friends into the life of violence and crime their parents bore them into.

All of this ends tonight. I'm going to make sure of it.

A consuming ache has crawled into my chest and made a home between my ribs, crowding out my heart and lungs. Building pressure until I can't take it anymore. It's a good thing it's almost time to leave, because my friends and I are counting on tonight to wrap up all of the loose ends and untangle the mess we're caught in up to our necks.

The ache started small when I found Janice standing like a

deer in headlights at the front of the department. It swelled to barely manageable when I got home and found a potted miniature rosebush sitting beside my completely functional and bullet-hole free Corvette. Rock finished it this morning after I left. All it needs is a new paint job and it'll be as good as new.

The watery gleam in my mom's eyes when I revved it up made the decision to switch cars easy. She took it to work and I have her car for the night.

It was probably for the best. If I drove the Corvette out to the bar where the Snakes are crowning their new leader tonight, that would basically be begging for a spotlight on myself and my friends and asking for trouble. It would be like flinging myself on the bonfire and handing the Snakes the lighter fluid.

I won't be the one going down tonight. The Snakes have had their day, but it's ending. Janice and I are sneaking into their den tonight with the express purpose of cutting off their head and smashing them under our heels.

After tonight, our town won't have a Snake problem anymore.

Janice is across town with Ty at the Smoothie Hut, so she's meeting me there. Destin and Leander insisted on meeting me there. I sure hope this doesn't go sideways and end with any of my friends hurt.

My phone chimes in my lap. A message from Janice. *Hurry. A ton of people just got here.*

Accelerating through a yellow light, I set my jaw when it turns red just as I reach the intersection.

Immediately, a squad car's lights flash on. Crapsicles. They were hiding behind a hedge. Should have known better.

Pulling over, I roll down my window and wait for the deputy to appear. Mom will hear about this, and I will be in deep crap. Later. Still have time to bring down the Snakes before I'm grounded for who knows how long.

Deputy Kelley clicks her tongue as she squares up with the passenger window. "I told you I didn't want to write your first ticket, Val."

"So don't write one?"

My phone buzzes again. And again.

"You ran a red right in front of me, and I'm not playing favorites."

"So I am your favorite?"

"I'll have to think about it. Leander was pretty helpful at the department this afternoon."

"I can promise you more hot apple cider."

The deputy eyes me as she pulls her notepad out of her belt and writes. She hands it over, and I frown down at it, knowing I'm looking at a hefty fine. "This is going to be expensive, isn't it?"

"The state has to make their budget square somehow. Now, this better be your first and your last ticket. No more running red lights. Got it?"

"Yes, ma'am." My phone screen finally goes dark, and I glance at it. I'm itching to check it, but not in front of Kelley. I don't want another ticket for touching my phone while driving.

She raises an eyebrow at me as if daring me to try her.

"See you tomorrow, deputy."

"Tomorrow, then." She retreats to her squad car, and I pull onto the road. I'll check my phone when I get to the bar. *Hurry.*

As soon as I turn a corner out of Kelley's line of sight, I gun it.

The bar parking lot is packed full of hot rods and vintage cars and motorcycles, so I end up parking down the alley away from streetlights and prying eyes. I creep along the narrow corridor, hoping to get inside without being noticed, but I can't even get near the place.

A hand landing on my shoulder makes me jump, barely stifling a scream. Janice, Leander, and Destin are right beside me, covering their amused smiles behind their hands. My heart squeezes at the sight of them. "You three sure you want to be here?" I wheeze.

"We're not leaving you, dummy." Destin snags my arm and pulls me in for a noogie. Which I can't escape from without making noise and drawing attention. I go limp, and he lets go.

"We're your backup," Leander puts in.

My eyes skip between them. "Thanks for coming. Seriously."

"Any time." Leander's sincerity makes me feel bad for the guy. Our lives would be a lot less complicated if I could just return his feelings. Instead, I've got it bad for someone who might never be attainable for me, even if I do manage to quash the Snakes's operation tonight.

Speaking of slimy reptiles, bunches of Snakes are gathered in the parking lot, drinking from bottles and cans and laughing uproariously. A current of celebration fills the air like a noxious cloud. Anything these hairless apes are celebrating cannot be good for this town. Or for my friends and me.

Night falls quickly as the sun runs to meet the horizon, even though it's only 5 o'clock. I half expected the gang to wait until midnight to begin their crowning ceremony, but maybe that's just me being dramatic.

Instead, it's barely evening and they're already deep in their cups. No wonder Janice asked me to hurry. The stench of expectation in the air is so thick I can practically see it.

Frankly, I'm shocked there are so many people here. The department has busted and arrested so many gang members over the past year that I have to wonder where all of these eager recruits are coming from. Nowhere good.

I whisper the question in Janice's ear, but she shakes her head. She doesn't know either.

A liquor bottle flies through the air, and all four of us duck behind a dingy car at the edge of the bar's parking lot. Another one flies past, and the idiots roar with laughter when it shatters against a tree growing out of the cracked sidewalk.

The four of us crouch low over the asphalt. We huddle together, because it's February and it's freaking cold outside.

"What now?" Destin asks, hovering at my side.

I survey the parking lot, aware of the three sets of eyes watching me. "We wait for everyone to go inside, and we get as close as we can. Hopefully they'll be doing something illegal, and we can call the sheriff down here to break it up and make some arrests. With any luck, the Snakes' new head honcho will be caught in the middle, and that will be the end of it."

"They've got to be running out of candidates," Leander says, patting the navy blue beanie covering his blonde hair.

"You'd think," Janice puts in, hand toying with her sleek ponytail.

"Where's Ty tonight?" Destin asks, eyes on the crowd beyond our hiding place.

"Still at work," she answers. She didn't tell Ty about our little plan for tonight, because she wanted to keep him out of it. To keep him safe. I get it. If I had my way, no one I cared about would be in danger tonight. But life has made it very clear that I don't always get my way.

Hopefully tonight goes my way.

I could use the win. So could Janice and Rock.

Which is why we're hiding outside a swanky bar, waiting to catch the Snakes with their hands painted red and bring the sheriff and his deputies down on their heads.

Slowly, the crowd works its way into the building. No wonder they chose this place. It's much bigger since the remodel, and there are so many gang members here they need every inch of space.

Darkness closes in, and so does the cold. All four of us are shivering and clumped together by the time the last of the Snakes elbows their way into the building.

Janice meets my eyes. "You ready?"

"Let's move."

The four of us tiptoe around the side to the back door. Destin goes first since he's the least likely to be recognized and connected to the gang's leaders or the department. Easing the door open, he sticks his head inside. Raucous noise spills out around his shoulders.

My hands are sweaty inside my winter gloves as I check my phone.

Still no word from Rock. Wherever he is tonight, I hope he's safe. Tucked away from the viper pit we're about to step into. We didn't tell him we were doing this precisely so he'd stay out of it.

Withdrawing from the open portal, Destin looks right at me. "Last chance to change your mind."

I look from him to Leander to Janice. I focus on Rock, who will never be free as long as the Snakes are a malevolent presence around town. "Let's go."

Tucking my hood around my face, I follow him inside. The place is so crowded with bodies, nobody notices us squeezing inside and pressing against the wall. I'm so short I can't see anything but the backs of people's heads.

Frenzied energy fills the room, zapping me with nervous anticipation. Something big is about to happen, I can feel it. A mix of dread and resolve hardens in my gut. This ends tonight.

I look around, hoping to spot some egregious flouting of the law that would allow Sheriff McCandles to bust up this party. There's nothing. Everyone here is drinking and munching on bar peanuts. We need a higher vantage point.

Skirting past a couple big guys in leather jackets, we slip up the stairs to the lofted balcony and make our way toward the railing. Up here, people cavort on couches in the dark. I don't look too closely because yuck. There's no trace of any drugs or illicit substances on the low tables. Disappointing.

The stench of alcohol and sweat is ripe, even up here above most of the crowd. I've only been inside for a few minutes but I already have a pounding headache. Annoyance grips me as sweat drips down my spine. The only violation at this gathering is the sheer number of people inside the building. The fire marshall would not be happy if he saw this, because this entire place is a fire hazard and a half.

Below, the crowd writhes with anticipation. Janice's eyes meet mine, shiny with warning. She looks as nervous as I feel.

Someone jumps onto the bar and stomps his feet. It's a middle-aged guy with graying hair and a beer belly. His leather jacket is emblazoned with snake patches up the arms and criss-crossing the back. He looks familiar.

"Isn't that the guy who owned the drug house?" I rasp in Janice's ear.

She nods, her face bloodless.

"What is he doing out of prison?"

Eyes glued on the man, she shakes her head.

Destin puts an arm around my shoulders and pulls me against him. Shielding me from the wave of bodies as it crashes against the railing and pushes us further into the corner.

"I've been a part of the brotherhood for a long time," the man on the bar yells.

Everyone hoots and cheers, raising glasses and bottles and cans in the air.

"I've been here a long time, and I never thought I'd see this day. When Dino and Angus Hill got arrested, I didn't know what would happen to our family. And then Leif got arrested, and I thought the Snakes were done. I thought the gang would break apart, and everyone would go their own ways."

The crowd boos, long and loud. A roar in my ears.

Dread blooms in my gut. I do not like where this is going.

"This is bad," Janice hisses in my ear, her face positively green in the low light. Leander puts an arm around her shoulders, and she accepts the support. A gang leader's daughter and a sheriff's son. That's one good thing to come out of tonight, at least.

"I know a lot of you were hoping Gabriel would take over as our leader. He has vision and the drive to get things done…" The man trails off, looking around the crowd. Meeting eyes with many of his fellow gang members.

They fall quiet, hushing. A moment of silence.

Wait. The gang members are acting like something happened to Gabriel. Like he's no longer here. Down on the dance floor, a young guy pours out his drink on the ground.

My chest hitches. If they're not crowning Gabriel tonight, then who?

Getting my phone out, I text Rock. Frantic. *Are you okay? Please answer. Please.*

Destin's phone lights up, too bright in the quiet, dim building. My eyes squeeze shut against the white glare. This is it. They're going to turn around, see us, and maul us right here and now. I hold my breath.

No one moves. Everyone in the bar is locked on to the man standing on the bartop. I don't know his name, but this guy knows how to hold a crowd. My hands dig into my pockets, clenched in fists.

My friend's phone appears under my nose, and I read the screen. It's a text from Jonesie. They found a body in the state park, dumped in the woods. Exactly where Rock told me his dad used to dump the bodies. I lock my knees to keep them from wobbling.

The man up front raises his glass. "Rest in peace, Gabriel. Let's take a drink in memory of our brother."

Everyone in the bar lifts their drink. Loud swallowing noises make my stomach churn. Janice isn't the only one feeling queasy. Gabriel is dead. *He won't be bothering you anymore.* He's dead, and Rock knew about it. My stomach lurches. Did Rock… is it possible he killed Gabriel in the brawl last night? Is that why he told me to stay out of it? Because he knew exactly what I would uncover if I pushed?

Even if that is exactly what happened, it had to be because REB picked a fight with Rock. Rock would never seek out anyone with the intention of killing them. Rock would never do that. He doesn't have a murderer's heart.

Deep down, doubt takes hold. Rock knew the Snake was a threat to me. The gangster proved it over and over. If he had gotten the chance, the crazy-pants Snake would have killed me.

Rock would never let that happen. Just like I was prepared to shoot him when I thought he was lurking in my house, lying in wait to kill me and make good on his threats.

The crowd ripples, and someone presses against Destin, squeezing our space even further. He pushes the guy back, keeping us from being stepped on. The Snake is so caught by what the man on the bar is saying that he doesn't spare us a glance.

Alarm builds in my gut, rising into my throat. Suddenly my

eyes are wide open. We should never have come here.

Janice and Leander and Destin and I are fools. We're surrounded by agitated, violent men who will absolutely hurt us if they realize who we are. If the Snakes discover who has snuck into their midst, they will kill us without remorse.

Finally, my self-preservation instincts kick in. Rock would be proud, wherever the freak he is tonight. Clearly he has more sense than I do and is lying low until this night is over.

We have to get out of this place. Now.

The man on the bar holds up his hands to quiet the rowdy mass. "Like I said, I never thought this night would come. I never thought this young man would lead the Snakes. Didn't think it would ever come to this, or that he would even want the title. But he proved me wrong last night. He proved all of us wrong, didn't he, fellas?"

Fear cuts off the flow of stale air into my lungs. I can't breathe. Can't move.

The gang goes absolutely wild, yelling and hooting like dogs on the scent of fresh blood.

Leander pulls me back into his chest, and whispers in my ear, "We have to get out of here."

Janice wraps a hand around mine. "This is bigger than we can handle, V. Let's go, before someone gets hurt."

I shake them off. My eyes are cemented to the man standing on the bar. Because climbing up beside him is someone I know top to bottom. Soul to soul. Someone I've spent lifetimes with. Someone I wanted to keep for lifetimes more. Someone who means so much to me I'd risk my life to protect him.

I owe my life to him, at least twice over. I wanted to return the favor.

I'll never be out, V.

Janice gasps, hands smothering the sound at her lips.

Everyone in the building screams so loud all the residents of hell can probably hear it as Rock stands tall on the bartop. A black leather jacket emblazoned with snakes covers his upper body. It's big in the shoulders. A bold of lightning hits me. It's his dad's jacket. Dark purpled bruises are stark against his skin, less than a day after he brawled and won.

My stomach bottoms out.

This cannot be happening. After everything we've been through, after all of the battles we fought, individually and together, so that neither of us would be dragged down by the Snakes. He went and became their new leader.

Rock's mouth is a grim line. His eyes are flat and dead. Nothing behind them. He is totally shut down. Locked tight. Until he scans the crowd and finds me standing, gripping the loft railing for all I'm worth. There's a flare behind his eyes that almost looks like tenderness, but then it's gone. Hardness takes its place. He glances from me to Leander, and wordless communication passes between them.

Leander wraps his arms around me and drags me toward the staircase. I'm frozen, staring at Rock. I want to kick and punch and bite, but if I do that the Snakes will hear the ruckus. They'll see me, and I don't know if Rock will be able to save me, even now.

I can't make a sound, even though every fiber of my being is aching with the need to scream.

Because I know Rock's motive behind this. The ugly hurts apparent on his skin. The hideous jacket wrapped around his shoulders. A mantle and a burden he never wanted to carry. Rock wouldn't have done this, taken up this crown of thorns, unless it was to protect someone he cared about. Unless there was no other way to save someone close to him.

Rock sacrificed himself, his life and future, to save me.

As Leander half carries me downstairs and out of the building, I don't fight him. I don't struggle. I know a losing hand when I see one.

But this game we're playing? It's not over. Rock may have folded in order to take the target off my back, but this isn't the end of our story. I refuse to accept it.

Rock saved me tonight, but he had to sacrifice himself to do it. He had to give in to his father's demand that he become something he hates in order to save my skin. The weight of Rock's choice sits low in my gut, twisting my stomach into anxious knots.

This isn't over. I won't let Rock set fire to his goals and dreams for me. I won't let him sacrifice everything he has worked for his entire life on the selfish and twisted altar of his father's expectations. I don't know how I'm going to pull it off, but I'm going to undo this mess.

Rock saved me, and I'm going to save him right back.

Acknowledgements

You would think after writing fourteen books, it would get easier. In some ways it does: I know what to expect. I know it will be difficult. I know that at some point I'm going to want to quit, and will have to lean on pure stubbornness to finish writing the darn book.

In some ways, writing doesn't get any easier. It takes determination to sit down in front of the computer enough days in a row to draft an entire story from start to finish. Then come editing, proofreading, formatting, designing, and more. None of these tasks is easy, but all of them are worth the effort.

After writing this, my fifteenth book, I can confidently say I still love crafting stories. There is something magical about taking a half-formed idea and turning it into three hundred pages of love, hate, fear, joy, twists, and turns. When Chuck Wendig called people magic skeletons, he was right.

Thank you to Hallie Christensen, Christina Kobel, and Brittany Radomski for reading this part of Val and Rock's story and giving critique and encouragement. This book wouldn't be what it is without your help.

Thank you to my local coffee shop, Pilgrim's Coffee, for consistently delicious drinks and a place to write away from all of the distractions my home holds.

Thank you to Autumn Krause for being a continual cheerleader on those coffee shop days. From writing to titles to marketing, you're always in my corner. Right back at you, Autumn.

Evangeline and Stella, I hope you see your mom chasing her dreams and are inspired to chase your own. It's a big world out there, with lots of opportunities. I hope you go after what you want, especially when the days are long and the work is tough.

Adam, thank you from the bottom of my heart. I couldn't write books without you. Thank you for being the best support system a writer could ask for. I'm so thankful you're my person.

About the Author

Emily Kazmierski lives in sunny Southern California with her husband and two daughters. When she's not in her book dragon form devouring books, she can be found in the kitchen making homemade ice cream or baking something delicious. In addition to reading and writing, Emily loves watching makeup videos on YouTube and cuddling with her two long-haired dachshunds, Nestlé and Kiefer.